The Young Oxford Book — *of* — Nasty Endings

The —
Young Oxford Book
— *of* —
Nasty Endings

DENNIS PEPPER

OXFORD UNIVERSITY PRESS
Oxford • New York • Toronto

Oxford University Press, Great Clarendon Street, Oxford OX2 6DP

Oxford New York

Athens Auckland Bangkok Bogota
Buenos Aires Calcutta Cape Town Chennai Dar es Salaam Delhi
Florence Hong Kong Istanbul Karachi Kuala Lumpur Madrid
Melbourne Mexico City Mumbai Nairobi Paris Sao Paulo
Singapore Taipei Tokyo Toronto Warsaw
and associated companies in
Berlin Ibadan

Oxford is a trade mark of Oxford University Press

01947

This selection and arrangement © Dennis Pepper 1997
First published 1997
First published in paperback 1998
Reprinted in paperback 1998

JF

Speyside HS

A CIP catalogue record for this book is available
from the British Library

ISBN 0 19 278151 0 (hardback)
ISBN 0 19 278158 8 (paperback)

Printed in Great Britain by
Biddles Ltd, Guildford & King's Lynn

Contents

Introduction

You know the story:

> . . . The search must have moved on. Cautiously she inched her way up the slope and peered over the top. The rutted field looked empty. She relaxed, resting her head in the tangle of weeds and grass that fringed the embankment. How long had it been since she last slept? Three days? Four? She jerked her attention back to the present. If she were going to get clear she had to keep moving. Clutching her throbbing arm she struggled to her knees. Behind her there was a deep, throaty chuckle. 'Well, now—' There was no mistaking the hated, jeering voice. 'Well, now, who do we have here?' As she turned to face her tormentor her foot twisted under her and she fell back towards him. Then . . .

Then, of course, she woke up. It had all been a bad dream and you feel, quite rightly, that you've been cheated.

I don't think you'll feel cheated by the stories in this book. When Cathy Palfrey in 'The Loony' wakes up she doesn't escape from her particular horror but finds herself more firmly entangled in it not knowing, in the end, what is real and what isn't. Ambrose Fennel's awakening, in 'We'll Look After You' is less horrific but the situation he finds himself in is decidedly unwelcome—and he can't escape from it. And when Graham Kraken is revived from his cryogenic sleep his unexpected but all too believable nightmare is just beginning. As the authors unravel their stories we see that they are not offering escape routes to the people in them nor are we, the readers, being reassured by comfortable endings but only by the fact that they are, after all, *stories*: what might have been, what could be, told with a greater or lesser degree of realism. Each story holds us in the author's imaginary world, and this is what happens there.

However, you are not being offered a collection of stories in which blood splatters the ceiling and dismembered limbs are stored in the freezer or dumped in a lay-by in black plastic bin-liners. Such stories do not usually excite those exquisite feelings of horror or terror that readers look for and they soon become tedious. Of course, nasty things happen to people in these stories and the stories themselves do have nasty endings—which isn't quite the same thing when you think about it—but more often than not the writers move aside when they think they have said enough and leave the final working out to us. Nowhere, in Roald Dahl's 'The Landlady', are we told what happens to Billy Weaver, but if you don't know then you need to read the story again.

Do the characters deserve what they get? Well, yes and no. Of course, Ned ought not to have broken into the old man's house just because he was curious about a phone call and wanted to prove himself to his fellow librarians, but he suddenly realizes, at the end of Ramsey Campbell's story, that his situation is desperate and he is about to be efficiently and nastily dealt with. He isn't a real baddy, like Alan in 'Mr Lupescu' or Phil in 'Cop for a Day', so is the nasty end we suppose is in store for him a fitting one? (The next question is, of course, is this a reasonable question to ask, about this or any other story?)

Along with the 'horror' stories you will find others that could be broadly classified as 'crime', or 'ghost', or 'science fiction' – or a combination of several of these. Some are realistic, others more tongue-in-the-cheek. Some are long, others very short, little more than anecdotes, with a twist or shock ending. Surprise endings, which occur in some of the long stories as well as in the shorter ones, are less of a surprise when you look at the stories closely. They have to be carefully prepared and seen to be appropriate when they come—which is why the 'then she woke up' story is so unsatisfactory. The ending doesn't belong.

As with previous collections in this series, I have gone out of my way to bring together stories by writers whose main interest is in writing for adults and those who write mainly for younger readers. It's a good mix. Don't expect to sleep easy.

Dennis Pepper
June 1997

The Landlady

ROALD DAHL

Billy Weaver had travelled down from London on the slow afternoon train, with a change at Swindon on the way, and by the time he got to Bath it was about nine o'clock in the evening and the moon was coming up out of a clear starry sky over the houses opposite the station entrance. But the air was deadly cold and the wind was like a flat blade of ice on his cheeks.

'Excuse me,' he said, 'but is there a fairly cheap hotel not too far away from here?'

'Try The Bell and Dragon,' the porter answered, pointing down the road. 'They might take you in. It's about a quarter of a mile along on the other side.'

Billy thanked him and picked up his suitcase and set out to walk the quarter-mile to The Bell and Dragon. He had never been to Bath before. He didn't know anyone who lived there.

But Mr Greenslade at the Head Office in London had told him it was a splendid city. 'Find your own lodgings,' he had said, 'and then go along and report to the Branch Manager as soon as you've got yourself settled.'

Billy was seventeen years old. He was wearing a new navy-blue overcoat, a new brown trilby hat, and a new brown suit, and he was feeling fine. He walked briskly down the street. He was trying to do everything briskly these days. Briskness, he had decided was *the* one common characteristic of all successful businessmen. The big shots up at Head Office were absolutely fantastically brisk all the time. They were amazing.

There were no shops on this wide street that he was walking along, only a line of tall houses on each side, all of them identical. They had porches and pillars and four or five steps going up to their front doors, and it was obvious that once upon a time they had been very swanky residences. But now, even in the darkness, he could see that the paint was peeling from the woodwork on their doors and windows, and that the handsome white façades were cracked and blotchy from neglect.

Suddenly, in a downstairs window that was brilliantly illuminated by a street-lamp not six yards away, Billy caught sight of a printed notice propped up against the glass in one of the upper panes. It said BED AND BREAKFAST. There was a vase of pussy-willows, tall and beautiful, standing just underneath the notice.

He stopped walking. He moved a bit closer. Green curtains (some sort of velvety material) were hanging down on either side of the window. The pussy-willows looked wonderful beside them. He went right up and peered through the glass into the room, and the first thing he saw was a bright fire burning in the hearth. On the carpet in front of the fire, a pretty little dachshund was curled up asleep with its nose tucked into its belly. The room itself, so far as he could see in the half-darkness, was filled with pleasant furniture. There was a baby-grand piano and a big sofa and several plump armchairs; and in one corner he spotted a large parrot in a cage. Animals were usually a good sign in a place like this, Billy told himself; and all in all, it looked to him as though it would be a pretty decent house to stay in. Certainly it would be more comfortable than The Bell and Dragon.

On the other hand, a pub would be more congenial than a boarding-house. There would be beer and darts in the evenings, and lots of people to talk to, and it would probably be a good bit cheaper, too. He had stayed a couple of nights in a pub once before and he had liked it. He had never stayed in any boarding-houses, and, to be perfectly honest, he was a tiny bit frightened of them. The name itself conjured up images of watery cabbage, rapacious landladies, and a powerful smell of kippers in the living-room.

After dithering about like this in the cold for two or three minutes, Billy decided that he would walk on and take a look at The Bell and Dragon before making up his mind. He turned to go.

And now a queer thing happened to him. He was in the act of stepping back and turning away from the window when all at once his eye was caught and held in the most peculiar manner by the small notice that was there. BED AND BREAKFAST, it said. BED AND BREAKFAST, BED AND BREAKFAST, BED AND BREAKFAST. Each word was like a large black eye staring at him through the glass, holding him, compelling him, forcing him to stay where he was and not to walk away from that house, and the next thing he knew, he was actually moving across from the window to the front door of the house, climbing the steps that led up to it, and reaching for the bell.

He pressed the bell. Far away in a back room he heard it ringing, and then *at once*—it must have been at once because he hadn't even had time to take his finger from the bell-button—the door swung open and a woman was standing there.

Normally you ring the bell and you have at least a half-minute's wait before the door opens. But this dame was like a jack-in-the-box. He pressed the bell—and out she popped! It made him jump.

She was about forty-five or fifty years old, and the moment she saw him, she gave him a warm welcoming smile.

'*Please* come in,' she said pleasantly. She stepped aside, holding the door wide open, and Billy found himself automatically starting forward into the house. The compulsion or, more accurately, the desire to follow after her into that house was extraordinarily strong.

'I saw the notice in the window,' he said, holding himself back.

'Yes, I know.'

'I was wondering about a room.'

'It's *all* ready for you, my dear,' she said. She had a round pink face and very gentle blue eyes.

'I was on my way to The Bell and Dragon,' Billy told her. 'But the notice in your window just happened to catch my eye.'

'My dear boy,' she said, 'why don't you come in out of the cold?'

'How much do you charge?'

'Five and sixpence a night, including breakfast.'

It was fantastically cheap. It was less than half of what he had been willing to pay.

'If that is too much,' she added, 'then perhaps I can reduce it just a tiny bit. Do you desire an egg for breakfast? Eggs are expensive at the moment. It would be sixpence less without the egg.'

'Five and sixpence is fine,' he answered. 'I should like very much to stay here.'

'I knew you would. Do come in.'

She seemed terribly nice. She looked exactly like the mother of one's best schoolfriend welcoming one into the house to stay for the Christmas holidays. Billy took off his hat, and stepped over the threshold.

'Just hang it there,' she said, 'and let me help you with your coat.'

There were no other hats or coats in the hall. There were no umbrellas, no walking-sticks—nothing.

'We have it *all* to ourselves,' she said, smiling at him over her shoulder as she led the way upstairs. 'You see, it isn't very often I have the pleasure of taking a visitor into my little nest.'

The old girl is slightly dotty, Billy told himself. But at five and sixpence a night, who gives a damn about that? 'I should've thought you'd be simply swamped with applicants,' he said politely.

'Oh, I am, my dear, I am, of course I am. But the trouble is that I'm inclined to be just a teeny weeny bit choosy and particular—if you see what I mean.'

'Ah, yes.'

'But I'm always ready. Everything is always ready day and night in this house just on the off-chance that an acceptable young gentleman will come along. And it is such a pleasure, my dear, such a very great pleasure when now and again I open the door and I see someone standing there who is just *exactly* right.' She was half-way up the stairs, and she paused with one hand on the stair-rail, turning her head and smiling down at him with pale lips. 'Like you,' she added, and her blue eyes travelled slowly all the way down the length of Billy's body, to his feet, and then up again.

On the first-floor landing she said to him, 'This floor is mine.'

They climbed up a second flight. 'And this one is *all* yours,' she said. 'Here's your room. I do hope you'll like it.' She took him into a small but charming front bedroom, switching on the light as she went in.

'The morning sun comes right in the window, Mr Perkins. It *is* Mr Perkins, isn't it?'

'No,' he said. 'It's Weaver.'

'Mr Weaver. How nice. I've put a water-bottle between the sheets to air them out, Mr Weaver. It's such a comfort to have a hot water-bottle in a strange bed with clean sheets, don't you agree? And you may light the gas fire at any time if you feel chilly.'

'Thank you,' Billy said. 'Thank you ever so much.' He noticed that the bedspread had been taken off the bed, and that the bedclothes had been neatly turned back on one side, all ready for someone to get in.

'I'm so glad you appeared,' she said, looking earnestly into his face. 'I was beginning to get worried.'

'That's all right,' Billy answered brightly. 'You mustn't worry about me.' He put his suitcase on the chair and started to open it.

'And what about supper, my dear? Did you manage to get anything to eat before you came here?'

'I'm not a bit hungry, thank you,' he said. 'I think I'll just go to bed as soon as possible because tomorrow I've got to get up rather early and report to the office.'

'Very well, then. I'll leave you now so that you can unpack. But before you go to bed, would you be kind enough to pop into the sitting-room on the ground floor and sign the book? Everyone has to do that because it's the law of the land, and we don't want to go breaking any laws at *this* stage in the proceedings, do we?' She gave him a little wave of the hand and went quickly out of the room and closed the door.

Now, the fact that his landlady appeared to be slightly off her rocker didn't worry Billy in the least. After all, she was not only harmless—there was no question about that—but she was also quite obviously a kind and generous soul. He guessed that she had probably lost a son in the war, or something like that, and had never got over it.

So a few minutes later, after unpacking his suitcase and washing his hands, he trotted downstairs to the ground floor and entered the living-room. His landlady wasn't there, but the fire was glowing in the hearth, and the little dachshund was still sleeping in front of it. The room was wonderfully warm and cosy. I'm a lucky fellow, he thought, rubbing his hands. This is a bit of all right.

He found the guest-book lying open on the piano, so he took out his pen and wrote down his name and address. There were only two other entries above his on the page, and, as one always does with guest-books, he started to read them. One was a Christopher Mulholland from Cardiff. The other was Gregory W. Temple from Bristol.

That's funny, he thought suddenly. Christopher Mulholland. It rings a bell.

Now where on earth had he heard that rather unusual name before?

Was he a boy at school? No. Was it one of his sister's numerous young men, perhaps, or a friend of his father's? No, no, it wasn't any of those. He glanced down again at the book.

Christopher Mulholland   *231 Cathedral Road, Cardiff*
Gregory W. Temple   *27 Sycamore Drive, Bristol*

As a matter of fact, now he came to think of it, he wasn't at all sure that the second name didn't have almost as much of a familiar ring about it as the first.

'Gregory Temple?' he said aloud, searching his memory. 'Christopher Mulholland? . . .'

'Such charming boys,' a voice behind him answered, and he turned and saw his landlady sailing into the room with a large silver tea-tray in her hands. She was holding it well out in front of her, and rather high up, as though the tray were a pair of reins on a frisky horse.

'They sound somehow familiar,' he said.

'They do? How interesting.'

'I'm almost positive I've heard those names before somewhere. Isn't that queer? Maybe it was in the newspapers. They weren't famous in any way, were they? I mean famous cricketers or footballers or something like that?'

'Famous,' she said, setting the tea-tray down on the low table in front of the sofa. 'Oh no, I don't think they were famous. But they were extraordinarily handsome, both of them, I can promise you that. They were tall and young and handsome, my dear, just exactly like you.'

Once more, Billy glanced down at the book. 'Look here,' he said, noticing the dates. 'This last entry is over two years old.'

'It is?'

'Yes, indeed. And Christopher Mulholland's is nearly a year before that—more than *three years* ago.'

'Dear me,' she said, shaking her head and heaving a dainty little sigh. 'I would never have thought it. How time does fly away from us all, doesn't it, Mr Wilkins?'

'It's Weaver,' Billy said. 'W-e-a-v-e-r.'

'Oh, of course it is!' she cried, sitting down on the sofa. 'How silly of me. I do apologize. In one ear and out the other, that's me, Mr Weaver.'

'You know something?' Billy said. 'Something that's really quite extraordinary about all this?'

'No, dear, I don't.'

'Well, you see—both of these names, Mulholland and Temple, I not only seem to remember each one of them separately, so to speak, but somehow or other, in some peculiar way, they both appear to be sort of connected together as well. As though they were both famous for the same sort of thing, if you see what I mean—like . . . well . . . like Dempsey and Tunney, for example, or Churchill and Roosevelt.'

'How amusing,' she said. 'But come over here now, dear, and sit down beside me on the sofa and I'll give you a nice cup of tea and a ginger biscuit before you go to bed.'

'You really shouldn't bother,' Billy said. 'I didn't mean you to do anything like that.' He stood by the piano, watching her as she fussed about with the cups and saucers. He noticed that she had small, white, quickly moving hands, and red finger-nails.

'I'm almost positive it was in the newspapers I saw them,' Billy said. 'I'll think of it in a second. I'm sure I will.'

There is nothing more tantalizing than a thing like this which lingers just outside the borders of one's memory. He hated to give up.

'Now wait a minute,' he said. 'Wait just a minute. Mulholland ... Christopher Mulholland ... wasn't *that* the name of the Eton schoolboy who was on a walking-tour through the West Country, and then all of a sudden—'

'Milk?' she said. 'And sugar?'

'Yes, please. And then all of a sudden—'

'Eton schoolboy?' she said. 'Oh no, my dear, that can't possibly be right because *my* Mr Mulholland was certainly not an Eton schoolboy when he came to me. He was a Cambridge undergraduate. Come over here now and sit next to me and warm yourself in front of this lovely fire. Come on. Your tea's all ready for you.' She patted the empty place beside her on the sofa, and she sat there smiling at Billy and waiting for him to come over.

He crossed the room slowly, and sat down on the edge of the sofa. She placed his teacup on the table in front of him.

'*There* we are,' she said. 'How nice and cosy this is, isn't it?'

Billy started sipping his tea. She did the same. For half a minute or so, neither of them spoke. But Billy knew that she was looking at him. Her body was half-turned towards him, and he could feel her eyes resting on his face, watching him over the rim of her teacup. Now and again, he caught a whiff of a peculiar smell that seemed to emanate directly from her person. It was not in the least unpleasant, and it reminded him—well, he wasn't quite sure what it reminded him of. Pickled walnuts? New leather? Or was it the corridors of a hospital?

'Mr Mulholland was a great one for his tea,' she said at length. 'Never in my life have I seen anyone drink as much tea as dear, sweet Mr Mulholland.'

'I suppose he left fairly recently,' Billy said. He was still puzzling his head about the two names. He was positive now that he had seen them in the newspapers—in the headlines.

'Left?' she said, arching her brows. 'But, my dear boy, he

never left. He's still here. Mr Temple is also here. They're on the third floor, both of them together.'

Billy set down his cup slowly on the table, and stared at his landlady. She smiled back at him, and then she put out one of her white hands and patted him comfortingly on the knee. 'How old are you, my dear?' she asked.

'Seventeen.'

'Seventeen!' she cried. 'Oh, it's the perfect age! Mr Mulholland was also seventeen. But I think he was a trifle shorter than you are, in fact I'm sure he was, and his teeth weren't *quite* so white. You have the most beautiful teeth, Mr Weaver, did you know that?'

'They're not as good as they look,' Billy said. 'They've got simply masses of fillings in them at the back.'

'Mr Temple, of course, was a little older,' she said, ignoring his remark. 'He was actually twenty-eight. And yet I never would have guessed it if he hadn't told me, never in my whole life. There wasn't a *blemish* on his body.'

'A what?' Billy said.

'His skin was *just* like a baby's.'

There was a pause. Billy picked up his teacup and took another sip of his tea, then he set it down again gently in its saucer. He waited for her to say something else, but she seemed to have lapsed into another of her silences. He sat there staring straight ahead of him into the far corner of the room, biting his lower lip.

'That parrot,' he said at last. 'You know something? It had me completely fooled when I first saw it through the window from the street. I could have sworn it was alive.'

'Alas, no longer.'

'It's most terribly clever the way it's been done,' he said. 'It doesn't look in the least bit dead. Who did it?'

'I did.'

'*You* did?'

'Of course,' she said. 'And have you met my little Basil as well?' She nodded towards the dachshund curled up so comfortably in front of the fire. Billy looked at it. And suddenly, he realized that this animal had all the time been just as silent and motionless as the parrot. He put out a hand and touched it gently on the top of its back. The back was hard and cold, and when he pushed the hair to one side with his fingers, he could see the skin underneath, greyish-black and dry and perfectly preserved.

'Good gracious me,' he said. 'How absolutely fascinating.' He turned away from the dog and stared with deep admiration at the little woman beside him on the sofa. 'It must be most awfully difficult to do a thing like that.'

'Not in the least,' she said. 'I stuff *all* my little pets myself when they pass away. Will you have another cup of tea?'

'No, thank you,' Billy said. The tea tasted faintly of bitter almonds, and he didn't much care for it.

'You did sign the book, didn't you?'

'Oh, yes.'

'That's good. Because later on, if I happen to forget what you were called, then I can always come down here and look it up. I still do that almost every day with Mr Mulholland and Mr . . . Mr . . .'

'Temple,' Billy said. 'Gregory Temple. Excuse my asking, but haven't there been *any* other guests here except them in the last two or three years?'

Holding her teacup high in one hand, inclining her head slightly to the left, she looked up at him out of the corners of her eyes and gave him another gentle little smile.

'No, my dear,' she said. 'Only you.'

Call First

RAMSEY CAMPBELL

It was the other porters who made Ned determined to know who answered the phone in the old man's house.

Not that he hadn't wanted to know before. He'd felt it was his right almost as soon as the whole thing had begun, months ago. He'd been sitting behind his desk in the library entrance, waiting for someone to try to take a bag into the library so he could shout after them that they couldn't, when the reference librarian ushered the old man up to Ned's desk and said 'Let this gentleman use your phone.' Maybe he hadn't meant every time the old man came to the library, but then he should have said so. The old man used to talk to the librarian and tell him things about books even he didn't know, which was why he let him phone. All Ned could do was feel resentful. People weren't supposed to use his phone, and even he wasn't allowed to phone outside the building. And it wasn't as if the old man's calls were interesting. Ned wouldn't have minded if they'd been worth hearing.

'I'm coming home now.' That was all he ever said; then he'd put down the receiver and hurry away. It was the way he said it that made Ned wonder. There was no feeling behind the words, they sounded as if he were saying them only because he had to, perhaps wishing he needn't. Ned knew people talked like that: his parents did in church and most of the time at home. He wondered if the old man was calling his wife, because he wore a ring on his wedding finger, although in the claw where a stone should be was what looked like a piece of yellow fingernail. But Ned didn't think it could be his wife; each day the old man came he left the library at the same time, so why would he bother to phone?

Then there was the way the old man looked at Ned when he phoned: as if he didn't matter and couldn't understand, the way most of the porters looked at him. That was the look that swelled up inside Ned one day and made him persuade one of the other porters to take charge of his desk while Ned waited to listen in on the old man's call. The girl who always smiled at Ned was on the switchboard, and they listened together. They heard the phone in the house ringing then lifted, and the old man's call and his receiver going down: nothing else, not even breathing apart from the old man's.

'Who do you think it is?' the girl said, but Ned thought she'd laugh if he said he didn't know. He shrugged extravagantly and left.

Now he was determined. The next time the old man came to the library Ned phoned his house, having read what the old man dialled. When the ringing began its pulse sounded deliberately slow, and Ned felt the pumping of his blood rushing ahead. Seven trills and the phone in the house opened with a violent click. Ned held his breath, but all he could hear was his blood thumping in his ears. 'Hello,' he said and after a silence, clearing his throat, 'Hello!' Perhaps it was one of those answering machines people in films used in the office. He felt foolish and uneasy greeting the wide silent metal ear, and put down the receiver. He was in bed and falling asleep before he wondered why the old man should tell an answering machine that he was coming home.

The following day, in the bar where all the porters went at lunchtime, Ned told them about the silently listening phone. 'He's weird, that old man,' he said, but now the others had finished joking with him they no longer seemed interested, and he had to make a grab for the conversation. 'He reads weird books,' he said. 'All about witches and magic. Real ones, not stories.'

'Now tell us something we didn't know,' someone said, and the conversation turned its back on Ned. His attention began to wander, he lost his hold on what was being said, he had to smile and nod as usual when they looked at him, and he was thinking: they're looking at me like the old man does. I'll show them. I'll go in his house and see who's there. Maybe I'll take something that'll show I've been there. Then they'll have to listen.

But next day at lunchtime, when he arrived at the address he'd seen on the old man's library card, Ned felt more like knocking at the front door and running away. The house was menacingly big, the end house of a street whose other windows were brightly bricked up. Exposed foundations like broken teeth protruded from the mud that surrounded the street, while the mud was walled in by a five-storey crescent of flats that looked as if it had been designed in sections to be fitted together by a two-year-old. Ned tried to keep the house between him and the flats, even though they were hundreds of yards away, as he peered in the windows.

All he could see through the grimy front window was bare floorboards; when he coaxed himself to look through the side window, the same. He dreaded being caught by the old man, even though he'd seen him sitting behind a pile of books ten minutes ago. It had taken Ned that long to walk here; the old man couldn't walk so fast, and there wasn't a bus he could catch. At last he dodged round the back and peered into the kitchen: a few plates in the sink, some tins of food, an old cooker. Nobody to be seen. He returned to the front, wondering what to do. Maybe he'd knock after all. He took hold of the bar of the knocker, trying to think what he'd say, and the door opened.

The hall leading back to the kitchen was long and dim. Ned stood shuffling indecisively on the step. He would have to decide soon, for his lunch-hour was dwindling. It was like one of the empty houses he'd used to play in with the other children, daring each other to go up the tottering stairs. Even the things in the kitchen didn't make it seem lived in. He'd show them all. He went in. Acknowledging a vague idea that the old man's companion was out, he closed the door to hear if they returned.

On his right was the front room; on his left, past the stairs and the phone, another of the bare rooms he'd seen. He tiptoed upstairs. The stairs creaked and swayed a little, perhaps unused to anyone of Ned's weight. He reached the landing, breathing heavily, feeling dust chafe his throat. Stairs led up to a closed attic door, but he looked in the rooms off the landing.

Two of the doors which he opened stealthily showed him nothing but boards and flurries of floating dust. The landing in front of the third looked cleaner, as if the door were often opened. He pulled it towards him, holding it up all the way so it didn't scrape the floor, and went in.

Most of it didn't seem to make sense. There was a single bed with faded sheets. Against the walls were tables and piles of old books. Even some of the books looked disused. There were black candles and racks of small cardboard boxes. On one of the tables lay a single book. Ned padded across the fragments of carpet and opened the book in a thin path of sunlight through the shutters.

Inside the sagging covers was a page which Ned slowly realized had been ripped from the Bible. It was the story of Lazarus. Scribbles that might be letters filled the margins, and at the bottom of the page: 'p. 491'. Suddenly inspired, Ned turned to that page in the book. It showed a drawing of a corpse sitting up in his coffin, but the book was all in the language they sometimes used in church: Latin. He thought of asking one of the librarians what it meant. Then he remembered that he needed proof he'd been in the house. He stuffed the page from the Bible into his pocket.

As he crept swiftly downstairs, something was troubling him. He reached the hall and thought he knew what it was. He still didn't know who lived in the house with the old man. If they lived in the back perhaps there would be signs in the kitchen. Though if it was his wife, Ned thought as he hurried down the hall, she couldn't be like Ned's mother, who would never have left torn strips of wallpaper hanging at shoulder height from both walls. He'd reached the kitchen door when he realized

what had been bothering him. When he'd emerged from the bedroom, the attic door had been open.

He looked back involuntarily, and saw a woman walking away from him down the hall.

He was behind the closed kitchen door before he had time to feel fear. That came only when he saw that the back door was nailed rustily shut. Then he controlled himself. She was only a woman, she couldn't do much if she found him. He opened the door minutely. The hall was empty.

Half-way down the hall he had to slip into the side room, heart punching his chest, for she'd appeared again from between the stairs and the front door. He felt the beginnings of anger and recklessness, and they grew faster when he opened the door and had to flinch back as he saw her hand passing. The fingers looked famished, the colour of old lard, with long yellow cracked nails. There was no nail on her wedding finger, which wore a plain ring. She was returning from the direction of the kitchen, which was why Ned hadn't expected her.

Through the opening of the door he heard her padding upstairs. She sounded barefoot. He waited until he couldn't hear her, then edged out into the hall. The door began to swing open behind him with a faint creak, and he drew it stealthily closed. He paced towards the front door. If he hadn't seen her shadow creeping down the stairs he would have come face to face with her.

He'd retreated to the kitchen, and was near to panic, when he realized she knew he was in the house. She was playing a game with him. At once he was furious. She was only an old woman, her body beneath the long white dress was sure to be as thin as her hands, she could only shout when she saw him, she couldn't stop him leaving. In a minute he'd be late for work. He threw open the kitchen door and swaggered down the hall.

The sight of her lifting the phone receiver broke his stride for a moment. Perhaps she was phoning the police. He hadn't done anything, she could have her Bible page back. But she laid the receiver beside the phone. Why? Was she making sure the old man couldn't ring?

As she unbent from stooping to the phone she grasped two uprights of the banisters to support herself. They gave a loud splintering creak and bent together. Ned halted, confused. He was still struggling to react when she turned towards him, and he saw her face. Part of it was still on the bone.

He didn't back away until she began to advance on him, her nails tearing new strips from both walls. All he could see was her eyes, unsupported by flesh. His mind was backing away faster than he was, but it had come up against a terrible insight. He even knew why she'd made sure the old man couldn't interrupt until she'd finished. His calls weren't like speaking to an answering machine at all. They were exactly like switching off a burglar alarm.

We'll Look After You

ROBIN KLEIN

I t wasn't a particularly dramatic accident. The car just skidded in gravel, tipped neatly off the road and slid a little way down the mountainside, coming to rest in thick scrub. But Ambrose Fennel struck his head against the dashboard and lost consciousness.

When he woke up, he found himself in bed with a pounding forehead and both arms bandaged from fingers to elbows. There was a cradle arrangement under the bedclothes and his right leg seemed to be constricted in heavy strapping and a splint. Ambrose was the sort of person who couldn't bear illness or injury. Even with a cut finger, he always half-shut his eyes while he dabbed on antiseptic. So now he flinched in appalled horror at his terrible injuries and the realization that he must be in hospital, even though the room didn't look much like a hospital ward. Hospital beds weren't usually old-fashioned brass ones with crocheted woollen bedspreads.

There didn't seem to be any buzzer to summon assistance, either. 'Hey!' he called feebly. 'Anyone around? Would someone please . . .' It took several calls, and he was outraged that he should even be left unattended with such injuries. He prepared some cutting remarks about antiquated country nursing homes and their equally inefficient staff, but when the middle-aged woman came into the room, he found her rather intimidating and didn't utter any of them. She was tall and strong-looking in spite of her grey hair, and a thorough bossyboots judging by the brisk way she pushed his head firmly back on the pillows and tucked his arms under the blanket.

'You must lie still and keep very quiet, young man,' she said. 'That leg of yours is fractured, you know, and both arms have shocking abrasions. My word, you were lucky, all the same! No one ever uses that mountain road, so you could have been trapped there in your car for ever and not a soul knowing. It's fortunate that we just happened to hear the sound of the crash and went to investigate.'

'I took that road by mistake,' Ambrose explained groggily. The pain lurking about behind his forehead confused him. It was difficult to remember things clearly. 'I didn't know it was in such bad condition and so dangerous. There should be a warning notice at the turn-off down by the highway.'

'There is a notice, but it got blown over in the wind. Mavis went down the mountain to check, and she's put the board back again so nobody else will make the same mistake.'

'Mavis?'

'She's my daughter, and you'll meet her by and by. My name's Mrs Burbage and there's just the two of us here, Mavis and me. *Three* of us now, counting you. You don't have to worry, we've set that leg of yours nicely and attended to your poor arms. Just lie there quietly like a good boy and let time do the healing—with Mavis and I helping it along, of course.'

'Mrs Burbage!' Ambrose cried, horrified. 'With all due respect —a broken leg needs professional attention! I'm sure you've done your best and I'm extremely grateful, but now you must telephone for a doctor, call an ambulance . . .'

'Oh no, dear, I can't do that. We don't have the telephone on at all, you see. We don't have a car, either, and I'm afraid yours can't possibly be got back on the road, even if Mavis or me could drive. But you mustn't worry . . .'

'Mustn't worry! Look, you don't seem to realize . . .'

'Mavis is cooking such a lovely supper for you. You'll really appreciate her cooking. I'm sure that some young man will come along some day and ask her to be his wife, all on the strength of her cooking.'

She drew up a chair and sat down cosily with a bag of knitting. Ambrose was devastated by her matter-of-factness. He watched her stealthily, wondering if she were, in fact, simpleminded. The daughter—Mavis, he thought with relief. She's probably organized an ambulance to come up here to fetch me, but couldn't get it across to her dim-witted old mum. Any minute now an ambulance will turn up . . . 'What are you knitting, Mrs Burbage?' he asked, smiling politely at the poor, silly old thing.

'I've just cast on the first row for a pullover. I hope you like this colour, because it's going to be for you, my dear. I've had this wool set by for ever such a long time, but it's still as good as new.'

'That's really very kind of you. Perhaps I'll be driving along this way again some time, and I'll certainly call in to say hello. And collect the sweater. I've never had a sweater hand-knitted specially for me before.' Best to humour her . . .

'I don't suppose any of the young ladies you know ever bothered to learn how to knit. I don't have much time for modern girls myself. Young hussies the lot of them, tinting their hair and wearing indecent clothes—it's not nice at all. My Mavis has been raised very differently, living up here right away from bad influences. Of course, I'd be the first to admit she's not a beauty, but looks aren't everything. She's refined and ladylike and wholesome, and that's what counts in a girl of marrying age, wouldn't you agree? But you'll see for yourself when she brings supper.'

'I'm looking forward to meeting her,' Ambrose said fervently, wanting to know just when the ambulance would arrive. Mavis, of course, would have that well in hand, she must be quite capable if she had to deal with such a peculiar old mother every day.

But when the girl came into the room with a tray, Ambrose looked at her and felt uneasy. He had expected an enterprising, self-sufficient country girl, but Mavis was so shy she couldn't even meet his eyes. She was homely to the point of ugliness, with blurred features like the contours of a badly printed topographic map. He even felt quite sorry for her, despite his own rising worries.

'Did you send for an ambulance?' he whispered as she set down the tray, but she blushed scarlet and shook her head. My God, they're *both* dim-witted! he thought.

'Look here,' he said severely. 'I'm very grateful that you got me out of the car and applied first aid, but I *insist* that one of you go and notify a neighbour immediately! Can't you see . . . with horrific injuries like this, first aid just isn't going to be sufficient! I need a doctor. Somehow you've got to get me to a doctor, or fetch one up here!'

'But we can't do that,' Mrs Burbage said gently. 'We haven't got the telephone, as I told you before, not to mention having no car. Ooops . . . careful, dear, don't try to hold the cup with your arms in the state they are—let Mavis give you little sips and spoonfuls. Delicious, isn't it? No one can make vegetable soup like Mavis! What was I saying . . . oh yes, we hardly ever go out, so we don't have any need of a car.'

'Surely you have some arrangement for shopping?'

'Oh, we're almost self-sufficient here with the vegie garden and the fowls. We've got a standing order for the few groceries we need, and every couple of months they leave a carton in a special place down by the highway. I walk down to fetch it up. I'm very strong for my age. But we just got our grocery delivery yesterday, so the van won't be coming out this way again for ever so long.'

'Well then, you could walk to the nearest neighbour. Or send Mavis . . .'

'But we haven't got any neighbours, not for miles and miles and miles. Besides, I wouldn't let Mavis go strolling about by herself after dark. She's been very carefully brought up, even though we do live here all by ourselves on top of this deserted mountain. Now, after that nice soup there's some lovely wine trifle . . .'

Ambrose struggled to make his requests composed and firm, as though instructing a pair of children. But his voice seemed to be coming from the far end of a long tunnel. 'Both of you could

... walk ... *must* walk down to the main road and wait for a passing motorist. Take a torch with you and wave them down. Give them your address and then tell them to drive as fast as possible to the nearest phone and ask for an ambulance to be sent up here. With a doctor ...'

'But you don't need a doctor, dear. We did all that was necessary. We set your poor broken leg and put ointment on your lacerations, and now we're going to nurse you back to health. Aren't we, Mavis?'

Mavis nodded and smiled moistly, showing all her gums. She had a terrible smile, poor unfortunate girl. Ambrose looked quickly away from the jackal grin, shuddering.

'You mustn't think it's any trouble for us, either,' Mrs Burbage said. 'Why, we're going to love having such a handsome young man around the house! All you have to do is lie there and be patient and quiet. We'll look after you. Don't you think we made a beautiful job of those bandages?'

Ambrose inspected his bandaged arms and was filled with new worries. Infection, he thought giddily. I could get some dreadful infection and need antibiotics, perhaps even a skin graft ... And pain-killers ... In proper hospitals they'd be giving me a course of injections to stop the pain after injuries like this!

Although he could feel no pain now, that was probably because he was still in shock. Being in shock was dangerous, a condition needing skilled medical care! And even if the shock abated, pain would eventually rush in to engulf him. All he could feel now, though, was a vast tiredness that spread through his body ...

When I don't turn up at the Lewishams they'll start to wonder, he thought. They'll notify the police and there'll be a search ... only a matter of holding out till ...

But hadn't there been a letter? Hadn't he, after all, decided not to go on that camping trip? He'd written to Darren and Nina saying he wanted to get right away from everything before he started looking around for a new job. Just driving around from place to place, not sure where, he'd be in touch sometime ...

No workmates now to miss him and make enquiries. No family. And his flat—he didn't even know any of the neighbours there, and was away so often they probably wouldn't even ... wouldn't ...

'That's right, dear,' said Mrs Burbage, pulling the sheet up under his chin. 'You go back to sleep and don't you fret about a thing. We'll take the very best care of you.'

He coasted in and out of sleep, losing track of time. Whenever he wakened, Mrs Burbage seemed to be knitting placidly by his bedside and Mavis bringing another meal on a tray. As soon as he opened his eyes, Mrs Burbage would pause in her knitting to boast to him about her daughter.

'She's such a jewel,' the voice murmured at him. 'You'll have noticed, of course, that she's a bit shy, but I think that's rather sweet in a young girl, myself. Shy because she doesn't think she's very pretty, but I keep telling her, "Beauty is as beauty does, Mavis. Beauty is in the eye of the beholder. One day some lovely young man is going to come along and really appreciate you for your sweet old-fashioned qualities." My word, she certainly has taken a liking to *you*. See how nicely she's ironed your shirt and trousers and jacket, all ready for you to step back into when we've finished nursing you back to health. Yes, she's really done them beautifully, a labour of love. They're spruce enough to wear to a wedding!'

Mrs Burbage's voice bumbled about inside his mind. He braced his body expecting pain every time he moved, but there was no pain. He just felt slow and muddled and craved sleep continually. Drugs . . . he thought suddenly. They're doping me with something in their damned food!

When the next tray came, he shook his head. 'I'm not hungry, Mavis,' he told the girl and closed his eyes and pretended to be drifting back to sleep.

'But Mavis made you such a nice little baked custard,' Mrs Burbage said. 'She made it specially for you!'

'That's very kind, but just leave the tray by the bed. I'll try to eat it later. And . . . I don't mean to sound rude, but do you mind not sitting there by the bedside quite so much? The knitting distracts me . . . I need quiet . . .'

'Of course, dear! You should have told me before. We only want to take the best possible care of you. Anything you want, you only have to ask.'

When they left the room, he sniffed at the custard suspiciously. It didn't look odd, and smelled blandly of milk and nutmeg, but he was sure it was drugged. He looked helplessly at the cradle over his splinted leg and at his bandaged arms. Firm, neat bandaging, but—surely dressings were supposed to be changed every day . . . Had Mrs Burbage and Mavis removed the original bandages at all yet? He couldn't remember them doing so, couldn't even remember how long he'd been lying here in this wretched bed. Should he call them back and ask? Those wounds could become infected if the dressings weren't changed . . . But he couldn't bear the thought of Mavis and her mother leaning over his bed, unrolling the bandages to check. He'd do it himself, distasteful though it would be . . .

He found the end of the bandage on his left arm, pulled it loose with his teeth and clumsily unwound it. Then he forced his apprehensive eyes to look at the bared skin, the horribly lacerated skin . . .

The arm was smooth and unmarked. He ripped the bandage from his other arm and that, too, was perfectly normal and undamaged. He shifted his splinted leg experimentally under the blanket. It felt cramped and uncomfortable but he could bend his toes, rotate his foot and flex his knee without discomfort. That leg, he thought furiously, wasn't even broken at all, and never had been! Nursing him back to health, indeed! He'd have them both arrested for abduction and fraud and keeping him here against his will! He heard footsteps and quickly pushed the loose bandages and his bare arms out of sight under the blankets.

'Mavis made you a nice cup of cocoa,' said Mrs Burbage.

'Thank you, Mavis. I'll drink it when it cools down a little. By the way, when can I get out of bed?' he asked casually. 'I feel much better, you know, and I can't inconvenience you two ladies much longer.'

'Oh, but broken legs take several weeks to mend, dear, and then there's your poor gashed arms. You can't rush these things, and you mustn't feel for one minute it's a bother to us. Mavis just adores cooking special little treats for you. I was only saying to her just now in the kitchen, "What a shame you never meet any nice young fellows, Mavis. It's about time you got engaged, really. Or . . . even married."'

Behind her back, Mavis simpered coyly. She had, he noticed, taken to wearing a battered silk flower pinned to her lank hair.

'I've suddenly realized ... what a sweet-looking young couple you make,' Mrs Burbage said, beaming. 'If I was superstitious I'd say it was Fate brought you both together!'

Mavis smirked.

'We've got a special little treat all lined up,' Mrs Burbage said. 'Mavis is going to sing for you! You didn't know she could sing, did you? There are such a lot of things Mavis can do. She's very accomplished. I raised her nicely so she would make an excellent wife for some fortunate young man. I keep telling her, "Don't despair, even if we do live in an out-of-the-way spot, there's still a chance that one day Mr Right will turn up like a knight in shining armour! You can't go against Fate!"'

'I'm sure she'll meet someone one day,' Ambrose said hurriedly. 'And yes, I'd certainly like to listen to her sing. Only—you don't mind if she sings in another room, do you? My head aches and I'm still very weak and sensitive to noise.'

'That's all right, we'll just go up the hall to the lounge-room and leave the doors open so you can hear,' said Mrs Burbage. 'I'll need her to turn the pages of the music for me at the piano, anyhow.'

Ambrose waited for the first sounds from the piano, then freed his leg. He worked at a hectic, urgent speed, though he felt giddy from his stay in bed. His imprisonment in bed! He swung his legs to the floor and rubbed frantically to bring back the circulation. Mavis was singing something about a girl waiting at the sliprails for her long-lost lover. She finished, and Ambrose called out loudly, 'That was very charming, Mavis! Please don't stop . . . sing something else. Sing all the songs you know. There's nothing I enjoy more than listening to nice long ballads.'

He pulled on his clothes, climbed out of the bedroom window and ran across a patch of untended lawn to the road. He reeled down the road feeling stiff and light-headed, with an eerie sensation creeping about between his shoulder blades. Evening was falling across the mountainside and he almost passed his car without seeing it. It was doubtful that anyone else passing by would notice it, either. Someone had brushed away any skid marks and covered the vehicle with branches and bracken. No use even climbing down to check the damage—it was obvious that a tow-truck would be needed to hoist it back on to the road.

He tried to recall just how far away the main highway was, hazily remembering bend after bend of this narrow, twisting road with no safe place to turn once he realized he'd made a mistake. Driving and driving, completely lost . . . There was probably a long walk ahead . . . He stumbled on, looking nervously over his shoulder, not even stopping to tie his shoelaces.

By now they would have gone into the bedroom to find out why he hadn't called out to ask for more music, found the open window and the discarded bandages and his clothes gone . . . Mavis, he shouldn't wonder, would be terribly upset. And her mother . . . Perhaps they'd even follow him down the darkening road! He broke into a panicky run, his feet scuffling about in loose stones. Eyes watching his flight like cats watching a maimed bird . . . He darted scared glances over his shoulder as he fled, fancying that he saw shadows moving secretively after him some way back, indistinct shapes, a pale shimmer that could have been an apron, something bobbing about that was perhaps an artificial flower pinned to hair . . .

'Go back! Go back to your own house . . . leave me *alone!*' he yelled at the shadows, then tripped and pitched heavily forward. He flung out an arm to break the agonizingly painful fall. Pain slammed at him as he tried to claw his way back on to his feet. But his leg—his injured, terribly injured leg—pinned him to the road's surface as though he were a butterfly fastened to a board. He cradled his head in his arms and wept with the pain.

'There, there,' a voice murmured as hands tenderly stroked his sweat-dampened hair. 'What a foolish young man, running down the mountainside in the twilight on such a steep, dangerous road! Why, you silly boy, you've gone and broken your other leg, now! My word, it's going to need a lot of nursing to get you shipshape again! But don't look so upset, dear, we can easily get you back to the house. It's no trouble at all. We don't mind a bit having to look after you. Do we, Mavis?'

Sweet Shop

MARC ALEXANDER

To the girl it seemed an age since the day her troubles had begun—Black Monday she called it—but in fact it was only the week before. On that afternoon she sat in Eng. Lit. class fiddling with her hair ribbon, which she always did when she was bored, while Mr South rambled on about fairy tales, of all things.

'There's a lot more to traditional fairy stories than you ever imagined when your teacher read "Jack and the Beanstalk" to you in the Infants,' he said, his specs flashing as they always did when he tried to get the class interested in his subject. 'What people thought of as magic in them was really glimpses of the future . . .'

'Do you believe in fairies, sir?' asked Hughie Cooper in a voice so respectful that some of the class could not help giggling.

'Oh yes, he does!' someone called out as they do in the panto.

'Oh no, he don't!' the class chorused, and this went on for a while. When it was quiet again Mr South said, 'Think of what I was saying—in the story of Snow White there was a magic mirror. What would that be today?'

'The telly, sir,' the class answered.

'And Seven-League Boots?'

Everyone shouted something different, and in the end Mr South agreed with those who said motor cars.

'And the Magic Carpet?'

'Please, sir,' said Hughie Cooper, 'isn't the Magic Carpet in *The Arabian Nights*, sir? Not in fairy tales, sir?'

Mr South pretended not to hear, and beamed when Betty Reynolds said, 'Concorde, sir?'

'What about "Puss in Boots", sir?' a boy asked from the back.

'That's a moggy in a chemist's shop,' said Hughie and there was a gale of laughter.

Mr South was getting angry but the buzzer saved the situation. It was home time and laughs were over for the day.

'Now think about fairy stories,' he shouted over the banging of desk tops. 'Next lesson you will write me an essay on fairy-tale things in modern life . . .'

In the playground the girl met her brother—being a year older than her he was in another class—and they walked home together. She told him about Mr South and his soppy fairy tales and he told her how someone had worked out a new video game in computer studies, and before long they were in their street which ran down to the canal.

'Hey, there's Dad's bike against the fence,' the boy said. 'Wonder why he's home?'

Even as he spoke the girl felt scared—she just knew that something was wrong, and as soon as they went inside she found out what it was. Their father was sitting at the kitchen table with a funny-not-ha-ha look on his face and a mug of tea in front of him.

'Your dad's been made redundant!' shouted Dora, their father's second wife. They could not bring themselves to call her 'mother'.

'Twenty-five years I've been at Holroyd's,' he said slowly. 'And even if I say so myself I was their best joiner in the hand-made furniture shop—and now I've been chucked out like an old boot. Seems there's no call for hand-made furniture any more, so the whole shop's being closed. They'll carry on making mass-produced rubbish—probably with robots!—but they don't need craftsmen any more. And in my day it took a five years' apprenticeship to learn the skills . . .'

'Pity you hadn't learned something more useful,' Dora said with her special sniff.

'Like what?' her husband demanded.

'Like being a clerk with the Council or a traffic warden—you don't hear of them being made redundant.'

'But I'm a joiner. Whatever ability God gave me is in my hands.'

Dora sniffed again and dabbed her eyes with the tea towel.

'Don't take on, love,' he said. 'I'll get something else.'

'You've no chance,' she replied angrily. 'Half the factories in this town are closed, so who do you think would want you at your age!'

'You can't blame me for the recession! I did think I might find some sympathy in my own home.'

'So it's sympathy you want! But what about me? Did you think about me when you let them sack you? How am I going to manage, answer me that—with those two not bringing in a penny and eating their heads off? . . . It's about time they made their own way in the world.'

'Dora, they're only school kids.'

'They cost as much as adults to keep. With you on the Unemployment I don't know what will happen.'

Their father stood up and said in a shaky voice, 'Well, I'll be off down to the Job Centre.' And he walked out.

The children exchanged a look and went outside but their father was already striding quickly down the long street.

'We'd better not go after him,' the girl said. 'He'll want to be alone for a bit.'

'Why the hell did he have to marry again?' demanded her brother.

'I suppose he was lonely.'

'He's got all the company he needs now. She could have laid off him on a day like this.'

Suddenly the girl laughed, a bitter, unsteady laugh. 'Now I know what old South was on about with his talk of fairy tales in the present day,' she said. 'There *are* still such things as witches!'

The boy looked bewildered so she said, 'Forget it—let's go down to the canal.'

When she was a little girl the canal bank had been her favourite place. In those days working boats tied up by the factories which backed on to the canal, but now a lot of them were empty and the boats did not come any more. The water was stagnant and people threw rubbish into it, but it was still peaceful. As the two children strolled along the old towpath they saw a silent angler with a fishing rod hoping to land a tiddler which had survived the pollution.

'As soon as I can I'm going away,' said the boy. Then he added, 'You can come with me, if you like.'

'Thanks.'

'I'm sick of it all—Dora's nagging, and the endless rows. We used to have such a good time. Seems like ages ago now.'

His sister took his hand but could think of nothing to say.

The canal ran through the town but as it was hidden away behind buildings most people had forgotten about it, which made it a secret way for the children to wander until they found they were in a part of the town which was strange to them.

'This must be the Old Town where the Council was going to build those new blocks of flats,' said the boy. 'Let's go and see what it's like.'

They went up a narrow passage between two warehouses and found themselves in a street where most of the houses had been knocked down. This had been done to make way for tower blocks but the Council had run out of money and the place looked like an old battlefield. Here and there a few houses, some lonely shops and a boarded-up church survived among the rubble. At the end of the street a building stood by itself and as the children drew nearer they gave whistles of surprise—it was a sweet shop. Its paint was bright, its glass shone in the sunlight, and it had a sign on which GINGERBREAD was painted in large golden letters.

They went up to the window and there was another surprise— it was crammed with the biggest assortment of sweets they had ever seen. The display was not made up of Mars bars and such-like but old-fashioned lollies in big glass jars, sweets that their mother—their real mother—told them she used to get when she was a girl, and which had to be weighed and put in little white paper bags.

'It can't do much business here,' said the boy. 'But look at those jelly babies . . .'

'There's a jar of aniseed balls . . .'

'Gob stoppers . . .'

'Chocolate fish . . .'

'If you're so interested, why not come inside,' said a soft voice, and they saw a plump white-haired old lady smiling at them from the door. The only odd thing about her was her spectacles, which magnified her eyes to twice their normal size, but the children soon got used to her appearance.

Inside the shop she gave them different sweets to try until the boy, feeling he should spend some money, bought a quarter of Pontefract cakes.

'Look, I have some gingerbread men,' said the old lady. 'Do you know the story of the Gingerbread Man?'

'My mum told me when I was small, and I cried at the way the Gingerbread Man kept losing pieces of himself as he ran away,' the girl said. 'It seemed so sad.'

'But not for those who were eating him,' chuckled the old lady. She was pleased to have someone to talk to because, as she told them, she had lost most of her customers when the houses were demolished but she loved her shop and did not want to leave it. They stayed chatting with her until it was twilight outside, and they had forgotten what had happened at home.

'Come back to Gingerbread any time,' she said as they left. 'My name is Hazel—the kiddies used to call me Aunt Hazel. You can if you like.'

When they got back to the towpath the girl found that the old lady had slipped a big bar of fruit-and-nut into her pocket.

'What a nice old dear,' she said as she shared it with her brother.

'Her shop reminds me of a picture I once saw in a storybook,' he said. 'I didn't think there were any shops like that left.'

'It's a find. Perhaps I will come back and see her.'

'You're just out for free chocolate,' he teased.

Next morning the two children did not wait to have breakfast but hurried out. They were sick of the quarrelling that had flared up the night before, when Dora had accused them of always plotting against her because she had the bad luck to be their stepmother. It was something that had not occurred to her until their father had been made redundant.

When they reached the corner the boy said, 'I'm going to cut school today.'

The girl nodded.

'Let's go for a walk.'

'Poor Dad, all those years at Holroyd's . . . and Dora going on as though it's his fault.'

Without either of them discussing where they were going, they arrived at the cemetery. In front of the gravestone with their mother's name on it was a bunch of carnations, and they realized that it was not to the Job Centre that their father had gone the night before.

Later they found themselves wandering along the canal bank, a place where they were less likely to be reported for playing truant.

'I know,' said the boy suddenly. 'Let's go and see Aunt Hazel—you might get given another bar of chocolate.'

They arrived at the shop called Gingerbread and had just enough money to buy a quarter of old-fashioned cough candy.

'You're not at school?' said Aunt Hazel, staring at them with her magnified eyes.

'We gave ourselves a holiday,' the girl said, and she laughed.

'I'm glad. I was feeling lonely. Sometimes I don't open the shop in the mornings because no one comes—my only customers are kids from the Council estate over there, and they come after school. But I'm glad I opened up today because you both look as though you have troubles.'

'We're all right,' said the boy quickly.

'Good, but as you are on holiday you can at least have a cup of tea with me.'

Having missed breakfast they were happy to follow her into her living-room which was just as quaint as the shop, and full of old-fashioned furniture which would have delighted their father. In front of an open fireplace dozed one of the biggest black cats they had ever seen, and there was a parrot in a big cage who chattered, 'Open the door—let me out.'

Aunt Hazel tapped the cage and said, 'Silly thing, you know Samkin would have your tailfeathers the moment you were outside.' But the parrot kept on saying 'Let me out' until she put a cloth over his cage and he thought it was night time.

'Why do you have bars at the window?' the boy asked.

'Now that I have no neighbours I'm nervous of burglars,' Aunt Hazel replied. 'The bars make me feel safe—a burglar would need a blowtorch to get in.'

'But he might come through the door.'

'Look.' She put a key into a keyhole close to the doorway and steel bars shot across it. 'I can operate the bars from the shop too, in case anyone tries to get through to the house in the daytime, and at night I'm as safe as a bank,' she said. 'It cost a lot to get them fitted but at my age you don't want to be worried each time the house creaks.

'That's enough of me—tell me about yourselves while you have your tea,' she added as she went to a cupboard which was stocked with cakes and biscuits.

She seemed so kind—rather like a nice granny—that the children found themselves telling her about their father being made redundant, how they did not get on with their stepmother, and how they would like to leave home. It was a great relief to talk about their problems to a sympathetic grown-up.

'She makes a change from Dora,' the boy whispered as they left her at the shop door, waving goodbye and telling them to visit her again.

'She likes you,' the girl said. 'All the time we were having tea and eating those gingerbread men she kept looking at you. Perhaps she wishes she'd been married and had a son.'

'I'm going to run away—to London,' he said suddenly.

The next few days were a nightmare for the girl. Her father looked ill and did not know what to do with himself except to go to the Job Centre each morning. Her brother was moody and silent and stayed away from school, and she was terrified that he would leave home without telling her.

One morning his stepmother found out that he was missing classes and there was an angry scene.

'You won't get any qualifications and you'll end up on the Unemployment like your father,' she yelled.

'Haven't we got enough trouble without you adding to it?' his father asked him.

The boy ran out of the house, slamming the door so hard that Dora's collection of china draught-horses rattled on the sideboard.

His sister left soon afterwards, and it seemed that the furious voices coming from the house followed her. She wanted to find her brother quickly because she knew how his mind worked, and she guessed that when he stormed out he had made his mind up never to return.

First she went to the cemetery, expecting that he would be paying a last visit before he hitch-hiked away from the grimy old town, but she found no one there. Then she was certain where he had gone, and in a few minutes she reached the canal.

The only living things she saw were two swans which, for some reason, made her think about Mr South and his fairy tales . . . something to do with the Swan Princess, she supposed. How she wished she lived in a fairy-tale land where all you had to worry about was dragons and ogres and wicked dwarfs—much better than real problems!

She was out of breath by the time she found herself in the demolished street where the sweet shop stood alone at the far end.

'Aunt Hazel,' she called when she went inside but there was no answer. It was the squawk of the parrot which made her open the door behind the counter and step into the living-room with its pretty furniture and barred windows.

To her horror she saw her brother in front of the open cupboard and he was *stealing*.

'How could you?' she gasped. 'And from such a nice old lady?'

'I'm not taking much,' he answered. 'Not money or anything —just some biscuits and scones to keep me going until I reach London.'

'It's still stealing,' she said. 'You should've asked.'

'I don't want anybody to talk me out of going,' he answered in a sulky voice. 'And that goes for you, too.'

She was about to give him an angry reply when there was a grating sound and the steel rods slid across the doorway behind her. Then Aunt Hazel appeared in the shop, her huge eyes peering at them through the bars as though they were animals in a zoo cage.

'Well, well, the chicks have returned to the gingerbread house,' she chuckled. 'Welcome back, Hansel and Gretel.'

Those Three Wishes

ROBERT SCOTT

Her name was Melinda Alice. She was clever and pretty and very, very nasty. She was so nasty that all the other kids wanted to be friends with her. After all, it was better to be her friend than one of her victims.

Once, back in the Junior School, a new girl arrived in the middle of term. She was small and shy and wore glasses and, of course, she didn't have any friends. 'Connie,' Melinda Alice christened her. 'Connie, Connie, Connie —Yuk!'

'That's not my name. It's—'

'Connie,' insisted Melinda Alice. 'Short for Contamination,' she added, turning to her circle of friends. Then she touched the new girl on the shoulder and looked at her hand in disgust. 'Yuk! It's contaminated!' She held her hand out for the others to see then wiped it vigorously on her fresh, clean handkerchief, which she immediately dropped in the rubbish bin.

After that everything the new girl touched had to be avoided or cleaned thoroughly before anyone else would use it. After that, Melinda Alice was called Melinda Malice—but not when she might hear you.

Melinda Alice's mother worried about her but her father thought it was all part of growing up. And look how well she was doing. Indeed, Melinda Alice always got good grades and that, her father insisted, was what school was all about.

On this day Melinda Alice left for school early. There was going to be a maths test and she wanted to find a quiet corner where she could go over her books again. Being the best mattered to her. It gave her more power, especially with the teachers.

She had just turned up the lane to take the back way to school when she almost stepped on a snail making its slimy way across the path.

'Yuk! Gross!' She stopped and looked round for something to squash it with. What, after all, was one snail more or less. If it didn't want to be flattened it shouldn't get in the way. Not finding anything, she lifted her foot to stamp on it.

'Please don't,' said the snail.

'What!'

'Please don't stamp on me. I'll give you three wishes if you let me go.'

'Oh, yes,' said Melinda Alice. 'And where's your magic wand?'

'Try me,' said the snail. 'If you don't you'll never know what you missed.'

'OK,' said Melinda Alice. She always went in for competitions, arguing that if you didn't enter you couldn't possibly win. And if the snail didn't deliver she could always get him later. 'My first wish is: I wish . . . I wish I had pierced ears and small gold ear-rings.'

Melinda Alice had been pestering her parents for months. Her mother told her to ask her father and her father told her to wait until she was older. He was very firm about it and he wouldn't be bribed. But now—she felt her ears gently—now she had them anyway. She looked round for the snail but it had already disappeared.

It was then that she realized what enormous power she had. I can find a cure for cancer, she thought. I can make sure everyone has enough to eat and a house to live in. I can even stop wars. Could she? Could the snail really grant wishes like that?

Melinda Alice thought for a moment, then said, 'My second wish is: I wish I had a pair of roller-blades.' And suddenly she sat down hard on the path. 'Not here, stupid!' she shouted. 'Put them in my cupboard at home.' They disappeared. She made a mental note to check when she got home, but there was little doubt that the snail could make some wishes come true. She picked herself up. I can get my own back on people, she thought. All her fine ideas about saving the world had disappeared. I can be captain of all the school teams, I can come first in all the exams. I can have anything—*anything*—I want.

Melinda Alice smirked to herself. She had read fairy stories when she was small and she knew exactly what her third wish would be. After all, she would need lots of wishes if she was going to do everything she wanted.

It was then that she heard the bell. She was late. She would never make it in time. But she did, sliding into her place as her form teacher waited, then called her name.

'Thought you'd decided to give it a miss,' said a voice behind her.

'What do you mean?' She was panting, trying to recover her breath.

'The maths test. Thought you weren't going to bother.'

Melinda Alice's heart sank. The snail had made her late and she hadn't had time to study.

'Oh, no!' she groaned. 'I'll blow it. Oh, I wish I was dead!'

The Loony

ALISON PRINCE

'Mama,' said Cathy, 'Lucy Claythorpe at school says the house Papa has bought used to have a lunatic woman shut up in it. The other girls say so, as well. The woman used to scream, they said, but nobody took any notice because they were used to it. The windows of her room were barred so that she couldn't get out, and at last she died in there but nobody knew.'

It was a relief to blurt it all out. Cathy had been wondering whether the dreadful story was true and, if so, whether her parents had heard it.

'My darling child,' said Mrs Palfrey, 'you must not listen to gossip.' She was always so beautiful, Cathy thought. Pearl buttons fastened the high neck of her blouse tightly round her throat, but she never looked hot or flustered. Cathy, who was often both of these things, envied her. 'Your father,' Mrs Palfrey continued, 'feels that we should have a house more in keeping with his status as a successful umbrella manufacturer. Blackstone Villa has a certain—distinction.'

Cathy thought of the house, standing in its yew-shrouded grounds on the edge of the town, backing on to the moor. It had tall windows, steep gables, and a stone path leading to its front door. A wall surrounded it, with a spiky pattern of wrought-iron along the top. It was on its own, not tucked between its neighbours like their present house. Perhaps that was what her mother meant by distinction. Cathy sighed.

'In any case,' Mrs Palfrey went on, 'people are absurdly superstitious about simple-mindedness. The very word, lunatic, shows a depth of ignorance. It comes from the Latin, *luna*, meaning moon. So lunatic is thought to mean moon-struck. As if the moon could have anything to do with it!' She laughed, then her face was again composed in its faint smile of unchallengeable good sense. 'Nobody in *this* family is likely to go mad,' she said.

Impulsively, Cathy flung her arms round her mother's neck and kissed her. She was so sensible and lovely—so utterly to be relied on.

'There, my pet,' said Mrs Palfrey, disentangling herself calmly after returning Cathy's kiss. 'Now, tea is ready in the dining-room.' She stood up gracefully. 'Your father says we should have a cook-housekeeper when we move into the new house,' she added. 'But I hardly feel that it is necessary.'

Cathy smiled as she followed her mother from the room. Of course it wasn't necessary. As well as being beautiful and wise, her mother was a wonderfully efficient housekeeper.

A week later, they moved into the new house. School had ended for the summer holidays, to Cathy's relief. She was tired of Lucy Claythorpe's taunts of 'Loo-ny! Loo-ny! Living in the mad-house!' People like Lucy, she tried to remind herself, could not be expected to understand about the Latin, *luna*. It was not Lucy's fault that she was absurdly superstitious. But the teasing hurt, and Cathy hoped that by next term the novelty of the Palfreys living in Blackstone Villa would have worn off.

It was very late by the time she got to bed. Her furniture looked strange, rearranged in the new room, and the curtains had not yet been hung at the tall window whose sills, Cathy had noticed, bore the scars of deep screw holes at approximately four-inch intervals. Her mother had fingered them lightly as she gazed round at the faded wallpaper.

'We will redecorate this room,' she had said. 'Ecru and ivory, I think. Very light. Very restrained.' Now, she bent to kiss Cathy. 'Good night, darling,' she said. 'Sleep tight.' She stood up and reached to turn off the gently-hissing gas lamp above Cathy's bed. 'No need to get up too early tomorrow,' she added. Her figure was still clearly visible in the moonlight which flooded in through the uncurtained window. 'I will bring you a cup of tea.'

'Thank you,' said Cathy, smiling. Then her mother went out.

I was silly to worry, Cathy thought as she gazed at the waxy face of the moon, whose roundness was still slightly flattened on one side. There is nothing malign about this house. The bars have been taken down from the window and all traces of the last people who lived here will soon have gone. The only reality is what is happening here and now. And everything is all right.

Filled with trust, she closed her eyes in the cool radiance of the moon, and fell asleep.

'Here is your tea.'

'Oh!' said Cathy sleepily. 'Thank you.'

It was broad daylight. The woman who stood by Cathy's bed with a cup and saucer in her hand was not Cathy's mother. She wore a long white apron over a black dress with the sleeves unbuttoned and pushed up over her mottled arms. Her wiry, reddish hair escaped from the white cap she wore, and her face was crumpled into angry grooves. A huge purple birthmark spread from her left eye down to her chin. Cathy stared at it in horrified fascination.

'Come along,' said the woman impatiently. 'Sit up and drink your tea.'

'Who are you?' asked Cathy. 'Where is Mama?'

'Don't start any of your nonsense,' said the woman. She put the cup of tea down on a chest of drawers that stood against the wall, then turned back to the bed. Without further words, she gripped Cathy by the arms and hauled her into a sitting position, punching the pillows into place behind her. Cathy uttered a cry of fright, and the woman said, 'Scream as much as you like. Everyone is used to it. If you were sane, poor creature, you would understand that it's useless. As it is—' She shrugged, then retrieved the cup of tea and thrust it into Cathy's hands. 'Now drink it,' she commanded. 'And don't you dare make a mess.'

Cathy sipped the tea. 'It's cold,' she said.

The woman laughed with contempt. 'Can't give hot tea to a loony,' she said. 'We don't want you scalding yourself, do we? Though I don't know why not,' she added bitterly.

Cathy drank the cold tea with a shudder, then pushed the bedclothes aside. She would go and find her mother and ask her to get rid of this person.

'And where are you going, miss?' enquired the woman.

Cathy tried to dodge past her but the woman caught her and flung her back on to the bed. This time Cathy did scream, again and again, loudly, kicking and wriggling as the woman held her down on the bed, her arms pinioned above her head.

The door opened and a man came in. Cathy, struggling, caught a glimpse of dark trousers, waistcoat and watch chain as he strode quickly to the head of the bed. She felt the woman shift her grasp to let the man pull some sort of garment over Cathy's head. It had endlessly long sleeves, as Cathy found when she was hauled again into a sitting position, the sleeves crossed and tied so that her arms were pulled tightly across her chest. Then they left her, trussed like a helpless parcel.

'Here is your tea,' said Cathy's mother.

'Oh!' said Cathy sleepily. 'Thank you.'

It was broad daylight.

'Are you feeling better now?' asked Mrs Palfrey. She did not smile.

'Better?' asked Cathy. She sipped her tea. It was lovely and hot. Why was she glad it was hot, she wondered? Tea was always hot.

'You had a bad dream,' said Mrs Palfrey. 'You were making such a noise in the night that I had to come and see what was the matter. You got out of bed, but I don't think you were awake. When I tried to persuade you to go back to bed you struggled and screamed like a mad thing. I had to call your father.'

Cathy frowned, vaguely disquieted. 'I don't remember,' she said. 'I think I dreamed about a cup of tea.'

'I hope it will not become a habit,' said Mrs Palfrey with some disapproval. 'Your father was not at all pleased to be so rudely awoken.'

Cathy's father was an impressive figure. The heavy formality of his clothes, the smell of the pomade he wore on his dark hair and the resounding boom of his voice combined to make Cathy feel a respect for him which bordered on fear. 'I'm very sorry,' she said, appalled to think what she must have done.

'We will say no more about it,' conceded her mother. She smiled kindly and added, 'It was probably the effect of the move. Tonight, things will not be so strange.'

In bed that night, Cathy stared at the bland face of the moon, almost a full circle tonight, and wondered what lay on the other side of sleep. What had happened last night to cause her parents to regard her so gravely today? And what lay in store in the unknown darkness of a dream? She tried hard to stay awake.

'Here is your tea,' said the woman.

Cathy opened her eyes and stared up at the purple-blotched face. This had happened before. They said it was a dream. 'No,' she said. 'It's not true.'

'Don't start any of your nonsense,' said the woman. 'Sit up.'

Cathy knew she must be careful. Obediently, she sat up.

'That's better,' said the woman. She put the cup of cold tea into Cathy's hands and said, 'Drink it.'

Cathy did so. It was very unpleasant. Opposition was useless, she knew. She had to be good and do as she was told until she hit on some way to break this nightmare and get back to real life.

'What must I do?' she asked meekly.

The woman laughed. '*Do*, you poor loony?' she said contemptuously. 'What do you think you can do? Put your clothes on, to start with, then sit on your chair by the window. That's what you *do*, isn't it?'

'Oh,' said Cathy. 'I see. Thank you.' She handed the woman her empty cup.

'We're having one of our good days, are we?' said the woman sarcastically. 'All right, clever miss, see if you can dress yourself while I take this cup to the kitchen. I'll be back in a minute to see what sort of muddle you've made of it. Then I'll take you for a walk to the bathroom.'

She went out, and Cathy heard the key being turned in the lock. There were clothes folded in a pile on the chair by the window. She got up and inspected them. A clumsy grey dress, thick black stockings and flannel underwear, and a knitted cardigan which had once been blue but was dirty and tea-stained. Holes in it had been roughly darned with ill-matched wool. A pair of heavy black lace-up shoes stood on the floor under the chair.

In a kind of desperate haste, Cathy struggled into the clothes, hating the idea that the woman would come and help her. It was bad enough without that. She stared out into the dew-wet garden as she buttoned the dress, and realized that the window was protected by vertical iron bars about four inches apart. This is a dream, she told herself fiercely, fighting down her panic. I must not worry about the bars. Or about these clothes I am wearing. It is all a dream. Soon it will stop.

Turning away from the window, Cathy ran her fingers through her hair. Her comb should be on the dressing-table with the silver-backed brushes and mirror, but the furniture in this room was different. She saw that there was a rather blotched unframed mirror standing on top of the chest of drawers, and crossed the room to look into it.

The face that looked back was not hers.

Cathy felt her mouth open in a scream of silent horror, and, as if mockingly, the mouth of the reflection opened also, dry lips parting in a gaunt face whose red-rimmed eyes stared out sense-lessly at a world which meant nothing. The hair which straggled through the fingers of the still-upraised hand was streaked with grey.

Sick horror flooded through Cathy and made her feel as if every joint had turned to water. Desperately, she assured herself again that this was merely a dream. She picked up the mirror in both hands and carried it to the barred window where, in the stronger early morning light, she stared again at the alien reflection. And again, the face that stared anxiously back was that of a middle-aged, demented woman.

To her own surprise, Cathy found within herself a cold ability to reason. Waking or sleeping, she argued, somewhere in this

house was the real world where her parents slept in their real bed. All she had to do was to break through this nightmare, then she would re-establish contact with normality. She thought carefully. The woman with the purple-marked face was a kind of gaoler. She would have to be destroyed.

A part of Cathy's mind recoiled from the plan she was formulating, but she reminded herself that this was only a dream. The face in the mirror proved it. And anything one did in a dream was unreal. One could not be held responsible, because these events were not really happening.

Very carefully, Cathy placed the mirror at an angle between the wall and the floor. Then she stood upright and kicked it with her heavily-shod foot. It was surprisingly difficult to break. She turned sideways to it and re-attacked it with a stamping action —and the mirror smashed into shards of splintered glass. Forgetting that she could not hurt herself in a dream, Cathy wrapped her hand in the blue cardigan before picking up a long sliver. She could hear footsteps coming up the stairs. She ran back to the bed and lay huddled on her side with the glass stiletto shrouded in its cardigan as she hugged it to her chest like a slender, lethal doll.

The door was unlocked. 'If she's turned violent,' the woman was saying to someone, 'it'll take both of us to restrain her. I certainly heard a crash.'

Cathy hoped that her nightgown, thrown over the back of the chair, would hide the evidence of the broken glass. It was odd how cool she felt. Mama would be proud of her, she thought.

'Now, what have you been up to?' demanded the woman, leaning over Cathy and shaking her roughly by the shoulder. Blindly, Cathy struck out with the splinter of glass. It met the resistance of a thick sleeve and she struck again and again. In the confusion of blows and shouting voices, she realized with angry satisfaction that blood was trickling over her hand. In a minute, she would be free.

There were voices downstairs. Cathy opened her eyes and saw that it was dawn. Grey light crept into the room, and birds were singing.

She sat up in bed. Why were people talking in the drawing-room below her at such an early hour? She noticed a dark stain on the patchwork quilt which covered her bed. She touched it and found that it was blood.

Dread and terror flooded through Cathy like some fatal weakness, and she lay back against her pillows feeling faint. What had happened? She tried to throw her mind back into the darkness of the sleep which had just ended, but was met by a baffling wall which defied her memory.

Slowly, she got out of bed and put on her dressing-gown. Then she saw that her hand-mirror lay smashed on the floor by the window, its silver frame twisted and broken. She almost put her foot on a long, pointed sliver of glass which lay by her bed. She gathered her dressing-gown round her in fresh horror, and pushed her feet into their slippers. Then she made her way across the room to her door. For some obscure reason, she was glad to find that it was not locked, and wondered why this should be so. Her bedroom door had never been locked.

Cathy crept down the carpeted stairs and crossed the hall to where the drawing-room door stood slightly ajar. She crouched down and peered through the crack.

Dr McClintock was bandaging Cathy's father's arm. Mrs Palfrey watched intently, sitting very upright in an armchair. She had evidently dressed hastily, and the unbraided mass of her dark hair hung almost to her waist. Even at this moment, Cathy thought it looked wonderful.

'I would not expect blood-poisoning from such clean slashes as these,' Dr McClintock remarked in his pleasant Scottish voice. 'Not in the ordinary way, that is. But after what happened in this house on a previous occasion, you understand, I feel it is necessary to be doubly vigilant. You must inform me at once if there is any sign of infection setting in.'

Cathy saw her parents look at each other. 'What *did* happen in this house?' enquired Mr Palfrey as he sat with his arm extended to the doctor's ministrations. A bowl of red-coloured water stood on the floor beside his chair.

Dr McClintock's hands were suddenly still. 'Had you not heard?' he asked, looking up from his bandaging. 'Oh, dear. I had stupidly assumed that you knew all about it, local gossip being what it is.'

'We do not gossip,' said Mrs Palfrey icily. 'But now that you have raised the subject, doctor, I think you had better tell us what you mean.'

The doctor's round face creased with distress. He tied the bandage neatly and clipped off its ends, then returned his scissors to the open bag which stood beside him. He sat back in his chair and sighed.

'It was a few years ago now,' he said. 'As you'll know, the house has stood empty a while. Mrs Knarr, who was house-keeper here, came banging on my door one night, saying that old Mr Grayson had cut his arm badly and she feared he would bleed to death. I was not Mr Grayson's regular doctor, you understand, but I was the nearest, and it was an emergency. So I came with her to this house where I found—' The doctor laughed in some embarrassment—'injuries very similar to your own, Mr Palfrey. Now, I know you and your wife have told me the truth concerning this brainstorm or whatever it was that afflicted your lassie—and we must decide what to do about that in a moment.'

Cathy, crouched at the door, took a deep, shuddering breath. But the doctor was going on. 'In Mr Grayson's case, however, I was told a doubtful story about the breaking of a wine glass. And then the housekeeper came in from the kitchen and, to Mr Grayson's very evident embarrassment, gave me an elaborate explanation concerning a slip on a polished floor which caused him to put his hand through a window. I had a strong feeling that both of them were lying, and wondered why. Anyway, dawn was breaking as I left the house. I was half-way to the gate when I heard a howling which made the hair stand up on the back of my neck.'

'Howling?' enquired Mr Palfrey. He sat with his dressing-gown sleeve rolled back over his bandaged arm, nursing his wrist in the other hand as if he was in considerable pain. 'A dog, you mean?'

'This was no dog,' said Dr McClintock. 'I looked back at the house and there, in the grey light of dawn, I saw a woman standing at the window of the room upstairs, directly above where we sit now. She was shaking the bars which guarded it and howling like an imprisoned animal. There was no doubt in my mind that it was she who had caused the injuries to old Mr

Grayson, and I could understand that he and his housekeeper were anxious to conceal the fact that they had temporarily lost control of her. Had I been at all indiscreet, the public outcry would have been considerable.'

Mr and Mrs Palfrey nodded in understanding, and Cathy, huddled miserably outside the door, shivered in dread.

'Anyway,' the doctor continued more rapidly, as if anxious to get the dreadful story finished, 'the arm turned gangrenous, and of course a man of Mr Grayson's age has little resistance. He was dead in a few weeks. His own doctor had taken over the case—to my relief, I can tell you. But the worst thing of all was yet to come. Now, Mrs Knarr had never been a sociable woman, you must understand. Possibly she was acutely conscious of a disfiguring birthmark which covered the left side of her face, but at any rate, she was reclusive. As a result, nobody thought it strange that she was not seen about following Mr Grayson's death. But one day the postman knocked at the door with a letter too broad to go through the slot, and nobody answered. He looked through the letter-box and saw that a pile of letters lay uncollected on the mat, and raised the alarm. The police broke the door down eventually, and found the house empty. Then they discovered the poor, demented creature in the upstairs room, lying dead. It seemed that she had starved to death. The housekeeper had simply packed her bags and gone, leaving the unfortunate prisoner to her fate.'

Mrs Palfrey shuddered and said, 'How appalling!'

Her husband asked, 'Was the housekeeper ever brought to justice?'

'Fate provided its own justice,' said the doctor. 'The woman bought an isolated house on the moors with the money she had acquired from Mr Grayson—not entirely legally, I may add—and lived there under an assumed name. But the place was struck by lightning one stormy night and she was burnt to death. The subsequent investigations revealed her identity.'

'And who was the unfortunate creature upstairs?' enquired Mr Palfrey. 'A member of the family, I take it?'

'She was Mr Grayson's daughter,' said the doctor. 'I think he cared for her, in his way. But as he grew old, he became completely dependent on the housekeeper. His wife, I gather, had died in childbirth—and it is not easy to find domestic staff who are willing to take on the care of a lunatic.'

Cathy burst into the room, all caution abandoned. 'You mustn't say lunatic!' she cried incoherently. Tears were streaming down her face. Lucy Claythorpe's teasing had come back to make the nightmare finally intolerable. 'It's *luna*, for the moon. Mama said so.' Sobbing overwhelmed her and she dived to her mother's knees and buried her face in her lap. A small residue of sense in the centre of her tormented mind assured her that this was the only security. Mama was utterly to be relied on.

The room was terribly silent, and Cathy knew that her parents and the doctor were looking at each other in unspoken discussion. She could feel her hair being stroked in an absent sort of way.

Dr McClintock gently raised Cathy to her feet and led her to a chair. 'Sit down, Cathy,' he said kindly, 'and don't distress yourself, my dear. Tell me, did you have a dream tonight? Can you remember anything about it?'

Cathy struggled. Fragmented visions came back to mind.

'There was a woman,' she said. 'With a big purple mark on her face.'

The doctor smiled. 'Now, if you were listening at the door, lassie, you heard me say that,' he said. 'Try again. Just cast your mind back to what really happened.'

'Bars,' said Cathy wildly. She did not know if it was memory or imagination. 'Bars across the window. Someone brought me a cup of tea.' It was all very confusing.

Dr McClintock looked at Cathy's parents. Eyebrows were raised, heads shaken. Then he turned back to Cathy and said, 'I think what you need is a long sleep, Cathy. A proper sleep with no bad dreams. From what I hear, you've had some pretty disturbed nights lately.' Cathy nodded. Tears were still trickling down her face, and her mother handed her a hanky. Cathy mopped and blew, but the tears kept coming. The doctor was pouring something from a bottle into a small glass. 'We'll have a proper talk about it tonight, when you're feeling better,' he said, 'but just now I want you to drink this.' He handed Cathy the glass and she drank obediently.

Cathy's mother carried the bowl out to the kitchen, and her father talked to Dr McClintock about things to do with money and trade which Cathy did not understand. Tears continued to well up, and it seemed too much effort to try and stop them. Her arms and legs began to feel very heavy. She hardly remembered being led back to her room.

When Cathy woke, it was late at night. Her limbs felt heavy and inert, as if they were still sleeping. How strange it was, she thought, to wake up in the dark, yet feel as if it should be morning.

The moon shone fitfully through scudding clouds. It was totally circular tonight, as perfect as a great pearl, but a wind had sprung up, and the yew trees in the garden moved their branches, casting erratic shapes across the wall of Cathy's room. There was darkness for a moment as clouds covered the moon, then it sailed clear of them, and the shadows danced again.

Cathy stared at the great white circle which hung so serenely in the dark sky. '*Luna*,' she murmured aloud, dwelling on the word. It sounded smooth and calm, like the moonlight itself. And, quite suddenly, she understood it all. For the first time, the dream experiences were clear in her mind. Horrified, she lay and thought about it. The people of her nightmare must be the ghosts of dead Mr Grayson and the terrible housekeeper, Mrs Knarr. The two of them seemed to be treating her, Cathy Palfrey, as the imprisoned madwoman. But why? Cathy stared round her room with the moving shadows of the yew trees flickering across the walls, and began to feel afraid. What if it should happen again? She tried to quell the thought, assuring herself that the fact of understanding it all made her safe. She was here, in the real world. The dream could not overwhelm her again. Or could it? She felt desperately alone and vulnerable. 'Mama!' she called loudly. 'Mama!'

She was immensely glad to hear a door opening downstairs in response. She heard her mother go to the kitchen, then, after a pause, come up stairs, stopping at the door of Cathy's room to unlock it. Hearing the key turn, Cathy was in terror that it would be the woman with the blotched face who came in, for, in real life, her door was never locked. But when the door opened it was her mother who stood there, beautiful and real, with a cup of tea in her hand. She said, as if everything was quite ordinary, 'Here is your tea.' Cathy gave a small sigh of relief.

Her mother stood the cup and saucer on the dressing-table and added, 'I'll light the gas.'

Warm and comfortable, Cathy smiled up at her mother as she reached up in a graceful movement to light the gas lamp above the bed.

'There!' said Mrs Palfrey as the light flared up. 'That's better.' She waved the match out and placed it carefully in an ash tray beside the cup and saucer on the dressing-table. Then, with her hands clasped before her, she gazed down at Cathy and said, 'Darling, for your own safety, your father and I feel that it may be wise to replace the bars across your window for a while.'

Bars. Imprisonment. Lunacy. Suddenly, the intentions of dead Mr Grayson and dead Mrs Knarr were clear. They wanted it all to happen again. They had condemned Cathy Palfrey to be imprisoned in this room. Cathy gave a gasp of terror as the taunting words rose in her mind: 'Loony, loony, living in the mad-house.' Living in the mad-house for ever.

'No,' said Cathy unsteadily. 'Mama, you mustn't. Please.'

'You might hurt yourself, darling,' her mother explained. 'Walking in your sleep, you see, you might fall out of the window.'

Cathy turned among her pillows to follow her mother's gaze as she looked with concern at the long window. The full moon was obscured by silver-edged clouds which parted as she watched, letting the cool light beam out. Then Cathy gave a scream of terror. The face reflected in the window's glass was blotched with dark shadows. It was the housekeeper. The round moon hung in the centre of the ghostly purple-marked face like a pearl, grotesquely beautiful amid such ugliness.

'No!' Cathy screamed. 'No! Go away! Leave me alone!' The figure she had thought to be her mother leaned anxiously over the bed, and the face was blotched with dark shadows as the yew trees moved in the moonlight. 'Mama!' Cathy screamed to the closed door, convinced that her mother had somehow left the room when the terrible stranger had come in. She leapt up, still screaming, and pushed the terrifying person away with all her might.

The figure staggered back, caught off balance, and clutched at the embroidered runner on the dressing-table. It slipped off and brought brushes and combs, the ash tray and the still-hot cup of tea crashing to the floor—and the figure plunged through the window and fell outwards in a shower of sparkling shards, each one reflecting a tiny, shattered fragment of the full moon.

Cathy covered her face with her hands. She could hardly breathe. Where, oh, *where* was her mother? And how had the awful Mrs Knarr come into the room? A grain of common sense told her that ghosts had no need of doors. Downstairs, the french window had opened. Cathy's father and the doctor had run out on to the lawn. Peeping through her fingers, she moved to the window and forced herself to look down.

The woman who lay on the moonlit grass moved once, in a kind of slow convulsion, then was still. The white, upturned face of Cathy's mother was still beautiful, even in death. The doctor was bending over her. He looked up at Mr Palfrey and shook his head.

Cathy's father brought his clenched fists to his chest and stood with hunched shoulders in silent agony. Then, slowly, he raised his head and stared up to where his daughter stood at the shattered window. 'Dr McClintock,' he ground out, and his voice was terrible in Cathy's ears, 'kindly go to the carpenter's house. Get the man out of bed if necessary, and bring him here. That window must be barred. At once, and for ever.'

Upstairs, standing in the moonlight, framed by the jagged remains of the glass, Cathy thought that she was crying. But, even to her own ears, it sounded like the howl of an imprisoned animal.

Ghost Hunter

SYDNEY J. BOUNDS

Ît was already dark when Peter Matson turned into St Agnes
Road looking for a house named *Rosemont*. The bright
beam from his cycle headlamp swept across tall houses,
some down at heel and others given a lick of paint and turned
into flats.

Rosemont lurked behind leafless trees, a large, rambling
building with high brick chimney stacks and gables. It appeared
to have had a lot of extensions built on to it at different times.
Peter thought it an unusual house to find in a London suburb,
like something out of 'Dracula'.

A single light gleamed from a downstairs window as he
swung into the short drive. He saw a wooden porch and a large
black door and, carved into the stonework above, a date: 1882.

Peter dismounted and leaned his cycle against the porch. His
legs ached and a chill wind from the dark trees froze the sweat

on his body. It had been a long ride and his saddle-bags were weighted down with all his equipment.

He used the old brass knocker to announce his arrival. Footsteps echoed inside and the door opened.

Peter faced a tubby man in a tweed suit; his hair was a fringe of grey about an egg-bald head, and he looked worried.

'Mr Swann? I'm Peter Matson. Sorry I'm a bit late, but the ride took longer than I expected.'

'Better late than never. Come on in.' Swann glanced at his watch as Peter wheeled his bike inside. 'I'll have to leave almost immediately—my wife's waiting for me.'

Marble-blue eyes looked with curiosity at Peter's lanky frame, his studious expression and thick-lensed glasses. In windcheater and jeans he looked no more than sixteen.

'You'll be all right here, alone?'

Peter smiled as he shut the door. 'I'm not afraid, if that's what you mean.'

'No, I suppose not—or you wouldn't be a member of a ghost hunting agency. I'd thought of exorcism, of course, but we don't want that kind of publicity. We hope you'll be discreet.'

'Of course. We don't want publicity either.'

It was cold in the hall and dust had gathered in the corners.

'This place is a bit of a maze,' Swann said, leading the way. 'I've just time to show you around.'

A passage branched off to the right, turned left into a large bare room and continued again as a corridor. Swann switched on lights as he went.

'Here's the kitchen. Make tea or coffee if you like.'

Swann retraced his steps to the entrance hall. 'All the doors and windows are locked. There's a cellar downstairs—that's the boiler room.'

They went up the wide, sweeping staircase. At the top was an open door leading to other rooms, and a passageway branching away to the left.

'You can walk right round on this floor,' the estate agent said. 'All the rooms are connected.'

Peter tried to form a mental map of the building, but the place really did seem a maze. He followed Swann along a passage that went up a short flight of stairs and down again, through an L-shaped room that ended in another corridor.

Finally they arrived at the end of a branch passage and the bottom of a steep flight of stairs that angled off to the right.

Swann paused. 'I don't believe it myself, but I'm told that some people see things about here.'

Peter looked up the bare wooden staircase as Swann switched on a dim light. 'What's up there?'

'Just attics. I suppose they were servants' quarters. Junk rooms.' Swann's tone of voice changed. 'I hope you can clear up this business. I can't get clients interested at all—the place has a bad name. Something so scared the previous tenants that they moved out.'

'I'm glad of the chance to investigate a haunting,' Peter said earnestly.

'So you do believe in ghosts?'

'I try to keep an open mind. Strange things happen . . . but ghosts, meaning spirits of the dead . . . ?' Peter shrugged. 'We're still looking for the evidence.'

His voice dropped to a murmur, as if he were speaking more to himself than to Swann. 'If ghosts are the spirits of the dead, how do they feel about the after-life? What does it feel like to be a ghost? Can a ghost feel anything at all?'

Swann wasn't interested. 'I've got to run. Just make yourself at home.'

'I'm curious,' Peter said quickly. 'Is there a story behind this haunting?'

'Nothing much. The whole thing's a mystery. A young girl committed suicide here, so they say. Nobody really knows.'

Peter followed him downstairs and the estate agent gave him a spare key. He made sure the front door was locked. Alone in the old house, he went round checking doors and windows. He sealed thread across them and left the passage lights on.

Then he unpacked his saddle-bags and assembled his ghost hunting equipment, setting up tape recorders and automatic cameras. He slipped a torch into his pocket.

He returned to the kitchen and made himself coffee. Relaxed in a chair, he sipped slowly and listened to the sounds of the house: the creaking of timbers and crack of water pipes, the rattle of a window.

Suddenly he sat up straight in his chair, sniffing the air. He put down his mug and stepped into the passage. No, he hadn't imagined it; he could smell a woman's perfume above the aroma of coffee. In the passage it appeared stronger. There was nothing subtle about it, just a reek of cheap scent.

Peter moved along the corridor, opening doors to make sure that each room was empty. He ended back in the main hallway. Here the perfume was almost overpowering, saturating the air.

He stared up the wide, curving staircase; in the bend he thought he detected something grey, some slight suggestion of movement. But he wasn't sure.

As he placed a foot on the lower step, the perfume vanished. His ears caught a soft laugh, so soft he couldn't be certain he hadn't imagined it.

Then there was nothing; no perfume, no hint of movement, no laughter. He froze for a long moment, then darted quickly up the stairs and searched each room. He found no one.

Peter hummed a happy tune. He was sure now that he wasn't wasting his time.

When Swann opened the door the next evening, he asked: 'Any luck?'

'Oh yes, we've got something here.'

The estate agent brightened at once. 'Then you'll be able to do something about it?'

'It depends,' Peter said cautiously. 'I can't guarantee anything.'

'It's like this,' Swann confided. 'I've got Head Office breathing down my neck. They're not interested in excuses, only sales. If I can't sell this place soon, it's going to count against me.'

'Stick it out,' Peter advised. 'A haunting of this kind doesn't usually last long.'

After Swann left, Peter arranged his tape recorders and cameras at the top and bottom of the main staircase. He filled a thermos flask with coffee and moved a chair into the hall, placing himself where he could watch the bend in the stairs.

The hours passed slowly before the soft laugh was repeated. Peter came alert immediately. He rose from his chair and padded to the foot of the stairs. The provocative sound came again from somewhere above, and he heard the tap-tap of high-heeled shoes going up.

And still he saw no one. The skin tightened on his scalp, lifting his hair, as the tapping sounds receded.

Peter found he had to take a grip on his nerves before he could go up but, finally, he forced himself to climb to the top of the stairs.

He looked down the branch passage to the left and, at the far end, glimpsed a wraithlike figure. It was an image of a girl of about seventeen or eighteen, and translucent—or so it seemed, because he could see the wall behind her. He hurried forward, and the image vanished as if a veil had dropped between them.

Peter studied the walls closely, rapping here and there. Solid. He inspected the adjoining rooms and found no sign of trickery. He went back downstairs and re-ran his tapes; the laughter and sound of high heels were there, faint but definitely recorded.

The following evening was a Friday, and Swann was going away for the weekend. Peter played the tapes for him and said: 'I've developed my film and there's nothing on it. But this sort of freak happening is not unusual.'

The estate agent regarded him with a curious expression. 'You do realize you'll be quite alone here till Monday morning? Are you sure you'll be all right?'

Peter nodded. 'I'm not worried. Perhaps, with peace and quiet for forty-eight hours, our ghost will reveal herself.'

Swann shrugged and left rather hurriedly.

Peter patrolled the building before taking up his post on the first floor, at the point where the ghost had vanished. But if he had expected any quick revelation he was disappointed. *Rosemont* cooled and creaked as he nodded in his chair.

He came to, startled, as a feminine voice purred in his ear. 'Soon . . . soon, now . . .'

He was cold, and his legs were stiff as broomsticks. He glimpsed the ghost-girl, distant, along the passage to the right. He rose and moved towards her. The image lingered as if waiting for him, then retreated, high heels tap-tapping, to the foot of the staircase leading to the attics. She seemed more solid than the previous night.

She went up the flight of steep narrow stairs, reached the top and paused to look down at him. As Peter started up after her, she disappeared.

He went up, holding tight to the banister rail. Moonlight, filtering through dusty windows, gave a pale glow that threw grey shadows. He had little doubt that she had deliberately led him up here, and wondered why. He made a quick search of the attics but discovered nothing out of the ordinary.

He spent most of Saturday searching the attics thoroughly. He carried his cameras and tape recorders to the top floor, tested and placed them carefully. He had the old house entirely to himself.

There were three small rooms with bare walls and floorboards thick with dust. The room furthest from the stairs still had some junk in it: broken furniture, ancient newspapers, a cracked mirror on the wall.

If the ghost had lured him to this topmost floor for some revelation, she had nowhere left to go.

Peter wrote a report for his agency and went out for a meal. He left it late before returning because, on the previous night, nothing much had happened before midnight. He let himself in and stood listening to the house. Then he went upstairs, switching on passage lights as he went.

He paused at the foot of the narrow stairs leading to the attics. Should he wait at the bottom? Or go straight up? He mentally tossed a coin, decided to play the game her way and allow her to lure him up the stairs.

He moved a chair into position and settled down for his vigil. This time he did not have long to wait for her; perhaps she, too, was eager for the final confrontation.

Her crude perfume came first, alerting him. Then the old house became silent; the hush had a peculiar deadness to it, as if any sound were no longer possible.

As he stared up the shadowed stairway she appeared at the top, smiling down at him. It was a smile of invitation. She seemed as real as any flesh-and-blood girl, and his pulse beat faster.

As he went carefully up the stairs, Peter told himself she was not real. The old treads were narrow and made no sound. She waited for him in silent stillness, allowing him to approach.

She was young, with an air of glamour, and her heavy scent acted like a drug.

When he reached the top, she backed away along the short passage to the last room of all. The moonlight was strong and bright, and she cast no shadow. Yet he saw her as plainly as any living girl.

She backed up against the far wall of the tiny room until she could go no further. Peter stood in the doorway and there were only yards between them.

The mirror showed only Peter's reflection. His breath made no sound.

Her eyes were dark pits in the pale oval of her face, and her gaze was riveted on him, compelling, almost hypnotic. He felt strangely reluctant to move as she left the wall and glided towards him.

She came closer, closer, till it seemed he sensed hot breath on his face. She wrapped her arms about him, and he felt the pressure of her embrace. Her hands pressed against his back, and he was engulfed in a cloud of sultry perfume.

take the place of the grudgingly sanctioned weekly interview—
because a certain rich uncle was visiting at her house, and her
mother was not the woman to acknowledge to a moneyed uncle,
who might 'go off' any day, a match so deeply ineligible as hers
with him.

So he waited for her, and the chill of an unusually severe May
evening entered into his bones.

The policeman passed him with but a surly response to his
'Goodnight'. The bicyclists went by him like grey ghosts with
fog-horns; and it was nearly ten o'clock, and she had not come.

He shrugged his shoulders and turned towards his lodgings.
His road led him by her house—desirable, commodious, semi-
detached—and he walked slowly as he neared it. She might,
even now, be coming out. But she was not. There was no sign of
movement about the house, no sign of life, no lights even in the
windows. And her people were not early people.

He paused by the gate, wondering.

Then he noticed that the front door was open—wide open—
and the street lamp shone a little way into the dark hall. There
was something about all this that did not please him—that
scared him a little, indeed. The house had a gloomy and deserted
air. It was obviously impossible that it harboured a rich uncle.
The old man must have left early. In which case—

He walked up the path of patent-glazed tiles, and listened. No
sign of life. He passed into the hall. There was no light anywhere.
Where was everybody, and why was the front door open? There
was no one in the drawing-room; the dining-room and the
study (nine feet by seven) were equally blank. Every one was
out, evidently. But the unpleasant sense that he was, perhaps,
not the first casual visitor to walk through that open door
impelled him to look through the house before he went away and
closed it after him. So he went upstairs, and at the door of the
first bedroom he came to he struck a wax match, as he had done
in the sitting-rooms. Even as he did so he felt that he was not
alone. And he was prepared to see *something*; but for what he
saw he was not prepared. For what he saw lay on the bed, in a
white loose gown—and it was his sweetheart, and its throat was
cut from ear to ear.

He doesn't know what happened then, nor how he got
downstairs and into the street; but he got out somehow, and the

policeman found him in a fit, under the lamp-post at the corner of the street. He couldn't speak when they picked him up, and he passed the night in the police-cells, because the policeman had seen plenty of drunken men before, but never one in a fit.

The next morning he was better, though still very white and shaky. But the tale he told the magistrate was convincing, and they sent a couple of constables with him to her house.

There was no crowd about it as he had fancied there would be, and the blinds were not down.

As he stood, dazed, in front of the door, it opened, and she came out.

He held on to the door-post for support.

'*She*'s all right, you see,' said the constable who had found him under the lamp. 'I told you you was drunk, but you *would* know best—'

When he was alone with her he told her—not all—for that would not bear telling—but how he had come into the commodious semi-detached, and how he had found the door open and the lights out, and that he had been into that long back room facing the stairs, and had seen something—in even trying to hint at which he turned sick and broke down and had to have brandy given him.

'But, my dearest,' she said, 'I dare say the house was dark, for we were all at the Crystal Palace with my uncle, and no doubt the door was open, for the maids *will* run out if they're left. But you could not have been in that room, because I locked it when I came away, and the key was in my pocket. I dressed in a hurry and I left all my odds and ends lying about.'

'I know,' he said; 'I saw a green scarf on a chair, and some long brown gloves, and lot of hairpins and ribbons, and a prayer book, and a lace handkerchief on the dressing-table. Why, I even noticed the almanac on the mantelpiece—October 21. At least it couldn't be that, because this is May. And yet it was. Your almanac is at October 21, isn't it?'

'No, of course it isn't,' she said, smiling rather anxiously; 'but all the other things were just as you say. You must have had a dream, or a vision, or something.'

He was a very ordinary, commonplace, City young man, and he didn't believe in visions, but he never rested day or night till he got his sweetheart and her mother away from that commodious semi-detached, and settled them in a quite distant suburb. In the course of the removal he incidentally married her, and the mother went on living with them.

His nerves must have been a good bit shaken, because he was very queer for a long time, and was always enquiring if any one had taken the desirable semi-detached; and when an old stockbroker with a family took it, he went to the length of calling on the old gentleman and imploring him by all that he held dear, not to live in that fatal house.

'Why?' said the stockbroker, not unnaturally.

And then he got so vague and confused, between trying to tell why and trying not to tell why, that the stockbroker showed him out, and thanked his God he was not such a fool as to allow a lunatic to stand in the way of his taking that really remarkably cheap and desirable semi-detached residence.

Now the curious and quite inexplicable part of this story is that when his wife came down to breakfast on the morning of the 22nd of October she found him looking like death, with the morning paper in his hand. He caught hers—he couldn't speak, and pointed to the paper. And there she read that on the night of the 21st a young lady, the stockbroker's daughter, had been found, with her throat cut from ear to ear, on the bed in the long back bedroom facing the stairs of that desirable semi-detached.

A Face in the Night

RUSKIN BOND

It may give you some idea of rural humour if I begin this tale with an anecdote that concerns me. I was walking alone through a village at night when I met an old man carrying a lantern. I found, to my surprise, that the man was blind. 'Old man,' I asked, 'if you cannot see, why do you carry a lantern?'

'I carry this,' he replied, 'so that fools do not stumble against me in the dark.'

This incident has only a slight connection with the story that follows, but I think it provides the right sort of tone and setting. Mr Oliver, an Anglo-Indian teacher, was returning to his school late one night, on the outskirts of the hill station of Simla. The school was conducted on English public school lines and the boys, most of them from well-to-do Indian families, wore blazers, caps, and ties. *Life* magazine, in a feature on India, had once called this school the 'Eton of the East'. Mr Oliver had been teaching in the school for several years. (He is no longer there.) The Simla bazaar, with its cinemas and restaurants, was about two miles from the school; and Mr Oliver, a bachelor, usually strolled into the town in the evening, returning after dark, when he would take a short cut through a pine forest.

When there was a strong wind, the pine trees made sad, eerie sounds that kept most people to the main road. But Mr Oliver was not a nervous or imaginative man. He carried a torch and, on the night I write of, its pale gleam—the batteries were running down—moved fitfully over the narrow forest path. When its flickering light fell on the figure of a boy, who was sitting alone on a rock, Mr Oliver stopped. Boys were not supposed to be out of school after 7 p.m., and it was now well past nine.

'What are you doing out here, boy?' asked Mr Oliver sharply, moving closer so that he could recognize the miscreant. But even as he approached the boy, Mr Oliver sensed that something was wrong. The boy appeared to be crying. His head hung down, he held his face in his hands, and his body shook convulsively. It was a strange, soundless weeping, and Mr Oliver felt distinctly uneasy.

'Well—what's the matter?' he asked, his anger giving way to concern. 'What are you crying for?' The boy would not answer or look up. His body continued to be racked with silent sobbing.

'Come on, boy, you shouldn't be out here at this hour. Tell me the trouble. Look up!'

The boy looked up. He took his hands from his face and looked up at his teacher. The light from Mr Oliver's torch fell on the boy's face—if you could call it a face.

He had no eyes, ears, nose, or mouth. It was just a round smooth head—with a school cap on top of it. And that's where the story should end—as indeed it has for several people who have had similar experiences and dropped dead of inexplicable heart attacks. But for Mr Oliver it did not end there.

The torch fell from his trembling hand. He turned and scrambled down the path, running blindly through the trees and calling for help. He was still running towards the school buildings when he saw a lantern swinging in the middle of the path. Mr Oliver had never before been so pleased to see the night-watchman. He stumbled up to the watchman, gasping for breath and speaking incoherently.

'What is it, *Sahib*?' asked the watchman. 'Has there been an accident? Why are you running?'

'I saw something—something horrible—a boy weeping in the forest—and he had no face!'

'No face, *Sahib*?'

'No eyes, nose, mouth—nothing.'

'Do you mean it was like this, *Sahib*?' asked the watchman, and raised the lamp to his own face. The watchman had no eyes, no ears, no features at all—not even an eyebrow!

The wind blew the lamp out, and Mr Oliver had his heart attack.

Such a Sweet Little Girl

LANCE SALWAY

It was at breakfast on a bright Saturday morning that Julie first made her announcement. She put down her spoon, swallowed a last mouthful of cornflakes and said, 'There's a ghost in my bedroom.'

No one took any notice. Her mother was writing a shopping list, and her father was deep in his newspaper. Neither of them heard what she said. Her brother Edward heard but he ignored her, which is what he usually did. Edward liked to pretend that Julie didn't exist. It wasn't easy, but he did his best.

Julie tried again. She raised her voice and said, 'There's a ghost in my bedroom.'

Mrs Bennett looked up from her list. 'Is there, dear? Oh, good. Do you think we need more marmalade? And I suppose I'd better buy a cake or something if your friends are coming to tea.'

Edward said sharply, 'Friends? What friends?'

'Sally and Rachel are coming to tea with Julie this afternoon,' his mother said.

Edward gave a loud theatrical groan. 'Oh, no. Why does she have to fill the house with her rotten friends?'

'You could fill the house with *your* friends, too,' Julie said sweetly. 'If you had any.'

Edward looked at her with loathing. 'Oh, I've got friends all right,' he said. 'I just don't inflict them on other people.'

'You haven't got any friends,' Julie said quietly. 'You haven't got any friends because no one likes you.'

'That's enough,' Mr Bennett said, looking up from his paper. There was silence then, broken only by the gentle rumble-slush, rumble-slush of the washing machine in the corner.

Edward chewed a piece of toast and thought how much he hated Julie. He hated a lot of people. Most people, in fact. But there were some he hated more than others. Mr Jenkins, who taught Maths. And that woman in the paper shop who'd accused him of stealing chewing gum, when everyone knew he never touched the stuff. And Julie. He hated Julie most of all.

He hated her pretty pale face, and her pretty fair curls, and her pretty little lisping voice. He hated the grown-ups who constantly fluttered round her, saying how enchanting she was, and so clever for her age, and wasn't Mrs Bennett lucky to have such a sweet little girl. What they didn't say, but he knew they were thinking behind their wide, bright smiles, was: poor Mrs Bennett with that lumpy sullen boy. So different from his sister. So different from lovely little Julie.

Lovely little Julie flung her spoon on the table. 'I *said* there's a ghost in my bedroom.'

Mrs Bennett put down her shopping list and ballpoint in order to give Julie her full attention. 'Oh dear,' she said. 'I do hope it didn't frighten you, darling.'

Julie smiled and preened. 'No,' she said smugly. '*I* wasn't frightened.'

Edward tried to shut his ears. He knew this dialogue by heart. The Bennett family spent a great deal of time adjusting their habits to suit Julie's fantasies. Once, for a whole month, they had all been forced to jump the bottom tread of the staircase because Julie insisted that two invisible rabbits were sleeping there. For a time she had been convinced, or so she said, that a pink dragon lived in the airing cupboard. And there had been a terrible few weeks the year before when all communication with her had to be conducted through an invisible fairy called Priscilla who lived on her left shoulder.

And now there was a ghost in her bedroom.

Try as he might, Edward couldn't shut out his sister's voice. On and on it whined: '. . . I was really very brave and didn't run away even though it was so frightening, and I said . . .'

Edward looked at his parents with contempt. His father had put down the newspaper and was gazing at Julie with a soppy smile on his face. His mother was wearing the mock-serious expression that adults often adopt in order to humour their young. Edward hated them for it. If he'd told them a story about a ghost when *he* was seven, they'd have told him to stop being so silly, there's no such thing as ghosts, why don't you grow up, be a man.

'What sort of ghost is it?' he asked suddenly.

Julie looked at him in surprise. Then her eyes narrowed. 'It's a frightening ghost,' she said, 'with great big eyes and teeth and horrible, nasty claws. Big claws. And it smells.'

'Ghosts aren't like that,' Edward said scornfully. 'Ghosts have clanking chains and skeletons, and they carry their heads under their arms.'

'This ghost doesn't,' Julie snapped.

'Funny sort of ghost, then.'

'You don't know anything about it.'

Julie's voice was beginning to tremble. Edward sighed. There'd be tears soon and he'd get the blame. As usual.

'Come now, Edward,' his father said heartily. 'It's only pretend. Isn't it, lovey?'

Lovey shot him a vicious glance. 'It's *not* pretend. It's a real ghost. And it's in my bedroom.'

'Of course, darling.' Mrs Bennett picked up her shopping list again. 'How are we off for chutney, I wonder?'

But Edward wasn't going to let the matter drop. Not this time. 'Anyway,' he said, 'ghosts don't have claws.'

'This one does,' Julie said.

'Then you're lying.'

'I'm not. There *is* a ghost. I saw it.'

'Liar.'

'I'm not!' She was screaming now. 'I'll show you I'm not. I'll tell it to *get* you. With its claws. It'll come and get you with its claws.'

'Don't make me laugh.'

'*Edward!* That's *enough!*' His mother stood up and started to clear the table. 'Don't argue.'

'But there isn't a ghost,' Edward protested. 'There can't be!'

Mrs Bennett glanced uneasily at Julie. 'Of course there is,' she said primly. 'If Julie says so.'

'She's a liar, a nasty little liar.'

Julie kicked him hard under the table. Edward yelped, and kicked back. Julie let out a screech, and then her face crumpled and she began to wail.

'*Now* look what you've done,' Mrs Bennett snapped. 'Oh *really*, Edward. You're twice her age. Why can't you leave her alone?'

'Because she's a liar, that's why.' Edward stood up and pushed his chair aside. 'Because there isn't a ghost in her bedroom. And even if there is, it won't have claws.' And he turned, and stormed out of the kitchen.

He came to a stop in the sitting-room, and crossed over to the window to see what sort of day it was going to be. Sunny, by the look of it. A small tightly cropped lawn lay in front of the house, a lawn that was identical in size and appearance to those in front of the other identical square brick houses which lined the road. Edward laughed out loud. Any ghost worthy of the name would wither away from boredom in such surroundings. No, there weren't any ghosts in Briarfield Gardens; with or without heads under their arms; with or without claws.

He turned away from the window. The day had started badly, thanks to Julie. And it would continue badly, thanks to Julie and her rotten friends who were coming to tea. And there was nothing he could do about it. Or was there? On the coffee table by the television set there lay a half-finished jigsaw puzzle. Julie had been working on it for ages, her fair curls bent earnestly over the table day after day. According to the picture on the box, the finished puzzle would reveal a thatched cottage surrounded by a flower-filled garden. When it was finished. If . . .

Edward walked across to the table and smashed the puzzle with one quick, practised movement of his hand. Pieces fell and flew and scattered on the carpet in a storm of coloured card-board. And then he turned and ran upstairs to his room.

He hadn't long to wait. After a few minutes he heard the sounds that he was expecting. The kitchen door opening. A pause. Then a shrill, furious shriek, followed by loud sobbing. Running footsteps. A quieter comforting voice. Angry footsteps on the stairs. The rattling of the handle on his locked bedroom door. And then Julie's voice, not like a seven-year-old voice at all any more, but harsh and bitter with hate.

'The ghost'll get you, Edward. I'm going to tell it to get you. With its claws. With its horrible, sharp claws.'

And then, quite suddenly, Edward felt afraid.

The fear didn't last long. It had certainly gone by lunchtime, when Edward was given a ticking-off by his father for upsetting dear little Julie. And by the time Julie's friends arrived at four, he was quite his old self again.

'The ugly sisters are here!' he announced loudly as he opened the front door, having beaten Julie to it by a short head.

She glared at him, and quickly hustled Sally and Rachel up the stairs to her room.

Edward felt a bit guilty. Sally and Rachel weren't at all ugly. In fact, he quite liked them both. He ambled into the kitchen, where his mother was busy preparing tea.

She looked up when he came in. 'I do hope you're going to behave yourself this evening,' she said. 'We don't want a repetition of this morning's little episode, do we?'

'Well, she asked for it,' Edward said sullenly, and sneaked a biscuit from a pile on a plate.

'Hands off!' his mother said automatically. 'Julie did *not* ask for it. She was only pretending. You know what she's like. There was no need for you to be so nasty. And there was certainly no excuse for you to break up her jigsaw puzzle like that.'

Edward shuffled uneasily and stared at the floor.

'She *is* only seven, after all,' Mrs Bennett went on, slapping chocolate icing on a sponge cake as she did so. 'You must make allowances. The rest of us do.'

'She gets away with murder,' Edward mumbled. 'Just because she's such a sweet little girl.'

'Nonsense!' his mother said firmly. 'And keep your mucky paws off those ginger snaps. If anyone gets away with murder in this house, it's you.'

'But she can't really expect us to believe there's a ghost in her bedroom,' Edward said. 'Do *you* believe her? Come on, mum, do you?'

'I . . .' his mother began, and then she was interrupted by a familiar lisping voice.

'You *do* believe me, mummy, don't you?'

Julie was standing at the kitchen door. Edward wondered how long she'd been there. And how much she'd heard.

'Of course I do, darling,' Mrs Bennett said quickly. 'Now run along, both of you. Or I'll never have tea ready in time.'

Julie stared at Edward for a moment with her cold blue eyes, and then she went out of the kitchen as quietly as she'd entered it.

Tea passed off smoothly enough. Julie seemed to be on her best behaviour, but that was probably because her friends were there and she wanted to create a good impression. Edward followed her example. Julie didn't look at him or speak to him, but there was nothing unusual about that. She and the others chattered brightly about nothing in particular, and Edward said nothing at all.

It was dusk by the time they'd finished tea, and it was then that Julie suggested that they all play ghosts. She looked straight at Edward when she said this, and the proposal seemed like a challenge.

'Can anyone play?' he asked. 'Or is it just a game for horrible little girls?'

'Edward!' warned his mother.

'Of course you can play, Edward,' said Julie. 'You *must* play.'

'But not in the kitchen or the dining-room,' said Mrs Bennett. 'And keep out of our bedroom. I'll go and draw all the curtains and make sure the lights are switched off.'

'All right,' said Julie, and the other little girls clapped their hands with excitement.

'How do we play this stupid game?' asked Edward.

'Oh, it's easy,' said Julie. 'One of us is the ghost, and she has to frighten the others. If the ghost catches you and scares you, you have to scream and drop down on the floor. As if you were dead.'

'Like "Murder in the Dark"?' asked Sally.

'Yes,' said Julie. 'Only we don't have a detective or anything like that.'

'It sounds a crummy game to me,' said Edward. 'I don't think I'll play.'

'Oh, *do*!' chorused Sally and Rachel. 'Please!'

And Julie came up to him and whispered, 'You *must* play, Edward. And don't forget what I said this morning; about my ghost, and how it's going to get you with its claws!'

'You must be joking!' Edward jeered. 'And anyway, I told you. Ghosts don't have claws.' He looked her straight in the eyes. 'Of course I'll play.'

Julie smiled, and then turned to the others and said, 'I'll be the ghost to start with. The rest of you run and hide. I'll count up to fifty and then I'll come and haunt you.'

Sally and Rachel galloped upstairs, squealing with excitement. Edward wandered into the hall, and stood for a moment wondering where to hide. It wasn't going to be easy. Their small brick box of a house didn't offer many possibilities. After a while he decided on the sitting-room. It was the most obvious place, and Julie would never think of looking there. He opened the door quietly, ducked down behind an armchair, and waited.

Silence settled over the house. Apart from washing-up sounds from the kitchen, all was quiet. Edward made himself comfortable on the carpet, and waited for the distant screams that would tell him that Sally had been discovered, or Rachel. But no sounds came. As he waited, ears straining against the silence, the room grew darker. The day was fading and it would soon be night.

And then, suddenly, Edward heard a slight noise near the door. His heart leaped and, for some reason, his mouth went dry. And then the fear returned, the unaccountable fear he had felt that morning when Julie hissed her threat through his bedroom door.

The air seemed much colder now, but that could only be his imagination, surely. But he knew that he wasn't imagining the wild thumping of his heart, or the sickening lurching of his stomach. He remembered Julie's words and swallowed hard.

'The ghost'll get you, Edward. With its claws. With its sharp, horrible claws.'

He heard sounds again, closer this time. A scuffle. Whispering. Or was it whispering? Someone was there. Something. He tried to speak, but gave only a curious croak. 'Julie?' he said. 'I know you're there. I know it's you.'

Silence. A dark terrible silence. And then the light snapped on and the room was filled with laughter and shouts of, 'Got you! Caught you! The ghost has caught you!' He saw Julie's face alive with triumph and delight, and, behind her, Sally and Rachel grinning, and the fear was replaced by an anger far darker and more intense than the terror he'd felt before.

'Edward's scared of the ghost!' Julie jeered. 'Edward's a scaredy cat! He's frightened! He's frightened of the gho-ost!'

'I'm not!' Edward shouted. 'I'm not scared! There isn't a ghost!' He pushed past Julie and ran out of the room and up the stairs. He'd show her. He'd prove she didn't have a ghost. There were no such things as ghosts. She didn't have a ghost in her room. She didn't.

Julie's bedroom was empty. Apart from the furniture and the pictures and the toys and dolls and knick-knacks. He opened the wardrobe and pulled shoes and games out on to the floor. He burrowed in drawers, scattering books and stuffed animals and clothes around him. At last he stopped, gasping for breath. And turned.

His mother was standing in the doorway, staring at him in amazement. Clustered behind her were the puzzled, anxious faces of Sally and Rachel. And behind them, Julie, looking at him with her ice-blue eyes.

'What on earth are you doing?' his mother asked.

'See?' he panted. 'There isn't a ghost here. She hasn't got a ghost in her bedroom. There's nothing here. Nothing.'

'Isn't there?' said Julie. 'Are you sure you've looked properly?'

Sally—or was it Rachel?—gave a nervous giggle.

'That's enough,' said Mrs Bennett. 'Now I suggest you tidy up the mess you've made in here, Edward, and then go to your room. I don't know why you're behaving so strangely. But it's got to stop. It's got to.'

She turned and went downstairs. Sally and Rachel followed her. Julie lingered by the door and stared mockingly at Edward. He stared back.

'It's still here, you know,' she said at last. 'The ghost is still here. And it'll get you.'

'You're a dirty little liar!' he shouted. 'A nasty, filthy little liar!'

Julie gaped at him for a moment, taken aback by the force of his rage. Then, 'It'll get you!' she screamed. 'With its claws. Its

horrible claws. It'll get you tonight. When you're asleep. Because I hate you. I hate you. Yes, it'll *really* get you. Tonight.'

It was dark when Edward awoke. At first he didn't know where he was. And then he remembered. He was in bed. In his bedroom. It was the middle of the night. And he remembered, too, Julie's twisted face and the things she said. The face and the words had kept him awake, and had haunted his dreams when at last he slept.

It was ridiculous, really. All this fuss about an imaginary ghost. Why did he get in such a state over Julie? She was only a little kid after all. His baby sister. You were supposed to love your sister—not fear her. But no, he wasn't *really* afraid of her. How could he be? Such a sweet little girl with blue eyes and fair bouncing curls who was half his age. A little girl who played games and imagined things. Who imagined ghosts. A ghost in her bedroom.

But he *was* frightened. He knew that now. And as his fear mounted again, the room seemed to get colder. He shut his eyes and snuggled down under the blankets, shutting out the room and the cold. But not the fear.

And then he heard it. A sound. A faint, scraping sound, as though something heavy was being dragged along the landing. A sound that came closer and grew louder. A wet, slithering sound. And with it came a smell, a sickening smell of drains and dead leaves and decay. And the sound grew louder and he could hear breathing, harsh breathing, long choking breaths coming closer.

'Julie?' Edward said, and then he repeated it louder. 'Julie!'

But there was no answer. All he heard was the scraping, dragging sound coming closer, closer. Near his door now. Closer.

'I know it's you!' Edward shouted, and he heard the fear in his own voice. 'You're playing ghosts again, aren't you? Aren't you?'

And then there was silence. No sound at all. Edward sat up in bed and listened. The awful slithering noise had stopped. It had gone. The ghost had gone.

He hugged himself with relief. It had been a dream, that's all. He'd imagined it. Just as Julie imagined things. Imagined ghosts.

Then he heard the breathing again. The shuddering, choking breaths. And he knew that the thing hadn't gone. That it was still there. Outside his door. Waiting. Waiting.

And Edward screamed, 'Julie! Stop it! Stop it! Please stop it! I believe you! I believe in the ghost!'

The door opened. The shuddering breaths seemed to fill the room, and the smell, and the slithering wet sound of a shape. Something was coming towards him, something huge and dark and . . .

He screamed as the claws, yes, the claws tore at his hands, his chest, his face. And he screamed again as the darkness folded over him.

When Julie woke up and came downstairs the ambulance had gone. Her mother was sitting alone in the kitchen, looking pale and frightened. She smiled weakly when she saw Julie, and then frowned.

'Darling,' she said. 'I did so hope you wouldn't wake up. I didn't want you to be frightened . . .'

'What's the matter, mummy?' asked Julie. 'Why are you crying?'

Her mother smiled again, and drew Julie to her, folding her arms around her so that she was warm and safe. 'You must be very brave, darling,' she said. 'Poor Edward has been hurt. We don't know what happened but he's been very badly hurt.'

'Hurt? What do you mean, mummy?'

Her mother brushed a stray curl from the little girl's face. 'We don't know what happened, exactly. Something attacked him. His face . . .' Her voice broke then, and she looked away quickly. 'He has been very badly scratched. They're not sure if his eyes . . .' She stopped and fumbled in her dressing-gown pocket for a tissue.

'I expect my ghost did it,' Julie said smugly.

'What did you say, dear?'

Julie looked up at her mother. 'My ghost did it. I told it to. I told it to hurt Edward because I hate him. The ghost hurt him. The ghost in my bedroom.'

Mrs Bennett stared at Julie. 'This is no time for games,' she said. 'We're very upset. Your father's gone to the hospital with Edward. We don't know if . . .' Her eyes filled with tears. 'I'm in no mood for your silly stories about ghosts, Julie. Not now. I'm too upset.'

'But it's true,' Julie said. 'My ghost *did* do it. Because I told it to.'

Mrs Bennett pushed her away and stood up. 'All right, Julie, that's enough. Back to bed now. You can play your games tomorrow.'

'But it's not a game,' Julie persisted. 'It's true! My ghost . . .'

And then she saw the angry expression on her mother's face, and she stopped. Instead, she snuggled up to her and whispered, 'I'm sorry, mummy. You're right. I *was* pretending. I was only pretending about the ghost. There isn't a ghost in my room. I was making it all up. And I'm so sorry about poor Edward.'

Mrs Bennett relaxed and smiled and drew Julie to her once again. 'That's my baby,' she said softly. 'That's my sweet little girl. Of course you were only pretending. Of course there wasn't a ghost. Would I let a nasty ghost come and frighten my little girl? Would I? Would I?'

'No, mummy,' said Julie. 'Of course you wouldn't.'

'Off you go to bed now.'

'Good night, mummy,' said Julie.

'Sleep well, my pet,' said her mother.

And Julie walked out of the kitchen and into the hall and up the stairs to her bedroom. She went inside, and closed the door behind her.

And the ghost came out to meet her.

'She doesn't believe me, either,' Julie said. 'We'll have to show her, won't we? Just as we showed Edward.'

And the ghost smiled, and nodded. And they sat down together, Julie and the ghost, and decided what they would do.

Mr Lupescu

ANTHONY BOUCHER

T he teacups rattled, and flames flickered over the logs.
'Alan, I *do* wish you could do something about
Bobby.'

'Isn't that rather Robert's place?'

'Oh, you know *Robert*. He's so busy doing good in nice
abstract ways with committees in them.'

'And headlines.'

'He can't be bothered with things like Mr Lupescu. After all,
Bobby's only his *son*.'

'And yours, Marjorie.'

'And mine. But things like this take a *man*, Alan.'

The room was warm and peaceful; Alan stretched his long
legs by the fire and felt domestic. Marjorie was soothing even
when she fretted. The firelight did things to her hair and the
curve of her blouse.

A small whirlwind entered at high velocity and stopped only when Marjorie said, 'Bob-*by*! Say hello nicely to Uncle Alan.'

Bobby said hello and stood tentatively on one foot.

'Alan . . .' Marjorie prompted.

Alan sat up straight and tried to look paternal. 'Well, Bobby,' he said. 'And where are you off to in such a hurry?'

'See Mr Lupescu 'f course. He usually comes afternoons.'

'Your mother's been telling me about Mr Lupescu. He must be quite a person.'

'Oh gee, I'll say he is, Uncle Alan. He's got a great big red nose and red gloves and red eyes—not like when you've been crying but really red like yours're brown—and little red wings that twitch only he can't fly with them cause they're rudder-mentary he says. And he talks like—oh gee, I can't do it, but he's swell, he is.'

'Lupescu's a funny name for a fairy godfather, isn't it, Bobby?'

'Why? Mr Lupescu always says why do all the fairies have to be Irish because it takes all kinds, doesn't it?'

'*Alan!*' Marjorie said. 'I don't see that you're doing a *bit* of good. You talk to him seriously like that and you simply make him think it *is* serious. And you *do* know better, don't you, Bobby? You're just joking with us.'

'Joking? About *Mr Lupescu*?'

'Marjorie, you don't— Listen, Bobby. Your mother didn't mean to insult you or Mr Lupescu. She just doesn't believe in what she's never seen, and you can't blame her. Now, supposing you took her and me out in the garden and we could all see Mr Lupescu. Wouldn't that be fun?'

'Uh-uh.' Bobby shook his head gravely. 'Not for Mr Lupescu. He doesn't like people. Only little boys. And he says if I ever bring people to see him, then he'll let Gorgo get me. G'bye now.' And the whirlwind departed.

Marjorie sighed. 'At least thank heaven for Gorgo. I never can get a very clear picture out of Bobby, but he says Mr Lupescu tells the most *terrible* things about him. And if there's any trouble about vegetables or brushing teeth, all I have to say is *Gorgo* and hey presto!'

Alan rose. 'I don't think you need worry, Marjorie. Mr Lupescu seems to do more good than harm, and an active imagination is no curse to a child.'

'You haven't *lived* with Mr Lupescu.'

'To live in a house like this, I'd chance it,' Alan laughed. 'But please forgive me now—back to the cottage and the typewriter ... Seriously, why don't you ask Robert to talk with him?'

Marjorie spread her hands helplessly.

'I know. I'm always the one to assume responsibilities. And yet you married Robert.'

Marjorie laughed. 'I don't know. Somehow there's something *about* Robert ...' Her vague gesture happened to include the original Degas over the fireplace, the sterling tea service, and even the liveried footman who came in at that moment to clear away.

Mr Lupescu was pretty wonderful that afternoon, all right. He had a little kind of an itch like in his wings and they kept twitching all the time. Stardust, he said. It tickles. Got it up in the Milky Way. Friend of mine has a wagon route up there.

Mr Lupescu had lots of friends, and they all did something you wouldn't ever think of, not in a squillion years. That's why he didn't like people, because people don't do things you can tell stories about. They just work or keep house or are mothers or something.

But one of Mr Lupescu's friends, now, was captain of a ship, only it went in time, and Mr Lupescu took trips with him and came back and told you all about what was happening this very minute five hundred years ago. And another of the friends was a radio engineer, only he could tune in on all the kingdoms of faery and Mr Lupescu would squidgle up his red nose and twist it like a dial and make noises like all the kingdoms of faery coming in on the set. And then there was Gorgo, only he wasn't a friend—not exactly; not even to Mr Lupescu.

They'd been playing for a couple of weeks—only it must've been really hours, cause Mamselle hadn't yelled about supper yet, but Mr Lupescu says Time is funny—when Mr Lupescu screwed up his red eyes and said, 'Bobby, let's go in the house.'

'But there's people in the house, and you don't—'

'I know I don't like people. That's why we're going in the house. Come on, Bobby, or I'll—'

So what could you do when you didn't even want to hear him say Gorgo's name?

He went into father's study through the french window, and it was a strict rule that nobody *ever* went into father's study, but rules weren't for Mr Lupescu.

Father was on the telephone telling somebody he'd try to be at a luncheon but there was a committee meeting that same morning, but he'd see. While he was talking, Mr Lupescu went over to a table and opened a drawer and took something out.

When father hung up, he saw Bobby first and started to be very mad. He said, 'Young man, you've been trouble enough to your mother and me with all your stories about your red-winged Mr Lupescu, and now if you're to start bursting in—'

You have to be polite and introduce people. 'Father, this is Mr Lupescu. And see, he does too have red wings.'

Mr Lupescu held out the gun he'd taken from the drawer and shot father once right through the forehead. It made a little clean hole in front and a big messy hole in the back. Father fell down and was dead.

'Now, Bobby,' Mr Lupescu said, 'a lot of people are going to come here and ask you a lot of questions. And if you don't tell the truth about exactly what happened, I'll send Gorgo to fetch you.'

Then Mr Lupescu was gone through the french window.

'It's a curious case, lieutenant,' the medical examiner said. 'It's fortunate I've dabbled a bit in psychiatry; I can at least give you a lead until you get the experts in. The child's statement that his fairy godfather shot his father is obviously a simple flight mechanism, susceptible of two interpretations. A, the father shot himself; the child was so horrified by the sight that he refused to accept it and invented this explanation. B, the child shot the father, let us say by accident, and shifted the blame to his imaginary scapegoat. B has, of course, its more sinister implications: if the child had resented his father and created an ideal substitute, he might make the substitute destroy the reality. . . . But there's the solution to your eyewitness testimony; which alternative is true, lieutenant, I leave up to your researches into motive and the evidence of ballistics and fingerprints. The angle of the wound jibes with either.'

The man with the red nose and eyes and gloves and wings walked down the back lane to the cottage. As soon as he got inside, he took off his coat and removed the wings and the mechanism of strings and rubber that made them twitch. He laid them on top of the ready pile of kindling and lit the fire. When it was well started, he added the gloves. Then he took off the nose, kneaded the putty until the red of its outside vanished into the neutral brown of the mass, jammed it into a crack in the wall, and smoothed it over. Then he took the red-irised contact lenses out of his brown eyes and went into the kitchen, found a hammer, pounded them to powder, and washed the powder down the sink.

Alan started to pour himself a drink and found, to his pleased surprise, that he didn't especially need one. But he did feel tired. He could lie down and recapitulate it all, from the invention of Mr Lupescu (and Gorgo and the man with the Milky Way route) to today's success and on into the future when Marjorie —pliant, trusting Marjorie—would be more desirable than ever as Robert's widow and heir. And Bobby would need a *man* to look after him.

Alan went into the bedroom. Several years passed by in the few seconds it took him to recognize what was waiting on the bed, but then, Time is funny.

Alan said nothing.

'Mr Lupescu, I presume?' said Gorgo.

Thus I Refute Beelzy

JOHN COLLIER

'There goes the tea bell,' said Mrs Carter. 'I hope Simon hears it.'

They looked out from the window of the drawing room. The long garden, agreeably neglected, ended in a waste plot. Here a little summerhouse was passing close by beauty on its way to complete decay. This was Simon's retreat. It was almost completely screened by the tangled branches of the apple tree and the pear tree, planted too close together, as they always are in the suburbs. They caught a glimpse of him now and then, as he strutted up and down, mouthing and gesticulating, performing all the solemn mumbo jumbo of small boys who spend long afternoons at the forgotten ends of long gardens.

'There he is, bless him!' said Betty.

'Playing his game,' said Mrs Carter. 'He won't play with the other children any more. And if I go down there—the temper! And comes in tired out!'

'He doesn't have his sleep in the afternoons?' asked Betty.

'You know what Big Simon's ideas are,' said Mrs Carter. '"Let him choose for himself," he says. That's what he chooses, and he comes in as white as a sheet.'

'Look! He's heard the bell,' said Betty. The expression was justified, though the bell had ceased ringing a full minute ago. Small Simon stopped in his parade exactly as if its tinny dingle had at that moment reached his ear. They watched him perform certain ritual sweeps and scratchings with his little stick, and come lagging over the hot and flaggy grass towards the house.

Mrs Carter led the way down to the playroom, or garden-room, which was also the tea-room for hot days. It had been the huge scullery of this tall Georgian house. Now the walls were cream-washed, there was coarse blue net in the windows, canvas-covered armchairs on the stone floor, and a reproduction of Van Gogh's *Sunflowers* over the mantelpiece.

Small Simon came drifting in, and accorded Betty a perfunctory greeting. His face was an almost perfect triangle, pointed at the chin, and he was paler than he should have been. 'The little elf-child!' cried Betty.

Simon looked at her. 'No,' said he.

At that moment the door opened, and Mr Carter came in, rubbing his hands. He was a dentist, and washed them before and after everything he did. 'You!' said his wife. 'Home already!'

'Not unwelcome, I hope,' said Mr Carter, nodding to Betty. 'Two people cancelled their appointments; I decided to come home. I said, I hope I am not unwelcome.'

'Silly!' said his wife. 'Of course not.'

'Small Simon seems doubtful,' continued Mr Carter. 'Small Simon, are you sorry to see me at tea with you?'

'No, Daddy.'

'No, what?'

'No, Big Simon.'

'That's right. Big Simon and Small Simon. That sounds more like friends, doesn't it? At one time, little boys had to call their father "sir". If they forgot—a good spanking. On the bottom, Small Simon! On the bottom!' said Mr Carter, washing his hands once more with his invisible soap and water.

The little boy turned crimson with shame or rage.

'But now, you see,' said Betty, to help, 'you can call your father whatever you like.'

'And what,' asked Mr Carter, 'has Small Simon been doing this afternoon? While Big Simon has been at work.'

'Nothing,' muttered his son.

'Then you have been bored,' said Mr Carter. 'Learn from experience, Small Simon. Tomorrow, do something amusing, and you will not be bored. I want him to learn from experience, Betty. That is my way, the new way.'

'I have learned,' said the boy, speaking like an old, tired man, as little boys so often do.

'It would hardly seem so,' said Mr Carter, 'if you sit on your behind all the afternoon, doing nothing. Had *my* father caught me doing nothing, I should not have sat very comfortably.'

'He played,' said Mrs Carter.

'A bit,' said the boy, shifting on his chair.

'Too much,' said Mrs Carter. 'He comes in all nervy and dazed. He ought to have his rest.'

'He is six,' said her husband. 'He is a reasonable being. He must choose for himself. But what game is this, Small Simon, that is worth getting nervy and dazed over? There are very few games as good as all that.'

'It's nothing,' said the boy.

'Oh, come,' said his father. 'We are friends, are we not? You can tell me. I was a Small Simon once, just like you, and played the same games you play. Of course, there were no aeroplanes in those days. With whom do you play this fine game? Come on, we must all answer civil questions, or the world would never go round. With whom do you play?'

'Mr Beelzy,' said the boy, unable to resist.

'Mr Beelzy?' said his father, raising his eyebrows enquiringly at his wife.

'It's a game he makes up,' she said.

'Not makes up!' cried the boy. 'Fool!'

'That is telling stories,' said his mother. 'And rude as well. We had better talk of something different.'

'No wonder he is rude,' said Mr Carter, 'if you say he tells lies, and then insist on changing the subject. He tells you his fantasy; you implant a guilt feeling. What can you expect? A defence mechanism. Then you get a real lie.'

'Like in *These Three*,' said Betty. 'Only different, of course. *She* was an unblushing little liar.'

'I would have made her blush,' said Mr Carter, 'in the proper part of her anatomy. But Small Simon is in the fantasy stage. Are you not, Small Simon? You just make things up.'

'No, I don't,' said the boy.

'You do,' said his father. 'And because you do, it is not too late to reason with you. There is no harm in a fantasy, old chap. There is nothing wrong with a bit of make-believe. Only you must learn the difference between daydreams and real things, or your brain will never grow. It will never be the brain of a Big Simon. So, come on. Let us hear about this Mr Beelzy of yours. Come on. What is he like?'

'He isn't like anything,' said the boy.

'Like nothing on earth?' said his father. 'That's a terrible fellow.'

'I'm not frightened of him,' said the child, smiling. 'Not a bit.'

'I should hope not,' said his father. 'If you were, you would be frightening yourself. I am always telling people, older people than you are, that they are just frightening themselves. Is he a funny man? Is he a giant?'

'Sometimes he is,' said the little boy.

'Sometimes one thing, sometimes another,' said his father. 'Sounds pretty vague. Why can't you tell us just what he's like?'

'I love him,' said the small boy. 'He loves me.'

'That's a big word,' said Mr Carter. 'That might be better kept for real things, like Big Simon and Small Simon.'

'He is real,' said the boy, passionately. 'He's not a fool. He's real.'

'Listen,' said his father. 'When you go down the garden there's nobody there. Is there?'

'No,' said the boy.

'Then you think of him, inside your head, and he comes.'

'No,' said Small Simon. 'I have to make marks. On the ground. With my stick.'

'That doesn't matter.'

'Yes, it does.'

'Small Simon, you are being obstinate,' said Mr Carter. 'I am trying to explain something to you. I have been longer in the world than you have, so naturally I am older and wiser. I am

explaining that Mr Beelzy is a fantasy of yours. Do you hear?
Do you understand?'

'Yes, Daddy.'

'He is a game. He is a let's-pretend.'

The little boy looked down at his plate, smiling resignedly.

'I hope you are listening to me,' said his father. 'All you have
to do is to say, "I have been playing a game of let's-pretend. With
someone I make up, called Mr Beelzy." Then no one will say
you tell lies, and you will know the difference between dreams
and reality. Mr Beelzy is a daydream.'

The little boy still stared at his plate.

'He is sometimes there and sometimes not there,' pursued Mr
Carter. 'Sometimes he's like one thing, sometimes another. You
can't really see him. Not as you see me. I am real. You can't
touch him. You can touch me. I can touch you.' Mr Carter
stretched out his big, white dentist's hand, and took his little
son by the nape of the neck. He stopped speaking for a moment
and tightened his hand. The little boy sank his head still lower.

'Now you know the difference,' said Mr Carter, 'between a pretend and a real thing. You and I are one thing; he is another. Which is the pretend? Come on. Answer me. Which is the pretend?'

'Big Simon and Small Simon,' said the little boy.

'Don't!' cried Betty, and at once put her hand over her mouth, for why should a visitor cry, 'Don't!' when a father is explaining things in a scientific and modern way? Besides, it annoys the father.

'Well, my boy,' said Mr Carter, 'I have said you must be allowed to learn from experience. Go upstairs. Right up to your room. You shall learn whether it is better to reason, or to be perverse and obstinate. Go up. I shall follow you.'

'You are not going to beat the child?' cried Mrs Carter.

'No,' said the little boy. 'Mr Beelzy won't let him.'

'Go on up with you!' shouted his father.

Small Simon stopped at the door. 'He said he wouldn't let anyone hurt me,' he whimpered. 'He said he'd come like a lion, with wings on, and eat them up.'

'You'll learn how real he is!' shouted his father after him. 'If you can't learn it at one end, you shall learn it at the other. I'll have your breeches down. I shall finish my cup of tea first, however,' said he to the two women.

Neither of them spoke. Mr Carter finished his tea, and unhurriedly left the room, washing his hands with his invisible soap and water.

Mrs Carter said nothing. Betty could think of nothing to say. She wanted to be talking for she was afraid of what they might hear.

Suddenly it came. It seemed to tear the air apart. 'Good God!' she cried. 'What was that? He's hurt him.' She sprang out of her chair, her silly eyes flashing behind her glasses. 'I'm going up there!' she cried, trembling.

'Yes, let us go up,' said Mrs Carter. 'Let us go up. That was not Small Simon.'

It was on the second-floor landing that they found the shoe, with the man's foot still in it, much like that last morsel of a mouse which sometimes falls unnoticed from the side of the jaws of the cat.

A Sharp Attack of Something or Other

T. H. WHITE

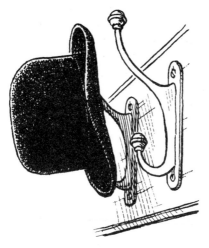

The senior partner claimed to be descended, on the wrong side of the blanket, from Talleyrand. To his sorrow, he was getting old.

He took out his gold watch from Cartier's, hardly thicker than a half-crown, and noted that it was 9.40. He telephoned.

'Susan?'

'Oh, Francis!'

'Henry left?'

'You know he always catches the same train.'

'I know. Well, honey?'

'Francis, I can't come. You musn't ring me up like this, honestly you musn't. It's quite a small exchange and you don't know what might get about. After all, I *am* a married woman: I am his wife: you know how he hates me going out with you.'

'He needn't know.'

'Of course he'll know. He's under my feet all the time. How won't he know? Honestly I can't come, Francis; I'd love to, but honestly. No wool.'

'Wool?'

'Over eyes.'

'Henry,' he said grimly, 'needs to be put away for a bit.'

When the junior partner reached the office, he was in a condescending humour.

'There's a hat for you,' he said, putting the black, immaculate object on the desk. 'Bought it this morning from So-and-So's. Best hatter in town. You want to smarten yourself up, Francis, now that you're getting on. Buy yourself a new hat and get your feet pedicured, ha, ha! It's wonderful what a new hat can do for an old man, old man. In the spring a young man's fancy, and all that. Curly brim. Latest fashion. Size six and seven-eighths. No less than five smackers at So-and-So's. The lot!'

He pulled off the size label and threw it in the wastepaper basket.

'You overwhelm me, Henry.'

'Nuts.'

The younger man hung it on the office hat-rack and went to the floor of the Stock Exchange, bareheaded.

Francis looked at it for a long time, disliking its bouncy assertiveness, its vulgarity, its meanness, its brim. For it was mean: meanly valued for having cost five guineas. It was a cad's hat.

He rang for the secretary; who came, flashing in rimless, octagonal spectacles, acidulous, efficient, devoted to the head of the firm.

'Mr Foster has bought himself a new tile.'

'So I see.'

'It is in the latest mode.'

'I hope it will be big enough for Mr Foster's head.'

His poker face, the heritage of Talleyrand, examined her with what seemed to be benevolence.

'Are we busy this morning, Miss Vine?'

'There's only Robinson and Peabody.'

'I can deal with them.'

'There are the letters to sign.'

'Yes.'

He put the long fingertips together.

'Miss Vine, would you mind taking a taxi to Messrs So-and-So's in Bond Street and buying me a hat exactly like Mr Foster's, size seven and a half? Take it with you, if you like, to be sure of the pattern.'

'Very well, Mr Marchand.'

'It will be a little secret between us.'

When it was time to go home, Henry took the superb headgear from its peg and put it on his head with a flourish. It sank to the bridge of his nose.

'Good heavens,' he said. 'Look at this thing. Only bought it this morning, and it's out of shape already. By God, I'll kick up a shindy with those baskets in Bond Street. You'd think that an expensive hat from So-and-So's . . . They'll have to change it for me, that's all. Bloody profiteers!'

He was late next morning, arriving with a grievance and a new hat, this time a midnight blue.

'They tried to say it was part worn because I pulled the ticket off. But I tore them off a strip. I gave them something to think about. They said that it couldn't have fitted in the first place, but it did. You saw me in it. Dirty crooks. Anyway, they changed it for this one in the end. I think it's better, don't you? You see the blue effect? It goes black in electric light, so you can wear it for a show. But I bloody well told them it was the last time I'd go to So-and-So's. You want to be firm with these people, or they take advantage. Insist on service, that's my motto, if you want to get it. However, as a matter of fact, I do prefer this model. It's kind of jaunty, no? Thought of getting yourself a new lid yet, old man? Just the job for the middle-aged spread.'

When he had gone about his business, Francis said to himself, with a faint exclamation mark between the eyebrows, 'Wear it for a show!' He rang for Miss Vine.

'Electric blue this time,' he said, 'please. Like the new one. Size seven and a half.'

'Very good, Mr Marchand.'

When the blue hat sank over his eyebrows that evening, Henry snatched it off with a start. He looked sidelong at his partner, to see whether he had noticed, and retreated to the washroom, where he put it on and off again several times in front of the mirror. He took it home with him furtively, carried under the arm.

Before business opened next day, Francis was sorry to notice that the young man seemed depressed.

'Are you feeling all right, Henry?'

'Why not?'

'I thought you looked different somehow. I don't know why.'

'Different how?'

'It's probably nothing.'

'Perhaps I am a little worried.'

'I mean, for the last couple of days, you seem to change.'

'Change?'

'Swell up or something. Puffy. But it may be my fancy.'

Henry asked abruptly, 'Did you deal with Robinson and Peabody?'

'Yes. There was no trouble.'

After a bit, he enquired, 'Can people's heads swell?'

Francis laughed.

'Not yours, anyway,' he said teasingly. 'Forget it, Henry. It was an idea that crossed my mind, an optical delusion or something.'

'If people's heads did swell, it would be pretty serious?'

'Nonsense. You are getting ideas because of the famous hat.'

Henry took himself to the market and Francis went to the rack. The band of the blue hat, size seven and a half, was heavily stuffed with brown paper. He took the original ($6\frac{7}{8}$) from the deep bottom drawer of his desk, transferred the brown paper to it, and hung it on the peg. Size $7\frac{1}{2}$ went into the drawer instead.

That evening, Henry did not don his headgear in the office, but went to the washroom, where Francis was too tactful to follow him.

He came out, dazed and pale, with the hat balanced on top of his curled hair like a dodgem car on the Witching Waves. He might have been an eastern houri carrying a pitcher to the well. He went down the stairs carefully, looking straight in front of him, without a word.

'What is dropsy?' asked Henry in the morning, after he had hung up the hat, now minus its padding. 'Can you have goitre on the top of your head?'

He looked pinched, as if he had a hangover due to some attempt to drown his sorrows.

'Of course not.'

'I looked up snake bite in a Boy Scout's Diary which I have, and it said there are two kinds of venom. They are called haemotoxin and neurotoxin. Viper bite is haemotoxin and it makes you swell up immediately. You have to suck it, and wash your mouth out with permanganate of potash. But how can I suck the top of my head?'

'What on earth are you talking about?'
'Besides, I don't think I have been bitten by a snake.'
'Henry, are you feverish?'
'Yes.'
'I thought you looked a bit queer.'
'Do mosquitoes have haemotoxin?'
'I'm sure I don't know. Look, Henry, you are evidently out of sorts. Why don't you take a day off, and go to bed?'
'I shall carry on,' he said bravely, 'to the end.'
While he was carrying on, Francis exchanged the fitting size for size seven and a half.

He came out of the washroom blindfold, the hat over his ears, like a horse in a straw bonnet. He groped his way down the stairs in awful silence, clutching a packet of permanganate of potash.

In the morning, the senior partner consulted his Cartier watch and lifted the telephone.
'Susan?'
'Oh, Francis!'
'Henry left?'
'Well, as a matter of fact, no. Or rather, yes. He's gone to a nursing home.'
'A nursing home! Good gracious, not ill I hope?'
'He thinks he is. It's too extraordinary. He says his head keeps swelling and shrinking. Do you think it could?'
'I wouldn't put anything past Henry.'
'So he can't come to the office.'
'Poor Henry!'
'And he's gone a sort of purple-brownish colour, like permanganate.'
'No wool?'
'Honestly.'
'My poor Susan, this must be very worrying for you. You ought to be taken out of yourself.'
No answer.
'Honey?'
'Well, Francis, I *could* come. If it didn't seem too heartless about Henry?'

Voodoo

FREDRIC BROWN

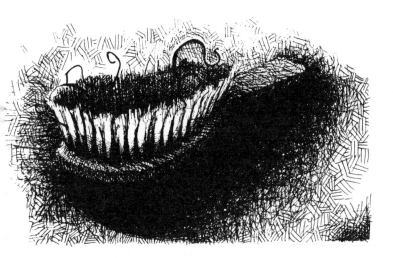

Mr Decker's wife had just returned from a trip to Haiti—a trip she had taken alone—to give them a cooling off period before they discussed a divorce.

It hadn't worked. Neither of them had cooled off in the slightest. In fact, they were finding now that they hated one another more than ever.

'Half,' said Mrs Decker firmly. 'I'll not settle for anything less than half the money plus half of the property.'

'Ridiculous!' said Mr Decker.

'Is it? I could have it all, you know. And quite easily, too. I studied voodoo while in Haiti.'

'Rot!' said Mr Decker.

'It isn't. And you should be glad that I am a good woman for I could kill you quite easily if I wished. I would then have *all* the money and *all* the real estate, and without any fear of consequences. A death accomplished by voodoo cannot be distinguished from a death by heart failure.'

'Rubbish!' said Mr Decker.

'You think so? I have wax and a hatpin. Do you want to give me a tiny pinch of your hair or a fingernail clipping or two—that's all I need—and let me show you?'

'Nonsense!' said Mr Decker.

'Then why are you afraid to have me try? Since *I* know it works, I'll make you a proposition. If it doesn't kill you, I'll give you a divorce and ask for nothing. If it does, I'll get it all automatically.'

'Done!' said Mr Decker. 'Get your wax and hatpin.' He glanced at his fingernails. 'Pretty short. I'll give you a bit of hair.'

When he came back with a few short strands of hair in the lid of an aspirin tin, Mrs Decker had already started softening the wax. She kneaded the hair into it, then shaped it into the rough effigy of a human being.

'You'll be sorry,' she said, and thrust the hatpin into the chest of the wax figure.

Mr Decker was surprised, but he was more pleased than sorry. He had not believed in voodoo, but being a cautious man he never took chances.

Besides, it had always irritated him that his wife so seldom cleaned her hairbrush.

The Candidate

HENRY SLESAR

A man's worth can be judged by the calibre of his enemies. Burton Grunzer, encountering the phrase in a pocket-sized biography he had purchased at a news-stand, put the book in his lap and stared reflectively from the murky window of the commuter train. Darkness silvered the glass and gave him nothing to look at but his own image, but it seemed appropriate to his line of thought. How many people were enemies of that face, of the eyes narrowed by a myopic squint denied by vanity the correction of spectacles, of the nose he secretly called patrician, of the mouth that was soft in relaxation and hard when animated by speech or smiles or frowns?

How many enemies? Grunzer mused. A few he could name, others he could guess. But it was their calibre that was important. Men like Whitman Hayes, for instance; there was a 24-carat opponent for you. Grunzer smiled, darting a sidelong glance at the seat-sharer beside him, not wanting to be caught indulging in a secret thought. Grunzer was thirty-four; Hayes was twice as old, his white hairs synonymous with experience, an enemy to be proud of. Hayes knew the food business, all right, knew it from every angle: he'd been a wagon jobber for six years, a broker for ten, a food company executive for twenty before the old man had brought him into the organization to sit on his right hand.

Pinning Hayes to the mat wasn't easy, and that made Grunzer's small but increasing triumphs all the sweeter. He congratulated himself. He had twisted Hayes's advantages into drawbacks, had made his long years seem tantamount to senility and out-lived usefulness; in meetings, he had concentrated his questions on the new supermarket and suburbia phenomena to demon-strate to the old man that times had changed, that the past was dead, that new merchandising tactics were needed, and that only a younger man could supply them . . .

Suddenly, he was depressed. His enjoyment of remembered victories seemed tasteless. Yes, he'd won a minor battle or two in the company conference room; he'd made Hayes's ruddy face go crimson, and seen the old man's parchment skin wrinkle in a sly grin. But what had been accomplished? Hayes seemed more self-assured than ever, and the old man more dependent upon his advice . . .

When he arrived home, later than usual, his wife Jean didn't ask questions. After eight years of a marriage in which, child-less, she knew her husband almost too well, she wisely offered nothing more than a quiet greeting, a hot meal, and the day's mail. Grunzer flipped through the bills and circulars, and found an unmarked letter. He slipped it into his hip pocket, reserving it for private perusal, and finished the meal in silence.

After dinner, Jean suggested a movie and he agreed; he had a passion for violent action movies. But first, he locked himself in the bathroom and opened the letter. Its heading was cryptic: *Society for United Action*. The return address was a post office box. It read:

Dear Mr Grunzer:
    Your name has been suggested to us by a mutual acquain-tance. Our organization has an unusual mission which cannot be

described in this letter, but which you may find of exceeding
interest. We would be gratified by a private discussion at your
earliest convenience. If I do not hear from you to the contrary in
the next few days, I will take the liberty of calling you at your
office.

It was signed, *Carl Tucker, Secretary*. A thin line at the
bottom of the page read: *A Nonprofit Organization*.

His first reaction was a defensive one; he suspected an oblique
attack on his pocketbook. His second was curiosity: he went to
the bedroom and located the telephone directory, but found no
organization listed by the letterhead name. *OK, Mr Tucker*, he
thought wryly, *I'll bite.*

When no call came in the next three days, his curiosity was in-
creased. But when Friday arrived, he forgot the letter's promise
in the crush of office affairs. The old man called a meeting with
the bakery products division. Grunzer sat opposite Whitman
Hayes at the conference table, poised to pounce on fallacies in
his statements. He almost had him once, but Eckhardt, the
bakery products manager, spoke up in defence of Hayes's views.
Eckhardt had only been with the company a year, but he had
evidently chosen sides already. Grunzer glared at him, and
reserved a place for Eckhardt in the hate chamber of his mind.

At three o'clock, Carl Tucker called.

'Mr Grunzer?' The voice was friendly, even cheery. 'I haven't
heard from you, so I assume you don't mind my calling today.
Is there a chance we can get together sometime?'

'Well, if you could give me some idea, Mr Tucker—'

The chuckle was resonant. 'We're not a charity organization,
Mr Grunzer, in case you got that notion. Nor do we sell
anything. We're more or less a voluntary service group: our
membership is over a thousand at present.'

'To tell you the truth,' Grunzer frowned, 'I never heard of
you.'

'No, you haven't, and that's one of the assets. I think you'll
understand when I tell you about us. I can be over at your office
in fifteen minutes, unless you want to make it another day.'

Grunzer glanced at his calendar. 'OK, Mr Tucker. Best time
for me is right now.'

'Fine! I'll be right over.'

Tucker was prompt. When he walked into the office, Grunzer's eyes went dismayed at the officious briefcase in the man's right hand. But he felt better when Tucker, a florid man in his early sixties with small, pleasant features, began talking.

'Nice of you to take the time, Mr Grunzer. And believe me, I'm not here to sell you insurance or razor blades. Couldn't if I tried; I'm a semi-retired broker. However, the subject I want to discuss is rather . . . intimate, so I'll have to ask you to bear with me on a certain point. May I close the door?'

'Sure,' Grunzer said, mystified.

Tucker closed it, hitched his chair closer and said:

'The point is this. What I have to say must remain in the strictest confidence. If you betray that confidence, if you publicize our society in any way, the consequences could be most unpleasant. Is that agreeable?'

Grunzer, frowning, nodded.

'Fine!' The visitor snapped open the briefcase and produced a stapled manuscript. 'Now, the society has prepared this little spiel about our basic philosophy, but I'm not going to bore you with it. I'm going to go straight to the heart of our argument. You may not agree with our first principle at all, and I'd like to know that now.'

'How do you mean, first principle?'

'Well . . .' Tucker flushed slightly. 'Put in the crudest form, Mr Grunzer, the Society for United Action believes that . . . *some* people are just not fit to live.' He looked up quickly, as if anxious to gauge the immediate reaction. 'There, I've said it,' he laughed, somewhat in relief. 'Some of our members don't believe in my direct approach; they feel the argument has to be broached more discreetly. But frankly, I've gotten excellent results in this rather crude manner. How do you feel about what I've said, Mr Grunzer?'

'I don't know. Guess I never thought about it much.'

'Were you in the war, Mr Grunzer?'

'Yes. Navy.' Grunzer rubbed his jaw. 'I suppose I didn't think the Japs were fit to live, back then. I guess maybe there are other cases. I mean, you take capital punishment, I believe in that. Murderers, rape-artists, perverts, hell, I certainly don't think *they're* fit to live.'

'Ah,' Tucker said. 'So you really accept our first principle. It's a question of category, isn't it?'

'I guess you could say that.'

'Good. So now I'll try another blunt question. Have you—personally—ever wished someone dead? Oh, I don't mean those casual, fleeting wishes everybody has. I mean a real, deep-down, uncomplicated wish for the death of someone *you* thought was unfit to live. Have you?'

'Sure,' Gunzer said frankly. 'I guess I have.'

'There are times, in your opinion, when the removal of someone from this earth would be beneficial?'

Grunzer smiled. 'Hey, what is this? You from Murder, Incorporated or something?'

Tucker grinned back. 'Hardly, Mr Grunzer, hardly. There is absolutely no criminal aspect to our aims or our methods. I'll admit we're a "secret" society, but we're no Black Hand. You'd be amazed at the quality of our membership; it even includes members of the legal profession. But suppose I tell you how the society came into being?

'It began with two men; I can't reveal their names just now. The year was 1949, and one of these men was a lawyer attached to the district attorney's office. The other man was a state psychiatrist. Both of them were involved in a rather sensational trial, concerning a man accused of a hideous crime against two small boys. In their opinion, the man was unquestionably guilty, but an unusually persuasive defence counsel, and a highly suggestible jury, gave him his freedom. When the shocking verdict was announced, these two, who were personal friends as well as colleagues, were thunderstruck and furious. They felt a great wrong had been committed, and they were helpless to right it . . .

'But I should explain something about this psychiatrist. For some years, he had made studies in a field which might be called anthropological psychiatry. One of these researches related to the voodoo practice of certain groups, the Haitian in particular. You've probably heard a great deal about voodoo, or Obeah as they call it in Jamaica, but I won't dwell on the subject lest you think we hold tribal rites and stick pins in dolls . . . But the chief feature of his study was the uncanny *success* of certain strange practices. Naturally, as a scientist, he rejected the supernatural explanation and sought the rational one. And, of course, there was only one answer. When the *vodun* priest decreed the punishment or death of a malefactor, it was the malefactor's own convictions concerning the efficacy of the death wish, his own faith in the voodoo power, that eventually made the wish come true. Sometimes, the process was organic—his body reacted psychosomatically to the voodoo curse, and he would sicken and die. Sometimes, he would die by "accident"—an accident prompted by the secret belief that once cursed, he *must* die. Eerie, isn't it?'

'No doubt,' Grunzer said, dry-lipped.

'Anyway, our friend, the psychiatrist, began wondering aloud if *any* of us have advanced so far along the civilized path that we couldn't be subject to this same sort of "suggested" punishment. He proposed that they experiment on this choice subject, just to see.

'How they did it was simple,' he said. 'They went to see this man, and they announced their intentions. They told him they were going to *wish him dead*. They explained how and why the wish would become reality, and while he laughed at their proposal, they could see the look of superstitious fear cross his face. They promised him that regularly, every day, they would be wishing for his death, until he could no longer stop the mystic juggernaut that would make the wish come true.'

Grunzer shivered suddenly, and clenched his fist. 'That's pretty silly,' he said softly.

'The man died of a heart attack two months later.'

'Of course. I knew you'd say that. But there's such a thing as coincidence.'

'Naturally. And our friends, while intrigued, weren't satisfied. *So they tried it again.*'

'Again?'

'Yes, again. I won't recount who the victim was, but I will tell you that this time they enlisted the aid of four associates. This little band of pioneers was the nucleus of the society I represent today.'

Grunzer shook his head. 'And you mean to tell me there's a *thousand* now?'

'Yes, a thousand and more, all over the country. A society whose one function is to *wish people dead*. At first, membership was purely voluntary, but now we have a system. Each new member of the Society for United Action joins on the basis of submitting one potential victim. Naturally, the society investigates to determine whether the victim is deserving of his fate. If the case is a good one, the *entire* membership then sets about to *wish him dead.* Once the task has been accomplished, naturally, the new member must take part in all future concerted action. That and a small yearly fee, is the price of membership.'

Carl Tucker grinned.

'And in case you think I'm not serious, Mr Grunzer—' He dipped into the briefcase again, this time producing a blue-bound volume of telephone directory thickness. 'Here are the facts. To date, two hundred and twenty-nine victims were named by our selection committee. Of those, *one hundred and four* are no longer alive. Coincidence, Mr Grunzer?

'As for the remaining one hundred and twenty-five—perhaps that indicates that our method is not infallible. We're the first to admit that. But new techniques are being developed all the time. I assure you, Mr Grunzer, *we will get them all.*'

He flipped through the blue-bound book.

'Our members are listed in this book, Mr Grunzer. I'm going to give you the option to call one, ten or a hundred of them. Call them and see if I'm not telling the truth.'

He flipped the manuscript toward Grunzer's desk. It landed on the blotter with a thud. Grunzer picked it up.

'Well?' Tucker said. 'Want to call them?'

'No.' He licked his lips. 'I'm willing to take your word for it, Mr Tucker. It's incredible, but I can see how it works. Just *knowing* that a thousand people are wishing you dead is enough to shake hell out of you.' His eyes narrowed. 'But there's one question. You talked about a "small" fee—'

'It's fifty dollars, Mr Grunzer.'

'Fifty, huh? Fifty times a thousand, that's pretty good money, isn't it?'

'I assure you, the organization is not motivated by profit. Not the kind you mean. The dues merely cover expenses, committee work, research and the like. Surely you can understand that?'

'I guess so,' he grunted.

'Then you find it interesting?'

Grunzer swivelled his chair about to face the window.

God! he thought.

God! If it *really* worked!

But how could it? If wishes became deeds, he would have slaughtered dozens in his lifetime. Yet, that was different. His wishes were always secret things, hidden where no man could know them. But this method was different, more practical, more terrifying. Yes, he could see how it might work. He could visualize a thousand minds burning with the single wish of death, see the victim sneering in disbelief at first, and then slowly, gradually, surely succumbing to the tightening, constricting chain of fear that it *might* work, that so many deadly thoughts could indeed emit a mystical, malevolent ray that destroyed life.

Suddenly, ghostlike, he saw the ruddy face of Whitman Hayes before him.

He wheeled about and said:

'But the victim has to *know* all this, of course? He has to know the society exists, and has succeeded, and is wishing for *his* death? That's essential, isn't it?'

'Absolutely essential,' Tucker said, replacing the manuscripts in his briefcase. 'You've touched on the vital point, Mr Grunzer. The victim must be informed, and that, precisely, is what I have done.' He looked at his watch. 'Your death wish began at noon today. The society has begun to work. I'm very sorry.'

At the doorway, he turned and lifted both hat and briefcase in one departing salute.

'Goodbye, Mr Grunzer,' he said.

The Near Departed

RICHARD MATHESON

The small man opened the door and stepped in out of the glaring sunlight. He was in his early fifties, a spindly, plain-looking man with receding grey hair. He closed the door without a sound, then stood in the shadowy foyer, waiting for his eyes to adjust to the change in light. He was wearing a black suit, white shirt, and black tie. His face was pale and dry skinned despite the heat of the day.

When his eyes had refocused themselves, he removed his panama hat and moved along the hallway to the office, his black shoes soundless on the carpeting.

The mortician looked up from his desk. 'Good afternoon,' he said.

'Good afternoon.' The small man's voice was soft.

'Can I help you?'

'Yes, you can,' the small man said.

The mortician gestured to the armchair on the other side of his desk. 'Please.'

The small man perched on the edge of the chair and set the panama hat on his lap. He watched the mortician open a drawer and remove a printed form.

'Now,' the mortician said. He withdrew a black pen from its onyx holder. 'Who is the deceased?' he asked gently.

'My wife,' the small man said.

The mortician made a sympathetic noise. 'I'm sorry,' he said.

'Yes.' The small man gazed at him blankly.

'What is her name?' the mortician asked.

'Marie,' the small man answered quietly. 'Arnold.'

The mortician wrote the name. 'Address?' he asked.

The small man told him.

'Is she there now?' the mortician asked.

'She's there,' the small man said.

The mortician nodded.

'I want everything perfect,' the small man said. 'I want the best you have.'

'Of course,' the mortician said. 'Of course.'

'Cost is unimportant,' said the small man. His throat moved as he swallowed drily. 'Everything is unimportant now. Except for this.'

'I understand,' the mortician said.

'I want the best you have,' the small man said. 'She's beautiful. She has to have the very best.'

'I understand.'

'She always had the best. I saw to it.'

'Of course.'

'There'll be many people,' said the small man. 'Everybody loved her. She's so beautiful. So young. She has to have the very best. You understand?'

'Absolutely,' the mortician reassured him. 'You'll be more than satisfied, I guarantee you.'

'She's so beautiful,' the small man said. 'So young.'

'I'm sure,' the mortician said.

The small man sat without moving as the mortician asked him questions. His voice did not vary in tone as he spoke. His eyes blinked so infrequently the mortician never saw them doing it.

When the form was completed, the small man signed and stood. The mortician stood and walked around the desk. 'I guarantee you you'll be satisfied,' he said, his hand extended.

The small man took his hand and gripped it momentarily. His palm was dry and cool.

'We'll be over at your house within the hour,' the mortician told him.

'Fine,' the small man said.

The mortician walked beside him down the hallway.

'I want everything perfect for her,' the small man said. 'Nothing but the very best.'

'Everything will be exactly as you wish.'

'She deserves the best.' The small man stared ahead. 'She's so beautiful,' he said. 'Everybody loved her. Everybody. She's so young and beautiful.'

'When did she die?' the mortician asked.

The small man didn't seem to hear. He opened the door and stepped into the sunlight, putting on his panama hat. He was half-way to his car when he replied, a faint smile on his lips, 'As soon as I get home.'

The Statuette

KENNETH IRELAND

Wayne remembered how, when he was little, he had been scared of his teddy bear. If he had stared at it, it seemed to be staring back angrily from its button eyes, as if ready to reach out and grab him.

He had the same feeling now about the little bronze statuette which his father had bought at a police auction, and which his mother had cleaned up and placed on the mantelpiece. It was a little model of an imp or a devil or something—anyway, it was a little figure of a man with horns, with one of its bronze arms down by its side and the other raised as if pointing at something. The bearded face was looking towards the direction that the right arm was pointing.

'I got it dirt cheap,' his father said. 'I just happened to go along, having heard that the police were auctioning off various things they'd collected, or found which nobody had come to claim—and then this came up for sale.'

'Doesn't it look nice on the mantelpiece?' Wayne's mother had said, and then she and Wayne's father had stood back to admire it.

Wayne did not admire it at all.

'Fancy somebody not claiming it!' exclaimed his mother.

'Well, they couldn't claim it,' Wayne's father explained. 'It was confiscated—as evidence. Something to do with devil-worship, they said at the auction. And nobody else wanted it, so I bought it.'

Wayne's mother turned it round so that the arm pointed towards the inside wall of the room. 'It looks better that way, I think,' she decided.

Wayne picked it up and looked at it. It was only about six inches high, and there was no base but the legs were so positioned that the statuette stood upright on them. He wondered how people had used it while they were worshipping the devil.

'Better put it down,' his father told him, 'before you drop it.'

So Wayne returned it to the shelf, and that was the end of the matter until the following morning. He was having his breakfast when his mother came in, glanced at the mantelpiece and at once made for the statuette and turned it to face the opposite way.

'I told you, I prefer it to be pointing to the left,' she said. 'It looks better that way.'

'I didn't move it,' said Wayne. He hadn't even looked at it, because he didn't like it.

'Well, I don't suppose your father did. You must have picked it up without thinking, before you had your breakfast, then put it down the wrong way.'

'I didn't,' protested Wayne. 'I haven't touched it.'

'There's no need to make a song and dance out of it,' said his mother, frowning. 'It doesn't matter.'

But when Wayne came home from school, and happened to glance at the mantelpiece, he noticed at once that the little imp was pointing towards the window again. Now that was odd, because he had only just arrived home, his father was still at work, and his mother had not returned from shopping. So he turned it back to the position which his mother wanted, and left it at that. The only thing was, when he went downstairs the next morning, it was turned round again—pointing straight out of the window.

'This statue's turned round again,' he called.

His mother came in with the tea pot. 'Yes, and pigs have wings,' she retorted. 'Look, what's so important about it looking out of the window? I mean, if you really want it like that, I don't mind. But it does seem a bit silly to have a little statue standing nicely up there with its back towards us all the time and just its head turned round.'

'I don't care which way we have it,' muttered Wayne.

'Then leave it the way it was.' And his mother poured his tea, then moved the imp back to its correct position.

At night-time, when the room had been left empty since he had finished his homework, Wayne switched on the light, just to check his suspicions before going to bed. As he had expected, the thing had turned the other way again. When he inspected more closely, there were even little scratch marks on the woodwork which fitted exactly where the feet would have gone had they dragged themselves round. Without a word to anyone, he put the statuette back the other way.

Something was very odd, he was certain of that now. Neither his father nor his mother had been in that room since he had come out to watch the television. He had been the last one, therefore nobody in the house could have moved it. So either something had caused the imp to move, some kind of vibration perhaps—or the imp had moved all by itself.

He did not like the feeling he was getting. It was the thought of devil-worship, no doubt, which was causing him to feel shivery down his back. Was it possible, he was wondering, that somehow the worshippers had endowed this horrible little statuette with a power of its own? Or could it be the other way round, that the statuette already had some powers and so had infected the worshippers?

Well, it was nonsense; it had to be, either way. But Wayne decided that he was going to find out, one way or the other. He set his alarm for half-past twelve, because he knew that his parents would both be in bed and asleep by then, and put the clock underneath his pillow. They would not hear it when it went off, but he would.

He stifled the sound as soon as he could reach his hand under the pillow, and sat up in bed. Then he took the torch which he had also hidden there, and by its light turned the hand round so that the clock would ring again at its usual time of half-past seven, in case he forgot when he came to bed again. Then he took the eiderdown and the torch and padded off down the stairs. He made himself comfortable sitting up against the wall furthest away from the mantelpiece, with the eiderdown wrapped round him, then switched on the torch and pointed it at the statuette.

It looked eerie with just a beam of light cutting through the dark to it, shining like a spotlight. He was glad he had decided to sit as far away from the statuette as possible. One thing was certain, it was still exactly as it had been when he had left it. Well, he would give it half an hour. If it hadn't moved by then he would go back to bed.

It was a bit frightening, just sitting there staring at this evil-looking piece of sculpture. It reminded him again of when he had once stared at his teddy bear. The torch flickered a little in his hand, and the effect was almost as if the statuette was moving. That was quite unnerving, just for a moment. He steadied his hand. Nothing was happening after all, so he switched off the torch and decided to save the battery and try again a few minutes later.

When he woke up, it was to hear a faint scraping noise. For a few seconds he remained quite still. He had not intended to go to sleep, but now that he realized what had happened, and had heard the scraping sound again, he switched on the torch and the beam stabbed through the darkness towards the imp.

He blinked. The scraping was of the bronze feet on the wooden shelf, turning slowly. In the light of the torch, there was no doubt about it at all. The imp, or devil, or whatever it was, was caught in the act of turning round to face the opposite way! The arm which had been upraised towards the pattern on the wallpaper was now beginning to point towards the window. In a matter of seconds it had turned right round.

Wayne did not believe it. The statuette was inanimate, just a chunk of metal, with no life in it at all. It could not have moved unless some force was moving it. Suppressing his fear, he let the eiderdown drop to the carpet and rose to his feet. He walked towards the mantelpiece, with the torch directed firmly towards it, but even then hesitated before touching this chunk of metal. Then he put his hand out, grabbed the statuette by its shoulders in the fingers of one hand, picked it up, and turned it back to its correct position. Then he let go.

At once the movement began again, right in front of him not a foot from his eyes. Slowly it twisted round, even while he was standing there watching it. The legs almost seemed to be walking round. And it finished up, as before, pointing towards the window.

Wayne wondered if this was some sort of dream. Well, he'd soon find out if he was dreaming or not. He went over to the door, and switched on the light. Then he went into the kitchen, switched the light on in there as well but was careful not to make any noise which would wake his parents, turned on the cold water tap and ran the water on to his hand.

It was real, cold water all right. He was definitely not in the grips of a nightmare. He dried his hand on the kitchen towel, switched off the kitchen light, and returned to the dining-room. He felt safer with the light left on in there, now. The best thing to do, no doubt, would be to go back upstairs keeping the stairs light on, go into his parents' room, wake them up, and tell them what was going on. He expected, though, that they would not believe him. They would be sure to think he was making it all up. He wondered himself, even now, if he had not imagined it all. All right, so now he was wide awake, but what if he had not been when the statuette was moving?

He decided to try one more thing, before he made up his mind about that. The devil-statuette was quite motionless now, still pointing at the curtains behind which lay the windows and beyond them the back garden. He took the statuette off the shelf and put it on to the carpet, standing upright. He picked it up by its outstretched arm and used that as a kind of handle, positioning the statuette so that it continued to point towards the curtains. It was slightly out of line, so he pushed the hand with his finger and moved the statuette round so that it faced exactly the same way as before.

The outstretched hand, with its pointing fingers, suddenly closed round his finger, and stayed there. Wayne tried to shake it off, but the grip was too tight. What was more, the thing seemed to be trying to pull him towards the windows. It was beginning to walk across the carpet, taking him slowly with it.

He tried raising his finger, but the statuette clung to him. He could just lift it on one finger—but he could not make it let go of him. Neither could he break the hand off, although he tried. He thought of running upstairs and showing his father and mother just what was happening, but did not fancy the thought of this thing loose upstairs, even if he could somehow get his finger free.

He lowered his hand so that the statuette had its legs on the floor again, and as soon as this happened they began to move, drawing him inexorably towards the window. When they arrived there, the movement ceased; except that he could feel the tiny fist which grasped his finger almost pushing him forward.

Wayne didn't know what to do. He could yell for help and perhaps his father could find his hacksaw and cut the hand off for him. But his parents were heavy sleepers. It might be a long time before they would wake to his shouts and come down to rescue him, and in that time anything might happen. Still the cold, bronze hand was urging him forward, squeezing harder into his flesh.

It was ridiculous! This just could not be happening at all. He had somehow, while he was half-asleep, got his finger stuck in the outstretched hand of this little monstrosity, so now it was up to him to get it out again, put the statuette back on the shelf where it belonged, and go back upstairs and into bed as soon as possible. Let someone else work out why the imp kept turning round, and in the meantime leave well alone.

It was then that the head of the statuette turned and looked at him, and the other hand rose also and pointed imperiously towards the closed curtains. The meaning was clear. Wayne drew them back. He was relieved to find nothing waiting for him outside—no monster, no evil shape, nothing. Just the blackness of the night, with the light from the room shining on to the paving slabs outside but barely illuminating the edge of the lawn beyond them. Then the hand let go.

Even while he rubbed his finger to ease the pain, the imp seemed to fling itself at the pane of glass nearest to the floor. The window broke, and the thing was outside the room, twisting and turning and trying to get itself to an upright position.

Wayne regarded the scene with astonishment. So all this time the thing, whatever it really was, had been pointing towards the way it wished to go. Also, now that it was outside, it seemed incapable of getting to its feet again.

Wayne wondered how he was going to explain the broken window in the morning. Then it occurred to him that he would not need to explain anything. Nobody knew that he was down there, so he could not be blamed. It could be burglars for all anyone would know. And in the mean-time the statuette was writhing on the stone slabs of the patio.

After a moment's thought, Wayne came to a decision. He returned to the kitchen, switched on the light again, opened the back door and stepped outside. The stone slabs felt cold to his feet, but he did not mind. Something had to be done. He could not leave the situation as it was, for fear of worse happening.

He approached the fallen statuette, but kept at a safe distance. He knew that it could not move very fast. If it wanted to go somewhere else, so much the better as far as he was concerned. It could go where it liked as long as it did not return to their house. Let his parents wonder what had really taken place when they came down in the morning to find the mess.

He found himself talking to it as if it was alive.

'All right,' he said softly, 'all right. I'll put you the right way up. Don't grab me, that's all.'

The thing became motionless. It was just a little statue lying on its side on the ground. Cautiously, just in case, Wayne stooped down and taking hold of its back, well away from those hands—just as he had seen a fisherman pick up a lobster so as to avoid its claws—he stood it on its feet. Then he watched it. After a moment, the movement began again, across the patio and on to the grass, across the lawn to where the flowerbeds began. As it moved, the arms remained stationary, one by its side and one pointing forwards. The head was back in its original position, too. It was rather like watching a tiny ballet dancer moving, Wayne thought as he followed it, more curious than scared now.

As soon as it was standing on the bare earth, a short distance from the edge of the lawn, it stopped again, then slowly turned. Slowly the fingers of the outstretched arm began to point downwards.

Something buried in the garden? Wayne wondered. That was hardly likely, but nevertheless he walked over to where the hand was directing him, waiting to see what happened next. The soil on his feet would soon wash off.

He heard the creaking noise almost at once. It seemed to be coming from all round him. Startled, he spun round, but could see nothing to cause it. Then he felt a gentle movement beneath his feet. He switched the torch on at once.

He was just in time to see the ground open up as the wooden board over the old, disused well finally gave way and he fell twenty feet down the shaft. There was water all round him. He never reached the bottom but rose to the surface again.

It was then that he began to shout. He knew it was no use. He was too far away now for his parents to be able to hear him, even if they did wake up. The last thing he saw in the faint light from the broken opening in the ground was the little bronze imp sneering down at him. Then that was gone, making its slow journey back towards the house. It was a long time to half-past seven.

The Meeting

ROBERT SCOTT

H ow is it that I send to the market a young man strong and fearless and full of health but he returns shaking like a leaf in the wind?'

'Master, I am afraid.'

'I need no prophet to tell me that.'

'Master, the market was full of jostling women and quarrelling servants but in the corner by the sherbet seller I saw one who glared at me, who pointed and nodded and showed his teeth. Master, it was Death who threatened me.'

'May Allah keep you safe.'

'It is as Allah wills, but, Master, you can help your servant. Lend me your swiftest horse and I will go to my brother in Samarra. Death will not look for me there.'

When his servant had left the merchant went himself to the market-place, where he saw one standing apart by the sherbet seller looking over the crowd.

'May Allah send you long life,' he said.

'It is as Allah wills.'

'This morning my servant came. He says you frowned upon him and threatened him.'

'Your servant is mistaken. I was astonished to see him here, in a Baghdad market-place, when I have a meeting with him tonight in Samarra.'

The Talking Head

ROBERT SCOTT

The hunter found a human head propped up by the roots of a tree. It was an old head, little more than a skull, with grinning jaws and gaping eye sockets. 'I wonder how that got here,' he muttered, half to himself.

'My big mouth brought me here,' the head answered.

The hunter dropped his weapons and ran back to his village, where he went straight to his chief.

'I've just seen a talking head,' he said.

'I can see one now,' said the chief, 'and it's wasting my time.'

'No,' the hunter protested. 'It's just a head and it's dead and rotten, but it speaks.'

'You are still wasting my time,' said the chief. 'What you say cannot be.'

'But it is. It does,' the hunter insisted. 'I can show you.'

'Very well,' the chief decided. 'You take three of my warriors with you and show them this head. If it speaks, you will bring it back and I will question it. If it doesn't, your own head will join it.'

The hunter led the chief's warriors to the tree. 'There,' he said. 'You see. There it is.'

'It doesn't speak.'

The hunter stood in front of the head. 'What brought you here?' he demanded.

There was no answer.

Again and again the hunter implored the head to speak to him, but it stayed silent. Finally the chief's warriors lost patience.

'This is foolish,' they said. 'You are wasting everyone's time.' And they chopped off his head, propped it by the side of the old one, and returned to the village.

'What brought you here?' the old head asked when they had gone.

'My big mouth brought me here,' the hunter's head replied.

Paths

JOHN CHRISTOPHER

Having decided to take the long way home through the fields, he found it easy to talk himself into the still longer route through the wood. When he had been little he had thought wild animals lived in it: wolves and bears. Later he heard tales of its being haunted. He didn't believe them, but even at eleven he could frighten himself at night by imagining being taken somehow from his bed and finding himself alone there. A summer afternoon was different, though.

Before entering the wood, he looked back. The new junior school from which he had just come lay in bright sunlight; it glittered especially from the solar panels on the south side of the tower. The panels extended outwards from the top, giving it a weird shape. The tower looked a bit like a bird with half-folded wings, getting ready to fly.

Trees crowded close. Usually there was birdsong, but today it was very quiet. All he heard were his footsteps on the soft earth, the occasional crackle of a twig. He came to the place, roughly at the wood's centre, where there was a grassy mound three or four metres across. The path skirted the mound, and normally the clearing would have been sunlit; surprisingly, the tree tops were lost in a mist. Two more things surprised him. Other paths he had never seen led into the clearing; and there was a girl sitting on the mound.

She wore funny clothes, and a lot of them: a white dress, white stockings, laced-up white boots. The dress was buttoned to the neck, with long sleeves and starched cuffs, and reached nearly to her ankles. She had long dark hair under a straw hat with blue ribbons. Her face was pale, eyes brown. Her nose was a bit long. She wouldn't have been pretty, he decided, even in normal clothes.

Going towards her, he asked, 'What's all this, then—fancy dress?'

She paused before answering. 'Who are you?' Her voice was light but sharp, and very precise. 'Are you a farmer's boy?'

She must be crackers: how could he be a farm worker, at his age?

'I'm Kevin Luscombe. I live in Southleigh. What's your name?'

She hesitated again. 'Arabella Cartwright. Where in Southleigh?'

'Cherrytree Road.'

She shook her head. 'There's no such place. Only London Road and Dover Road, and the Green.'

She spoke like someone describing a village. Those were all streets in the old part of the town: the Green was the main shopping centre.

She was staring at him suspiciously. 'What's that, written across your jersey?'

He glanced down at his T-shirt. 'You can read, can't you?'

'It says: "The Tripods are Coming". What does it mean?'

'It's a new TV serial—science fiction. My dad knows one of the cameramen.'

She said doubtfully, 'Science fiction? Teevy? Camera men?'

He looked at her dress again, remembering something else from television—about Victorian children living near a railway line. Feeling a bit foolish, he said, 'What year is it?'

'Don't be silly!'

'Go on. Tell me. What year?'

'Eighteen eighty-four. You know that.'

'No,' he said, 'I don't. And it isn't. It's nineteen. Nineteen eighty-four.'

They sat on the mound and talked, and came to a kind of understanding. If you thought of time as a spinning wheel, with the years as spokes, this was the hub. There was no way of knowing how or why each had got here. The wood had been spoken of in her time, Arabella said, as a magic place: the mound was said to hide a ruin from ancient times.

They were curious about each other's worlds; she more so, since while he knew something about hers from history, his was totally unknown to her. He spoke of flying machines, radio and television.

She said wistfully, 'I'd love to see some of it.'

He looked at her. 'Why not? Which path did you come by?' She pointed. 'That one's mine. I can take you along it, to my time.'

She said no at first—scared, he guessed. He kept on; she wavered, and eventually agreed. But as they slid off the mound, they saw someone approaching along one of the other paths.

It was a boy about their age, dressed in a tight-fitting green tunic with a padded front reaching to mid thigh. Puffed sleeves were slashed at elbow and shoulder to show a crimson shirt underneath. It looked like silk, as did the striped red and yellow stockings which covered his legs down to soft leather boots. He wore a pointed hat, with feathers at the back. He stopped when he saw them, and muttered something.

Kevin asked him, 'What year are you from?'

'Who art tha?'

It sounded part fearful, part angry. Kevin tried to explain, but he did not seem to understand.

'Who art tha?' he repeated. 'Frenchies? Spaniards, mayhap? 'Tis certain tha'rt not English.'

'Of course we're English!'

They both tried quizzing him, but did not get far. His accent was thick, Irish-sounding. Suddenly he said: 'My horse.' It sounded like 'hairse'. 'She's not well tethered. I mun see to it.'

He turned and went back along the path, almost running. Kevin said, 'From what time, do you think? Elizabethan?'

'His clothes would suggest it. And when I mentioned Mary Queen of Scots, he called her "that traitress", as though she were alive still. I was reading about her lately: she was beheaded in fifteen eighty-seven.'

'So he could be from fifteen eighty-four?'

'Yes, I would think so.'

'Then what about seventeen eighty-four, or sixteen eighty-four?'

'They may still come. Or perhaps no one went into the wood in those years.'

He shrugged. 'Anyway, I was taking you to nineteen eighty-four.'

She followed silently, obviously nervous. He reached the edge of the wood and stopped to let her come up with him; then saw she had stopped, too, a couple of metres back. In a low voice, she said: 'No.'

'There's nothing to be frightened of. We don't need to go into the town. You can look at things from a distance.'

'No, I'm sorry.'

She turned back, and he followed. She was a girl, of course; he ought not to be surprised at timidity being stronger than curiosity.

When they got back to the mound, a boy was there: younger and smaller than the one in Elizabethan finery, and looking little better than a savage. He wore a smock of coarse grey cloth, roughly stitched with twine, and nothing else. His hair was tousled; arms, legs, and feet thickly grimed. A bare sole of foot looked like a pad of black leather. He was playing with a pebble, and clenched it inside his fist when he saw them.

They tried questioning him, too, but with even less success. He spoke in a growling inarticulate voice. Kevin asked Arabella, 'Did you understand any of that?'

'A word, here and there. I'm sure he said "wood". Isn't that an old English word?'

'Is it?'

'He might be Saxon.'

From 984, Kevin wondered. Or 884? Wouldn't that be about the time Alfred the Great was trying to hold back the Danes?

He said, 'I don't fancy going along his path, whenever he's from.'

Arabella shivered. 'No, indeed.'

'On the other hand, I wouldn't mind taking a look into *your* time.'

She smiled. It was a nice smile; her nose wasn't really long. 'I'd like to show you.'

As he followed her, it occurred to him that they had no idea how long the wood might stay open to travellers from the different centuries. What if it closed up, and he was forced to stay in 1884? Well, he would miss his parents, sister, friends at school. On the other hand, it would certainly be exciting! And if he could remember details of one or two important inventions of the past hundred years, he might become famous, rich . . .

The shock hit him without warning as the trees thinned to show open space ahead: it brought sharp fear, a sickness in the stomach. He tried to force his way forward and managed a couple of steps, but no more. He was shivering.

Arabella turned round. 'What is it, Kevin?' She looked at him. 'You can't either, can you?'

He made an effort which brought sweat to his brow, and shook his head.

She said quietly, 'I wondered. I thought perhaps it wasn't just me. We can't get into any year except our own.'

He felt defeated and ashamed. 'I suppose we'd better go back, to the mound.'

'You must, to find your path.' Her voice was low. 'This is mine.'

'We can . . . talk.'

'We have talked.' She managed a shadowy smile. 'I'm glad we met.'

He said, 'Don't go yet!'

She came towards him, and he thought she had changed her mind. But all she did was lean forward and briefly kiss him. The straw hat was harsh against his skin, but her lips were soft.

'Goodbye, Kevin.'

In the field beyond the wood a man with a plough followed two horses. Kevin watched her out of sight, but she didn't look back. He walked down the path, wondering what would happen to her, and corrected himself: what *had* happened. There was no way of knowing—or was there? The old churchyard at the back of the Green . . . She could have moved away from Southleigh, of course, but she might not. It wasn't likely to be Arabella Cartwright; she would probably have married. But there weren't that many Arabellas, and he knew her year of birth. 'R.I.P. Arabella ——, born 1873, beloved wife of . . .' He let the thought go. He knew he wasn't going to look for that gravestone.

The clearing was empty, but he saw the savage boy on one of the paths, returning to whatever barbarous home he had come from. At least Arabella had gone back to a solid, comfortable world. Without TV or video, cars or aeroplanes or computers, but a hopeful world; good in itself and with better things to come. He and she had that in common.

He wondered about the savage boy's world. He had no temptation to go into it, even if that were possible, but it would do no harm to look. There might be knights riding across the hillside, or Vikings—Roman soldiers, even.

He followed, and caught sight of him again as he reached the edge of the wood. Just as the boy stepped into the open, he dropped the pebble he had been playing with. Kevin fought the same feeling of resistance and sickness as he walked the last few metres. He picked up the pebble and called out, but the boy walked on, unhearing. He walked across an empty untilled field: no knights, Vikings, Roman soldiers. No buildings, either.

Apart from a ruin of some sort, in the distance. It was overgrown, shapeless except for one bit that stood out. Ivy trailed from a shattered tower. The outline was blurred, yet he could still recognize it. A bird with a half-folded wing, getting ready to fly . . . long broken and abandoned.

Kevin looked at the pebble he had picked up. It wasn't a pebble, in fact, but a thin square of battered metal, with a panel of crazed plastic let in one side. Behind that it was just possible to make out the face of a digital watch.

He let it drop and ran down the path, heading for home.

The Veldt

RAY BRADBURY

'George, I wish you'd look at the nursery.'

'What's wrong with it?'

'I don't know.'

'Well, then.'

'I just want you to look at it, that's all, or call a psychologist in to look at it.'

'What would a psychologist want with a nursery?'

'You know very well what he'd want.' His wife paused in the middle of the kitchen and watched the stove busy humming to itself, making supper for four.

'It's just that the nursery is different now than it was.'

'All right, let's have a look.'

They walked down the hall of their soundproofed, Happylife Home, which had cost them thirty thousand dollars installed, this house which clothed and fed and rocked them to sleep and played and sang and was good to them. Their approach sensitized a switch somewhere and the nursery light flicked on when they came within ten feet of it. Similarly, behind them, in the halls, lights went on and off as they left them behind, with a soft automaticity.

'Well,' said George Hadley.

They stood on the thatched floor of the nursery. It was forty feet across by forty feet long and thirty feet high; it had cost half again as much as the rest of the house. 'But nothing's too good for our children,' George had said.

The nursery was silent. It was empty as a jungle glade at hot high noon. The walls were blank and two dimensional. Now, as George and Lydia Hadley stood in the centre of the room, the walls began to purr and recede into crystalline distance, it seemed, and presently an African veldt appeared, in three dimensions; on all sides, in colours reproduced to the final pebble and bit of straw. The ceiling above them became a deep sky with a hot yellow sun.

George Hadley felt the perspiration start on his brow.

'Let's get out of the sun,' he said. 'This is a little too real. But I don't see anything wrong.'

'Wait a moment, you'll see,' said his wife.

Now the hidden odorophonics were beginning to blow a wind of odour at the two people in the middle of the baked veldtland. The hot straw smell of lion grass, the cool green smell of the hidden water hole, the great rusty smell of animals, the smell of dust like a red paprika in the hot air. And now the sounds: the thump of distant antelope feet on grassy sod, the papery rustling of vultures. A shadow passed through the sky. The shadow flickered on George Hadley's upturned, sweating face.

'Filthy creatures,' he heard his wife say.

'The vultures.'

'You see, there are the lions, far over, that way. Now they're on their way to the water hole. They've just been eating,' said Lydia. 'I don't know what.'

'Some animal.' George Hadley put his hand up to shield off the burning light from his squinted eyes. 'A zebra or a baby giraffe, maybe.'

'Are you sure?' His wife sounded peculiarly tense.

'No, it's a little late to be *sure*,' he said, amused. 'Nothing over there I can see but cleaned bone, and the vultures dropping for what's left.'

'Did you hear that scream?' she asked.

'No.'

'About a minute ago?'

'Sorry, no.'

The lions were coming. And again George Hadley was filled with admiration for the mechanical genius who had conceived this room. A miracle of efficiency selling for an absurdly low price. Every home should have one. Oh, occasionally they frightened you with their clinical accuracy, they startled you, gave you a twinge, but most of the time what fun for everyone, not only your own son and daughter, but for yourself when you felt like a quick jaunt to a foreign land, a quick change of scenery. Well, here it was!

And here were the lions now, fifteen feet away, so real, so feverishly and startlingly real that you could feel the prickling fur on your hand, and your mouth was stuffed with the dusty upholstery smell of their heated pelts, and the yellow of them was in your eyes like the yellow of an exquisite French tapestry, the yellows of lions and summer grass, and the sound of the matted lion lungs exhaling on the silent noontide, and the smell of meat from the panting, dripping mouths.

The lions stood looking at George and Lydia Hadley with terrible green-yellow eyes.

'Watch out!' screamed Lydia.

The lions came running at them.

Lydia bolted and ran. Instinctively, George sprang after her. Outside, in the hall, with the door slammed, he was laughing and she was crying, and they both stood appalled at the other's reaction.

'George!'

'Lydia! Oh, my dear poor sweet Lydia!'

'They almost got us!'

'Walls, Lydia, remember; crystal walls, that's all they are. Oh, they look real, I must admit—Africa in your parlour—but it's all dimensional superactionary, supersensitive colour film and mental tape film behind glass screens. It's all odorophonics and sonics, Lydia. Here's my handkerchief.'

'I'm afraid.' She came to him and put her body against him and cried steadily. 'Did you see? Did you *feel*? It's too real.'

'Now, Lydia . . .'

'You've got to tell Wendy and Peter not to read any more on Africa.'

'Of course . . . of course.' He patted her.

'Promise?'

'Sure.'

'And lock the nursery for a few days until I get my nerves settled.'

'You know how difficult Peter is about that. When I punished him a month ago by locking the nursery for even a few hours— the tantrum he threw! And Wendy too. They *live* for the nursery.'

'It's got to be locked, that's all there is to it.'

'All right.' Reluctantly he locked the huge door. 'You've been working too hard. You need a rest.'

'I don't know . . . I don't know,' she said, blowing her nose, sitting down in a chair that immediately began to rock and comfort her. 'Maybe I don't have enough to do. Maybe I have time to think too much. Why don't we shut the whole house off for a few days and take a vacation?'

'You mean you want to fry my eggs for me?'

'Yes.' She nodded.

'And darn my socks?'

'Yes.' A frantic, watery-eyed nodding.

'And sweep the house?'

'Yes, yes . . . oh, yes.'

'But I thought that's why we bought this house, so we wouldn't have to do anything?'

'That's just it. I feel like I don't belong here. The house is wife and mother now and nursemaid. Can I compete with an African veldt? Can I give a bath and scrub the children as efficiently or quickly as the automatic scrub bath can? I can not. And it isn't just me. It's you. You've been awfully nervous lately.'

'I suppose I have been smoking too much.'

'You look as if you didn't know what to do with yourself in this house, either. You smoke a little more every morning and drink a little more every afternoon and need a little more sedative every night. You're beginning to feel unnecessary too.'

'Am I?' He paused and tried to feel into himself to see what was really there.

'Oh, George!' She looked beyond him, at the nursery door. 'Those lions can't get out of there, can they?'

He looked at the door and saw it tremble as if something had jumped against it from the other side.

'Of course not,' he said.

At dinner they ate alone, for Wendy and Peter were at a special plastic carnival across town and had televised home to say they'd be late, to go ahead eating. So George Hadley, bemused, sat watching the dining-room table produce warm dishes of food from its mechanical interior.

'We forgot the ketchup,' he said.

'Sorry,' said a small voice within the table, and ketchup appeared.

As for the nursery, thought George Hadley, it won't hurt for the children to be locked out of it a while. Too much of anything isn't good for anyone. And it was clearly indicated that the children had been spending a little too much time on Africa. That *sun*. He could feel it on his neck, still, like a hot paw. And the *lions*. And the smell of blood. Remarkable how the nursery caught the telepathic emanations of the children's minds and created life to fill their every desire. The children thought lions, and there were lions. The children thought zebra, and there were zebra. Sun—sun. Giraffe—giraffes. Death and death.

That *last*. He chewed tastelessly on the meat that the table had cut for him. Death thoughts. They were awfully young, Wendy and Peter, for death thoughts. Or, no, you were never too young, really. Long before you knew what death was you were wishing it on someone else. When you were two years old you were shooting people with cap pistols.

But this—the long, hot African veldt—the awful death in the jaws of a lion. And repeated again and again.

'Where are you going?'

He didn't answer Lydia. Preoccupied, he let the lights glow softly on ahead of him, extinguish behind him as he padded to the nursery door. He listened against it. Far away, a lion roared.

He unlocked the door and opened it. Just before he stepped inside, he heard a faraway scream. And then another roar from the lions, which subsided quickly.

He stepped into Africa. How many times in the last year had he opened this door and found Wonderland. Alice, the Mock Turtle, or Aladdin and his Magical Lamp, or Jack Pumpkinhead of Oz, or Dr Doolittle, or the cow jumping over a very real-appearing moon—all the delightful contraptions of a make-believe world. How often had he seen Pegasus flying in the sky ceiling, or seen fountains of red fireworks, or heard angel voices singing. But now, this yellow hot Africa, this bake oven with murder in the heat. Perhaps Lydia was right. Perhaps they needed a little vacation from the fantasy which was growing a bit too real for ten-year-old children. It was all right to exercise one's mind with gymnastic fantasies, but when the lively child mind settled on *one* pattern . . .? It seemed that, at a distance, for the past month, he had heard lions roaring, and smelled their strong odour seeping as far away as his study door. But, being busy, he had paid it no attention.

George Hadley stood on the African grassland alone. The lions looked up from their feeding, watching him. The only flaw to the illusion was the open door through which he could see his wife, far down the dark hall, like a framed picture, eating her dinner abstractedly.

'Go away,' he said to the lions.

They did not go.

He knew the principle of the room exactly. You sent out your thoughts. Whatever you thought would appear.

'Let's have Aladdin and his lamp,' he snapped.

The veldtland remained; the lions remained.

'Come on, room! I demand Aladdin!' he said.

Nothing happened. The lions mumbled in their baked pelts.

'Aladdin!'

He went back to dinner. 'The fool room's out of order,' he said. 'It won't respond.'

'Or—'

'Or what?'

'Or it *can't* respond,' said Lydia, 'because the children have thought about Africa and lions and killing so many days that the room's in a rut.'

'Could be.'

'Or Peter's set it to remain that way.'

'*Set* it?'

'He may have got into the machinery and fixed something.'

'Peter doesn't know machinery.'

'He's a wise one for ten. That IQ of his—'

'Nevertheless—'

'Hello, Mom. Hello, Dad.'

The Hadleys turned. Wendy and Peter were coming in the front door, cheeks like peppermint candy, eyes like bright blue agate marbles, a smell of ozone on their jumpers from their trip in the helicopter.

'You're just in time for supper,' said both parents.

'We're full of strawberry ice-cream and hot dogs,' said the children, holding hands. 'But we'll sit and watch.'

'Yes, come tell us about the nursery,' said George Hadley.

The brother and sister blinked at him and then at each other. 'Nursery?'

'All about Africa and everything,' said the father with false joviality.

'I don't understand,' said Peter.

'Your mother and I were just travelling through Africa with rod and reel; Tom Swift and his Electric Lion,' said George Hadley.

'There's no Africa in the nursery,' said Peter simply.

'Oh, come now, Peter. We know better.'

'I don't remember any Africa,' said Peter to Wendy. 'Do you?'

'No.'

'Run see and come tell.'

She obeyed.

'Wendy, come back here!' said George Hadley, but she was gone. The house lights followed her like a flock of fireflies. Too late, he realized he had forgotten to lock the nursery door after his last inspection.

'Wendy'll look and come tell us,' said Peter.

'She doesn't have to tell *me*. I've seen it.'

'I'm sure you're mistaken, father.'

'I'm not, Peter. Come along now.'

But Wendy was back. 'It's not Africa,' she said breathlessly.

'We'll see about this,' said George Hadley, and they all walked down the hall together and opened the nursery door.

There was a green, lovely forest, a lovely river, a purple mountain, high voices singing, and Rima, lovely and mysterious, lurking in the trees with colourful flights of butterflies, like animated bouquets, lingering in her long hair. The African veldtland was gone. The lions were gone. Only Rima was here now, singing a song so beautiful that it brought tears to your eyes.

George Hadley looked in at the changed scene. 'Go to bed,' he said to the children.

They opened their mouths.

'You heard me,' he said.

They went off to the air closet, where a wind sucked them like brown leaves up the flue to their slumber rooms.

George Hadley walked through the singing glade and picked up something that lay in the corner near where the lions had been. He walked slowly back to his wife.

'What is that?' she asked.

'An old wallet of mine,' he said.

He showed it to her. The smell of hot grass was on it and the smell of a lion. There were drops of saliva on it, it had been chewed, and there were blood smears on both sides.

He closed the nursery door and locked it, tight.

In the middle of the night he was still awake and he knew his wife was awake. 'Do you think Wendy changed it?' she said at last, in the dark room.

'Of course.'

'Made it from a veldt into a forest and put Rima there instead of lions?'

'Yes.'

'Why?'

'I don't know. But it's staying locked until I find out.'

'How did your wallet get there?'

'I don't know anything,' he said, 'except that I'm beginning to be sorry we bought that room for the children. If children are neurotic at all, a room like that—'

'It's supposed to help them work off their neuroses in a healthful way.'

'I'm starting to wonder.' He stared at the ceiling.

'We've given the children everything they ever wanted. Is this our reward—secrecy, disobedience?'

'Who was it said, "Children are carpets, they should be stepped on occasionally"? We've never lifted a hand. They're insufferable—let's admit it. They come and go when they like; they treat us as if *we* were offspring. They're spoiled and we're spoiled.'

'They've been acting funny ever since you forbade them to take the rocket to New York a few months ago.'

'They're not old enough to do that alone, I explained.'

'Nevertheless, I've noticed they've been decidedly cool towards us since.'

'I think I'll have David McClean come tomorrow morning to have a look at Africa.'

'But it's not Africa now, it's Green Mansions country and Rima.'

'I have a feeling it'll be Africa again before then.'

A moment later they heard the screams.

Two screams. Two people screaming from downstairs. And then a roar of lions.

'Wendy and Peter aren't in their rooms,' said his wife.

He lay in his bed with his beating heart. 'No,' he said. 'They've broken into the nursery.'

'Those screams . . . they sound familiar.'

'Do they?'

'Yes, awfully.'

And although their beds tried very hard, the two adults couldn't be rocked to sleep for another hour. A smell of cats was in the night air.

'Father?' said Peter.

'Yes.'

Peter looked at his shoes. He never looked at his father any more, nor at his mother. 'You aren't going to lock up the nursery for good, are you?'

'That all depends.'

'On what?' snapped Peter.

'On you and your sister. If you intersperse this Africa with a little variety—oh, Sweden perhaps or Denmark or China—'

'I thought we were free to play as we wished.'

'You are, within reasonable bounds.'

'What's wrong with Africa, father?'

'Oh, so now you admit you have been conjuring up Africa, do you?'

'I wouldn't want the nursery locked up,' said Peter coldly. 'Ever.'

'Matter of fact, we're thinking of turning the whole house off for about a month. Live sort of a carefree one-for-all existence.'

'That sounds dreadful! Would I have to tie my own shoes instead of letting the shoe tier do it? And brush my own teeth and comb my hair and give myself a bath?'

'It would be fun for a change, don't you think?'

'No, it would be horrid. I didn't like it when you took out the picture painter last month.'

'That's because I wanted you to learn to paint all by yourself, son.'

'I don't want to do anything but look and listen and smell; what else *is* there to do?'

'All right, go play in Africa.'

'Will you shut off the house sometime soon?'

'We're considering it.'

'I don't think you'd better consider it any more, father.'

'I won't have any threats from my son!'

'Very well.' And Peter strolled off to the nursery.

'Am I on time?' said David McClean.

'Breakfast?' asked George Hadley.

'Thanks, had some. What's the trouble?'

'David, you're a psychologist.'

'I should hope so.'

'Well, then, have a look at our nursery. You saw it a year ago when you dropped by; did you notice anything peculiar about it then?'

'Can't say I did; the usual violences, a tendency towards a slight paranoia here or there, usual in children because they feel persecuted by parents constantly, but, oh, really nothing.'

They walked down the hall. 'I locked the nursery up,' explained the father, 'and the children broke back into it during the night. I let them stay so they could form the patterns for you to see.'

There was a terrible screaming from the nursery.

'There it is,' said George Hadley. 'See what you make of it.'

They walked in on the children without rapping.

The screams had faded. The lions were feeding.

'Run outside a moment, children,' said George Hadley. 'No, don't change the mental combination. Leave the walls as they are. Get!'

With the children gone, the two men stood studying the lions clustered at a distance, eating with great relish whatever it was they had caught.

'I wish I knew what it was,' said George Hadley. 'Sometimes I can almost see. Do you think if I brought high-powered binoculars here and—'

David McClean laughed drily. 'Hardly.' He turned to study all four walls. 'How long has this been going on?'

'A little over a month.'

'It certainly doesn't *feel* good.'

'I want facts, not feelings.'

'My dear George, a psychologist never saw a fact in his life. He only hears about feelings; vague things. This doesn't feel good, I tell you. Trust my hunches and my instincts. I have a nose for something bad. This is very bad. My advice to you is to have the whole damn room torn down and your children brought to me every day during the next year for treatment.'

'Is it that bad?'

'I'm afraid so. One of the original uses of these nurseries was so that we could study the patterns left on the walls by the child's mind, study at our leisure, and help the child. In this case, however, the room has become a channel towards—destructive thoughts, instead of a release away from them.'

'Didn't you sense this before?'

'I sensed only that you had spoiled your children more than most. And now you're letting them down in some way. What way?'

'I wouldn't let them go to New York.'

'What else?'

'I've taken a few machines from the house and threatened them, a month ago, with closing up the nursery unless they did their homework. I did close it for a few days to show I meant business.'

'Ah, ha!'

'Does that mean anything?'

'Everything. Where before they had a Santa Claus now they have a Scrooge. Children prefer Santas. You've let this room and this house replace you and your wife in your children's affections. This room is their mother and father, far more important in their lives than their real parents. And now you come along and want to shut it off. No wonder there's hatred here. You can feel it coming out of the sky. Feel that sun. George, you'll have to change your life. Like too many others, you've built it around creature comforts. Why, you'd starve tomorrow if something went wrong with your kitchen. You wouldn't know how to tap an egg. Nevertheless, turn everything off. Start new. It'll take time. But we'll make good children out of bad in a year, wait and see.'

'But won't the shock be too much for the children, shutting the room up abruptly, for good?'

'I don't want them going any deeper into this, that's all.'

The lions were finished with their red feast.

The lions were standing on the edge of the clearing watching the two men.

'Now *I'm* feeling persecuted,' said McClean. 'Let's get out of here. I never have cared for these damned rooms. Make me nervous.'

'The lions look real, don't they?' said George Hadley. 'I don't suppose there's any way—'

'What?'

'—that they could *become* real?'

'Not that I know.'

'Some flaw in the machinery, a tampering or something?'

'No.'

They went to the door.

'I don't imagine the room will like being turned off,' said the father.

'Nothing ever likes to die—even a room.'

'I wonder if it hates me for wanting to switch it off?'

'Paranoia is thick around here today,' said David McClean. 'You can follow it like a spoor. Hello.' He bent and picked up a bloody scarf. 'This yours?'

'No.' George Hadley's face was rigid. 'It belongs to Lydia.'

They went to the fuse box together and threw the switch that killed the nursery.

The two children were in hysterics. They screamed and pranced and threw things. They yelled and sobbed and swore and jumped at the furniture.

'You can't do that to the nursery, you can't!'

'Now, children.'

The children flung themselves on to a couch, weeping.

'George,' said Lydia Hadley, 'turn on the nursery, just for a few moments. You can't be so abrupt.'

'No.'

'You can't be so cruel.'

'Lydia, it's off, and it stays off. And the whole damn house dies as of here and now. The more I see of the mess we've put ourselves in, the more it sickens me. We've been contemplating our mechanical, electronic navels for too long. My God, how we need a breath of honest air!'

And he marched about the house turning off the voice clocks, the stoves, the heaters, the shoe shiners, the shoe lacers, the body scrubbers and swabbers and massagers, and every other machine he could put his hand to.

The house was full of dead bodies, it seemed. It felt like a mechanical cemetery. So silent. None of the humming hidden energy of machines waiting to function at the tap of a button.

'Don't let them do it!' wailed Peter at the ceiling, as if he was talking to the house, the nursery. 'Don't let father kill everything.' He turned to his father. 'Oh, I hate you!'

'Insults won't get you anywhere.'

'I wish you were dead!'

'We were, for a long while. Now we're going to really start living. Instead of being handled and massaged, we're going to *live*.'

Wendy was still crying and Peter joined her again. 'Just a moment, just one moment, just another moment of nursery,' they wailed.

'Oh, George,' said his wife, 'it can't hurt.'

'All right . . . all right, if they'll only just shut up. One minute, mind you, and then off forever.'

'Daddy, Daddy, Daddy!' sang the children, smiling with wet faces.

'And then we're going on a vacation. David McClean is coming back in half an hour to help us move out and get to the airport. I'm going to dress. You turn the nursery on for a minute, Lydia, just a minute, mind you.'

And the three of them went babbling off while he let himself be vacuumed upstairs through the air flue and set about dressing himself. A minute later Lydia appeared.

'I'll be glad when we get away,' she sighed.

'Did you leave them in the nursery?'

'I wanted to dress too. Oh, that horrid Africa. What can they see in it?'

'Well, in five minutes we'll be on our way to Iowa. Lord, how did we ever get in this house? What prompted us to buy a nightmare?'

'Pride, money, foolishness.'

'I think we'd better get downstairs before those kids get engrossed with those damned beasts again.'

Just then they heard the children calling, 'Daddy, Mommy, come quick . . . quick!'

They went downstairs in the air flue and ran down the hall. The children were nowhere in sight. 'Wendy? Peter!'

They ran into the nursery. The veldtland was empty save for the lions waiting, looking at them. 'Peter, Wendy?'

The door slammed.

'Wendy, Peter!'

George Hadley and his wife whirled and ran back to the door.

'Open the door!' cried George Hadley, trying the knob. 'Why, they've locked it from the outside! Peter!' He beat at the door. 'Open up!'

He heard Peter's voice outside, against the door.

'Don't let them switch off the nursery and the house,' he was saying.

Mr and Mrs George Hadley beat at the door. 'Now, don't be ridiculous, children. It's time to go. Mr McClean'll be here in a minute and . . .'

And then they heard the sounds.

The lions on three sides of them, in the yellow veldt grass, padding through the dry straw, rumbling and roaring in their throats.

The lions.

Mr Hadley looked at his wife and they turned and looked back at the beasts edging slowly forward, crouching, tails stiff.

Mr and Mrs Hadley screamed.

And suddenly they realized why those other screams had sounded familiar.

'Well, here I am,' said David McClean in the nursery doorway. 'Oh, hello.' He stared at the two children seated in the centre of the open glade eating a little picnic lunch. Beyond them was the water hole and the yellow veldtland; above was the hot sun. He began to perspire. 'Where are your father and mother?'

The children looked up and smiled. 'Oh, they'll be here directly.'

'Good, we must get going.' At a distance Mr McClean saw the lions fighting and clawing and then quieting down to feed in silence under the shady trees.

He squinted at the lions with his hand up to his eyes.

Now the lions were done feeding. They moved to the water hole to drink.

A shadow flickered over Mr McClean's hot face. Many shadows flickered. The vultures were dropping down the blazing sky.

'A cup of tea?' asked Wendy in the silence.

The Old Burying Place . . .

GERALD KERSH

T he old man said: 'Once, when I was no older than you,
I went as far away as the Old Burying Place.'

'Where is that?' asked the little girl.

'Far away, across the plains and through the forest. Ha, we
were *men*, we were *hunters*. But these young men? Bah. They
have good bows and the best of everything, yet they have been
away for a day and a night, and where is the meat? All I ask is a
bit of meat to suck. I have lived through as many winters as
there are fingers on eight men's hands. In my day we had no

iron-tipped arrows. We chipped a sharp flint, bound it firm, and—psst! Iron! Bah! Women they are: not men.'

'Tell me about the Old Burying Place.'

'It's a long, long way away, but I went there when I was a boy. It was one winter, a terrible winter. There was no food. Even the acorns were rotten. All the pigs had gone away into the forests, so we followed them with our bows and our spears—my father, and his father, and myself.

'It was very cold. We walked for five days before we found the tracks of a pig. We followed them all day, our arrows on our bowstrings. Towards nightfall we caught up with him—a very old one, rooting under the snow for food. My father's arrow struck him in the flank. Then, when he ran away again, we followed. There was blood—'

'Tell me about the Old Burying Place.'

'Ssh! What am I telling you, then? I was saying: we followed the pig. I was tired, but dared not rest: they would have left me to die in the snow.

'At last we came to a part of the forest full of broken stones. "We are coming to the Old Burying Place," said my father's father. "There are bad things here. Let us go back." But my father said: "I fear only hunger," and drove us forward.

'Soon there were no trees, only stones—the Old Burying Place. This is a place of death and darkness. Nothing grows there—not a weed; nothing. There we found the pig, lying dead.

'We took out his liver and ate it before it got cold. Then we lay down to sleep, having lit a fire to keep away the cats. Only my father's father would not sleep. He said: "It is not lucky to sleep here. People sometimes do not wake up after sleeping here. There are things walking here that should not be walking." At dawn I awoke and saw him, still sitting, watching.

'Then my father said: "Let us open one of these burying places. I knew a man who found good cooking-pots in one of them." But his father said: "No. It is not good. There is bad air in these tombs. Why does nothing grow here, not even the grass?" But my father was already striking with his axe at the door of one of the tombs, at a place where the earth had fallen away.

'The door was of iron, but soft. It fell to a red dust. Then there was another door, and a deep pit. We took firesticks, and shouted to frighten away evil spirits, and climbed down, until we reached a great cave. Who could have dug such caves? They go deeper than man can follow, and are lined with smooth white stones, so that the sound of your voice comes back to you again and again, no matter how low you speak.

'We walked for a great distance. The cave was very cold and dark, and our firesticks were burning low. At last we saw bones. They must have been the bones of common people. They had all been buried together; thrown in a pile at one of the doorways —more bones than you could count if you had ten times ten fingers and toes—bones and bones and bones. No cooking-pots; nor iron; nothing except their death-masks.'

'Death-masks?' asked the little girl.

'Yes. The buried People who lived here when the world was young used to cover the faces of their dead.'

'Why?'

'Who knows why? So; we turned back. The bones of three people lay in a corner; a man, a woman, and a child, holding together still, even in death. Nearby there was a doll, such as you yourself might play with.'

'You should have brought it for me.'

'Fool! When you were not yet even born? My father said: "I shall not go away with empty hands." And he tore down a sheet of iron fixed to the wall. My father's father took a death-mask.

'As for me, I picked up a chain of yellow metal that hung on the dead woman's arm. It must have been a powerful talisman, because even as I pulled at it the bones fell apart and tumbled to the ground in a heap like all the rest. Then we went back. The pig—'

'And what was the chain like?'

'Tah! A chain. On the end of it there hung a thing like this—' the old man crossed his forefingers—'with the image of a man hanging on it, fastened by the hands and feet.'

'Oh, how pretty. And the mask?'

'I don't know . . . It looked like the bones of a man's head, but instead of eye-holes there were round plates of something you could see through; and instead of a nose there was a long tube and a bag. As for the iron plate, that is all I have left, and it hangs behind you now.'

'Oh, is that it?' asked the little girl. She looked. The plate was long and rectangular; much cracked; eaten up by time. It had been enamelled. Still legible on its surface was one word:

'PICCADILLY'

The girl said: 'I wish you had saved the chain.'

The old man rose, laughing, as three young men came into the cave, dragging the corpse of a goat.

Hey, You Down There!

HAROLD ROLSETH

Calvin Spender drained his coffee cup and wiped his mouth with the back of his hand. He belched loudly and then proceeded to fill a corncob pipe with coarsely shredded tobacco. He scratched a match across the top of the table and, holding it to his pipe, he sucked noisily until billows of acrid smoke poured from his mouth.

Dora Spender sat across the table from her husband, her breakfast scarcely touched. She coughed lightly, and then, as no frown appeared on Calvin's brow, she said, 'Are you going to dig in the well this morning, Calvin?'

Calvin fixed his small red-rimmed eyes upon her and, as if she had not spoken, said, 'Git going at the chores right away. You're going to be hauling up dirt.'

'Yes, Calvin,' Dora whispered. Calvin cleared his throat, and the action caused his Adam's apple to move convulsively under the loose red folds of skin on his neck. He rose from the table and went out the kitchen door, kicking viciously at the tawny cat which had been lying on the doorstep.

Dora gazed after him and wondered for the thousandth time what it was that Calvin reminded her of. It was not some other person. It was something else. Sometimes it seemed as though the answer was about to spring to her mind, as just now when Calvin had cleared his throat. But always it stopped just short of her consciousness. It was disturbing to know with such certainty that Calvin looked like something other than himself and yet not know what that something was. Someday though, Dora knew, the answer would come to her. She rose hurriedly from the table and set about her chores.

Half-way between the house and the barn a doughnut-shaped mound of earth surrounded a hole. Calvin went to the edge of the hole and stared down into it distastefully. Only necessity could have forced him to undertake this task, but it was either this digging or the hauling of barrels and barrels of water each day from Nord Fisher's farm a half mile down the road.

Calvin's herd of scrub cattle was small, but the amount of water it consumed was astonishing. For two weeks now, ever since his well had gone dry, Calvin had been hauling water, and the disagreeable chore was becoming more unpleasant because of neighbour Nord's clumsy hints that some form of payment for the water would not be amiss.

Several feet back from the edge of the hole Calvin had driven a heavy iron stake into the ground, and to this was attached a crude rope ladder. The rope ladder had become necessary when the hole had reached a depth well beyond the length of any wooden ladder Calvin owned.

Calvin hoped desperately that he would not have to go much deeper. He estimated that he was now down fifty or sixty feet, a common depth for many wells in the area. His greatest fear was that he would hit a stratum of rock which would call for the services of a well-drilling outfit. For such a venture both his funds and his credit rating were far too low.

Calvin picked up a bucket to which was attached a long rope and lowered it into the hole. It was Dora's backbreaking task to haul the bucket up hand over hand after Calvin had filled it from the bottom of the hole.

With a mumbled curse Calvin emptied his pipe and started down the rope ladder. By the time he got to the bottom of the hole and had filled the bucket, Dora should be there to haul it up. If she weren't, she would hear about it.

From the house Dora saw Calvin prepare to enter the well, and she worked with desperate haste to complete her chores. She reached the hole just as a muffled shout from below indicated that the bucket was full.

Summoning all her strength, Dora hauled the bucket up. She emptied it and then lowered it into the hole again. While she waited for the second bucketload, she examined the contents of the first. She was disappointed to find it had only the normal moistness of underground earth. No water seeped from it.

In her own fashion, Dora was deeply religious and at each tenth bucket she pulled up she murmured an urgent prayer that it would contain more water in it than earth. She had settled at praying at every tenth bucketload because she did not believe it in good taste to pester God with every bucket. Also, she varied the wording of each prayer, feeling that God must become bored with the same petition repeated over and over.

On this particular morning as she lowered the bucket for its tenth loading, she prayed, 'Please God, let something happen this time . . . let something really and truly happen so I won't have to haul up any more dirt.'

Something happened almost immediately. As the rope slackened in her hands indicating that the bucket had reached the bottom, a scream of sheer terror came up from the hole, and the rope ladder jerked violently. Whimpering sounds of mortal fear sounded faintly, and the ladder grew taut with heavy strain.

Dora fell to her knees and peered down into the darkness. 'Calvin,' she called, 'are you all right? What is it?'

Then, with startling suddenness, Calvin appeared, literally shooting out of the hole. At first Dora was not sure it was Calvin. The peeled redness of his face was gone; now it was a yellowish green. He was trembling violently and had trouble breathing.

It must be a heart attack, Dora thought, and tried mightily to suppress the surge of joy that swept over her.

Calvin lay upon the ground panting. Finally he gained control of himself. Under ordinary circumstances Calvin did not converse with Dora, but now he seemed eager to talk. 'You know what happened down there?' he said in a shaky voice. 'You know what happened? The complete bottom dropped right out of that hole. All of a sudden it went, and there I was, standing on nothing but air. If I hadn't grabbed aholt of the last rung of the ladder . . . Why, that hole must be a thousand feet the way the bottom dropped out of it!'

Calvin babbled on, but Dora did not listen. She was filled with awe at the remarkable way in which her prayer had been answered. If the hole had no more bottom, there would be no more dirt to haul up.

When Calvin had regained his strength, he crept to the edge of the hole and peered down.

'What are you going to do, Calvin?' Dora asked timidly.

'Do? I'm going to find out how far down that hole goes. Get the flashlight from the kitchen.'

Dora hurried off. When she returned, Calvin had a large ball of binder twine he had gotten from the tool shed.

He tied the flashlight securely to the end of the line, switched it on, and lowered it into the hole. He paid out the line for about a hundred feet and then stopped. The light was only a feeble glimmer down below and revealed nothing. Calvin lowered the light another hundred feet and this time it was only a twinkling speck as it swung at the end of the line. Calvin released another long length of twine and another and another and now the light was no longer visible, and the large ball of twine had shrunk to a small tangle.

'Almost a full thousand feet,' he whispered in awe. 'And no bottom yet. Might as well pull it up.'

But the line did not come up with Calvin's pull. It stretched and grew taut, but it did not yield to his tugging.

'Must be caught on something,' Calvin muttered, and gave the line a sharp jerk. In response there was a downward jerk that almost tore the line from his hands.

'Hey,' yelled Calvin. 'The line . . . it jerked!'

'But, Calvin,' Dora protested.

'Don't Calvin me. I tell you there's something on the end of this line.'

He gave another tug, and again the line was almost pulled from his hands. He tied the line to the stake and sat down to ponder the matter.

'It don't make sense,' he said, more to himself than to Dora. 'What could be down underground a good thousand feet?'

Tentatively he reached over and pulled lightly on the line. This time there was no response, and rapidly he began hauling it up. When the end of the line came into view, there was no flashlight attached to it. Instead, there was a small white pouch of a leatherlike substance.

Calvin opened the pouch with trembling fingers and shook into his palm a bar of yellow metal and a folded piece of parchment. The bar of metal was not large but seemed heavy for its size. Calvin got out his jackknife and scratched the point of the blade across the metal. The knife blade bit into it easily.

'Gold,' said Calvin, his voice shaky. 'Must be a whole pound of it . . . and just for a measly flashlight. They must be crazy down there.'

He thrust the gold bar into his pocket and opened the small piece of parchment. One side was closely covered with a fine script. Calvin turned it this way and that and then tossed it on the ground.

'Foreigners,' he said. 'No wonder they ain't got any sense. But it's plain they need flashlights.'

'But, Calvin,' said Dora. 'How could they get *down* there? There ain't any mines in this part of the country.'

'Ain't you ever heard of them secret government projects?' asked Calvin scornfully. 'This must be one of them. Now I'm going to town and get me a load of flashlights. They must need them bad. Now, mind you watch that hole good. Don't let no one go near it!'

Calvin strode to the battered pick-up which was standing near the barn, and a minute later was rattling down the highway towards Harmony Junction.

Dora picked up the bit of parchment which Calvin had thrown away. She could make nothing of the writing on it. It was all very strange. If it were some secret government undertaking, why would foreigners be engaged in it? And why would they need flashlights so urgently as to pay a fortune for one?

Suddenly it occurred to her that possibly the people down below didn't know there were English-speaking people up above. She hurried into the house and rummaged through Calvin's rickety desk for paper and pencil. In her search she found a small, ragged dictionary, and she took this with her to the kitchen table. Spelling did not come easy to Dora.

Her note was a series of questions. Why were they down there? Who were they? Why did they pay so much for an old flashlight?

As she started for the well it occurred to her that possibly the people down there might be hungry. She went back to the kitchen and wrapped a loaf of bread and a fair-sized piece of ham in a clean dish towel. She added a postscript to her note apologizing for the fact that she had nothing better to offer them. Then the thought came to her that since the people down below were obviously foreigners and possibly not too well versed in English, the small dictionary might be of help to them in answering her note. She wrapped the dictionary with the food in the towel.

It took Dora a long while to lower the bucket, but finally the twine grew slack in her hands, and she knew the bucket had reached the bottom. She waited a few moments and then tugged the line gently. The line held firm below, and Dora seated herself on the pile of soil to wait.

The warm sunlight felt good on her back, and it was pleasant to sit and do nothing. She had no fear that Calvin would return soon. She knew that nothing on earth—or under it—could keep Calvin from visiting a number of taverns once he was in town, and that with each tavern visited time would become more and more meaningless to him. She doubted that he would return before morning.

After a half hour Dora gave the line a questioning tug, but it did not yield. She did not mind. It was seldom that she had time to idle away. Usually when Calvin went to town, he burdened her with chores to be done during his absence, coupling each order with a threat of what awaited her should his instructions not be carried out.

Dora waited another half hour before giving the line another tug. This time there was a sharp answering jerk, and Dora began hauling the bucket upward. It seemed much heavier now, and twice she had to pause for a rest. When the bucket reached the surface, she saw why it was heavier.

'My goodness,' she murmured as she viewed the dozen or so

yellow metal bars in the bucket. 'They must be real hungry down there!'

A sheet of the strange parchment was also in the bucket, and Dora picked it out expecting to see the strange script of the first note.

'Well, I declare,' she said when she saw that the note was in English. It was in the same print as the dictionary, and each letter had been made with meticulous care.

She read the note slowly, shaping each word with her lips as she read.

Your language is barbaric, but the crude code book you sent down made it easy for our scholars to decipher it. We, too, wonder about you. How have you overcome the problem of living in the deadly light? Our legends tell of a race living on the surface, but intelligent reasoning has forced us to ridicule these old tales until now. We would still doubt that you are surface dwellers except for the fact that our instruments show without question that the opening above us leads to the deadly light.

The clumsy death ray which you sent us indicates that your scientific development is very low. Other than an artifact of another race it has no value to us. We sent gold as a courtesy payment only.

The food you call bread is not acceptable to our digestive systems, but the ham is beyond price. It is obviously the flesh of some creature, and we will exchange a double weight of gold for all that you can send us. Send more immediately. Also send a concise history of your race and arrange for your best scientists, such as they are, to communicate with us.

Glar, the Master

'Land sakes,' said Dora. 'Real bossy they are. I've a good mind not to send them *anything*. I don't dast send them more ham. Calvin would notice if any more is gone.'

Dora took the gold bars to her petunia bed beside the house and buried them in the loose black soil. She paid no heed to the sound of a car coming down the highway at high speed until it passed the house and wild squawking sounded above the roar of the motor. She hurried around to the front of the house, knowing already what had happened. She stared in dismay at the four white leghorns which lay along the road.

Now Calvin would charge her with negligence and beat her into unconsciousness.

Fear sharpened her wits. Perhaps if she could dispose of the bodies Calvin would think foxes had got them. Hastily she gathered up the dead chickens and feathers which lay scattered about. When she was finished, there was no evidence of the disaster.

She carried the chickens to the back of the house wondering how she could best dispose of them. Suddenly, as she glanced towards the hole, the answer came to her.

An hour later the four chickens were dressed and neatly cut up. Ignoring the other instructions in the note, she sent the bulky parcel of chicken down into the hole.

She sat down again to enjoy the luxury of doing nothing. When, an hour later, she picked up the line, there was an immediate response from below. The bucket was exceedingly heavy this time, and she was fearful that the line might break. She was dizzy with fatigue when she finally hauled the bucket over to the edge of the hole. This time there were several dozen bars of gold in it and a brief note in the same precise lettering as before.

Our scientists are of the opinion that the flesh you sent down is that of a creature you call chicken. This is the supreme food. Never have we eaten anything so delicious. To show our appreciation we are sending you a bonus payment. Your code book indicates that there is a larger creature similar to chicken called turkey. Send us turkey immediately. I repeat, send us turkey immediately.

Glar, the Master

'Land sakes,' gasped Dora. 'They must have et that chicken raw. Now where in tarnation would I get a turkey?'

She buried the gold bars in another part of her petunia bed.

Calvin returned about ten o'clock the next morning. His eyes were bloodshot, and his face was a mottled red. The loose skin on his neck hung lower than usual and more than ever he reminded Dora of something which eluded her.

Calvin stepped down from the pick-up, and Dora cringed, but he seemed too tired and preoccupied to bother with her. He surveyed the hole glumly, then got back into the truck and backed it to the edge of the mound of earth. On the back of the truck was a winch with a large drum of steel cable.

'Fix me something to eat,' he ordered Dora.

Dora hurried into the house and began preparing ham and eggs. Each moment she expected Calvin to come in and demand to know, with a few blows, what was holding up his meal. But Calvin seemed very busy in the vicinity of the hole. When Dora went out to call him to eat, she found he had done a surprising amount of work. He had attached an oil drum to the steel cable. This hung over a heavy steel rod which rested across the hole. Stakes driven into the ground on each side of the hole held the rod in place.

'Your breakfast is ready, Calvin,' said Dora.

'Shut up,' Calvin answered.

The winch was driven by an electric motor, and Calvin ran a cable from the motor to an electric outlet on the yard lightpost.

From the cab he took a number of boxes and placed them in the oil drum.

'A whole hundred of them,' he chuckled, more to himself than to Dora. 'Fifty-nine cents apiece. Peanuts . . . one bar of gold will buy thousands.'

Calvin threw the switch which controlled the winch, and with sickening force Dora suddenly realized the terrible thing that would soon happen. The creatures down below had no use or regard for flashlights.

Down went the oil drum, the cable screeching shrilly as it passed over the rod above the hole. Calvin got an oil can from the truck and applied oil generously to the rod and cable.

In a very short while the cable went slack and Calvin stopped the winch.

'I'll give them an hour to load up the gold,' he said and went to the kitchen for his delayed breakfast.

Dora was practically in a state of shock. What would happen when the flashlights came back up with an insulting note in English was too horrible to contemplate. Calvin would learn about the gold she had received and very likely kill her.

Calvin ate his breakfast leisurely. Dora busied herself with household tasks, trying with all her might to cast out of her mind the terrible thing which was soon to happen.

Finally Calvin glanced at the wall clock, yawned widely, and tapped out his pipe. Ignoring Dora he went out to the hole. In spite of her terrible fear Dora could not resist following him. It was as if some power outside herself forced her to go.

The winch was already reeling in the cable when she got to the hole. It seemed only seconds before the oil drum was up. The grin on Calvin's face was broad as he reached out over the hole and dragged the oil drum to the edge. A look of utter disbelief replaced the grin as he looked into the drum. His Adam's apple seemed to vibrate, and once again part of Dora's mind tried to recall what it was that Calvin reminded her of.

Calvin was making flat, bawling sounds like a lost calf. He hauled the drum out of the hole and dumped its contents on the ground. The flashlights, many of them dented and with lenses broken, made a sizeable pile.

With a tremendous kick Calvin sent flashlights flying in all directions. One, with a note attached, landed at Dora's feet. Either Calvin was so blinded by rage that he didn't see it, or he assumed it was written in the same unreadable script as the first note.

'You down there,' he screamed into the hole. 'You filthy swine. I'll fix you. I'll make you sorry you ever double-crossed me. I'll . . . I'll . . .'

He dashed for the house, and Dora hastily snatched up the note.

You are even more stupid than we thought [she read]. *Your clumsy death rays are useless to us. We informed you of this. We want turkey. Send us turkey immediately.*

Glar, the Master

She crumpled the note swiftly as Calvin came from the house with his double-barrelled shotgun. For a moment Dora thought that he knew everything and was about to kill her.

'Please, Calvin,' she said.

'Shut up,' Calvin said. 'You saw me work the winch. Can you do it?'

'Why, yes, but what . . .?'

'Listen, you stupid cow. I'm going down there and fix those dirty foreigners. You send me down and bring me up.' He

seized Dora by the shoulder. 'And if you mess things, I'll fix you, too! I'll really and truly fix you.'

Dora nodded dumbly.

Calvin put his gun in the oil drum and pushed it to the centre of the hole. Then, hanging on to the cable, he carefully lowered himself into the drum.

'Give me just one hour to run those dirty rats down, then bring me back up,' he said.

Dora threw the switch and the oil drum went down. When the cable slackened, she stopped the winch. She spent most of the hour praying that Calvin would not find the people down below and become a murderer.

Exactly an hour later Dora started the oil drum upward. The motor laboured mightily as though under a tremendous strain, and the cable seemed stretched almost to the breaking point.

Dora gasped when the oil drum came into view. Calvin was not in it! She shut off the motor and hastened to the drum, half expecting to find Calvin crouching down inside. But Calvin was not there. Instead there were scores of gold bars and on top of them a sheet of the familiar white parchment.

'Land sakes,' Dora said, as she took in a full view of the drum's contents. She had no idea of the value of the treasure upon which she gazed. She only knew it must be immense. Carefully, she reached down and picked out the note, which she read in her slow, precise manner:

Not even the exquisite flavour of the chicken compares to the incomparable goodness of the live turkey you sent down to us. We must confess that our concept of turkey was quite different, but this is of no consequence. So delectable was the turkey that we are again sending you a bonus payment. We implore you to send us more turkey immediately.

Glar, the Master

Dora read the note a second time to make sure she understood it fully. 'Well, I declare,' she said in considerable wonder. 'I declare.'

A Hundred Steps

ROBERT SCOTT

John paused in his descent, hand against the worn stone wall, and smiled grimly. It had been their first quarrel. No, not quarrel. Difference. Their first difference.

'A hundred steps to heaven or a thousand steps to hell,' the old woman had said if he understood her correctly. So he had insisted on driving out to the tower even though Janet complained bitterly that climbing derelict old towers wasn't her idea of heaven, especially on the last day of their honeymoon.

'Loosen up,' he had said. 'It'll only take half an hour and we'll get a marvellous view from the top. Then we can drive on to the coast.'

'It'll be too late.'

'A hundred steps to the top,' he had reminded her. 'That's what the old woman said. A hundred steps for lovers to see their heaven.' He was sure she had said '*their* heaven'.

'I'll wait here,' she insisted, smiling brightly and opening her copy of *True Romances*. And she stayed in the car, shoes off, feet tucked under her.

There had been no view of heaven from the top, only a thick, blanketing mist. And now? Well, now . . . He drew a deep breath, refusing to let his brain admit the terror that was ready to overwhelm him. A hundred steps to heaven or a thousand steps to hell. He had counted the steps on his way up and now he was counting them again on the way down.

'Nine hundred and eighty-two,' he muttered. 'Nine hundred and eighty-three. Nine hundred and . . . '

Death's Murderers

GERALDINE McCAUGHREAN

The man Grab was slumped over a table at the Tabard Inn in Southwark—(you may know the place). He had wetted his brain in beer, and it weighed heavy. The clanging of the church bell registered dully in his ears. 'Who are they burying?' he asked.

Old Harry, the landlord, who was wiping tables close by, said, 'Don't you know? I wondered why you weren't at the funeral —him being a friend of yours. It's Colley the Fence. Caught it last Wednesday and gone today. Him and his wife and his two boys.'

'Caught what?' demanded Grab, grasping Harry's arm.

'The Black Death, of course!'

Then another customer chimed in. 'Ay, they do say the Plague came to Combleton over yonder, and Death laid hands on every man, woman, and child and carried 'em off.'

'Where? Carried them off where?' demanded Grab, fighting his way through drink-haze like a ghost through cobwebs.

'Who knows where Death carries men off to,' said a deeply hooded character sitting in the corner of the bar, 'but he sure enough comes for every man in the end. And he's taken twice his share recently, thanks to the Plague.'

Tears of indignation started into Grab's eyes. 'I don't see what gives Death the right to go carrying off anyone!' he slurred. 'And if you ask me, it's about time some brave soul stood up to Death and put an end to his carryings-on—his carryings-off I mean. Dip! Cut! Where are you?' And he stumbled off into the sunlight to look for his two closest friends.

Dip was at home in bed, but not for long. Grab knocked him up and called him into the street. They met with Cut coming home from a card-game and cursing his empty pockets.

Grab threw an arm over each friend's shoulder. 'Have you heard? Old Colley the Fence is dead. Death carried off him and all his family in a couple of days. Let's take an oath, friends, not to rest until we've tracked down this "Death" fellow and stuck a knife between his ribs. Think what the mayor and parish would pay if we brought in Death's dead body. Besides—how many purses do you think he's emptied on the dark highway, eh? Death must have made himself quite a walletful by now.'

Cut fingered his sharp penknife—the one he used for cutting purses. Dip felt his fingers itch at the promise of rich pickings. 'We're with you, neighbour Grab!' they cried, and off they reeled, not the sum total of one brain between the three of them.

They looked for Death in the graveyard, but decided he must be out hunting the living instead. They looked for Death in the fields, but he had always gone before they arrived, leaving the flowers doomed to wither and the leaves, sooner or later, to fall.

Then, as the daylight failed, they saw a small figure on the road ahead. 'We've caught him up!' cried Grab, and they fell on the man, with flailing fists.

'Wait a minute! This isn't Death at all!' said Cut, letting his penknife fall. 'He's just some silly old duffer. Look at him—he's older than Methuselah!'

The old man peered at them out of the dark recesses of his hood. His face was as white and bony as a skull, with purse-string lips and eyes sunk deep in red whorls of wrinkled skin. His hands were as brown as vinegar-paper, and his back hunched over like a turtle's shell. 'What do you want with me? Don't I have enough to put up with? Can't you leave a poor blighted old creature in peace?'

'You're no good to us!' Dip said in disgust. 'We wanted Death, not some wrinkled old prune on legs!'

A bitter laugh creaked out through the creature's gappy ribs. '*You* want Death! Ah, not half as much as I do! I'm the one poor beast alive that Death can't carry off. I'm condemned to live for ever and to creep about the Earth in this worn-out old body, getting older and older and older. As for Death—I've just left him under that oak tree yonder. If you hurry, you'll find him still there.'

Cut's knife was raised again. 'So! You've had dealings with him. We'll kill you anyway!'

The fossil of a man let go a sigh that seemed to break through his brittle skin. 'Aaah, I wish you could rob me of this tedious burden, Life. You should pity me, even if you have no respect for my old age. But don't bother to batter on this prison my soul calls a body: you can't free me from it.' He shuffled out from under their raised blades, muttering, 'You're the lucky ones— you might die today!'

'Get to bed with the maggots and mould, you old relic of the Devil,' Grab cursed. 'We're on our way to kill Death. Then no one will have to die any more!' As soon as the old man was out of sight, the three accomplices forgot him completely.

Under the oak tree, there was no sign of Death. But there was a pot of money as big as any crock of gold at the rainbow's end.

Cut tipped the jar over with his foot, and the wealth of seven lifetimes spilled out on to the grass. They looked around. No one was even in sight. And there had been no attempt to hide the gold. It lay there, just inviting them to keep it. Grab and Dip and Cut were suddenly rich!

'Rich! We're rich, rich, rich!' As the gold coins spilled out of the jar, so all thought of their plot to kill Death dropped out of their minds.

'Dip, your legs are youngest,' said Grab. 'Run into town and fetch us some wine. We've got to celebrate luck like this!'

'Why is it always me?' Dip threw a sulky look at the gold, but was given only one coin to buy the makings of a party.

'We'll both stay and guard it, don't you worry,' Grab assured him. 'Be quick, lad. When you get back we'll decide what we're to do with it all—what mansions we'll build, who to bribe, what monks we'll pay to have done in. We don't have to do our own dirty work from now on, boy! We'll be the Three Kings of the Thieves.'

Full of such thoughts, Dip set off into the dusk to buy cakes and wine. The sun was behind him, and his shadow stretched long and spidery ahead, so that he was all the time stepping into his own darkness.

Grab and Cut watched him go, then sat down on either side of the pot of gold. They counted the coins. Somehow it always came to a different number: 848 or 916 or 772. Grab scowled. 'Of course you realize we can't divide it three ways.'

'We can't?'

'You take my word for it. It won't share out evenly.'

'It won't?'

'Two ways, yes. Not three. One of us will have to take less.'

'Oh!'

Cut decided at once that since Dip was the youngest, he should take the smallest share. They both nodded to themselves and settled back to counting the gold. This time there seemed to be 999—or 783, or perhaps 870. But it did not change their opinion that Dip should have less.

'Of course it won't go far between the *three* of us,' Grab mused. 'Not with the cost of living how it is. And you know how Dip squanders money.'

'No?'

'He'll soon have spent all his, and he'll be asking to borrow from us.'

'But I can't spare any of mine!' said Cut anxiously.

'No more can I. There's little enough to share out between two, let alone three.' They lapsed into silence, and above them the oak's heavy branches groaned while the gold coins clinked between their fingers. 'Supposing . . .' said Cut, 'just supposing Dip was to meet with an accident on his way back from town . . .'

'So many thieves these days . . .' said Grab nodding sadly. 'So many ruffians and murderers.'

Meanwhile, Dip was watching his shadow move ahead of him on the roadway like a black plough. How big it was—much bigger than him. When he had his share of the money, he would be a bigger man in every way. No more creeping through the crowds at fairs, cutting purses and catching the pennies that dropped. He could walk tall and stately, in fur-trimmed robes, and people would touch their forelocks and step aside. Beggars would fight for the chance to plead with him. And if he felt like it, he could drive them away with a pelting of money, and see them grovel in his wake.

Ah, but if he was going to start giving money away, there would be less for the true necessities—drink and women and gambling. In fact he could think of so many good uses for the gold that it seemed a pity Cut and Grab had been with him when he had found the jar. Really, the more he thought about it, the less fair it seemed that they had bunked in on his good fortune.

As he reached the outskirts of the town, he noticed an apothecary's sign hanging over a door. He did not remember ever having seen it before, but he knocked without hesitation.

'What's your trouble, young man, that you rouse me from my bed?' An ancient, hairless head poked out of an upstairs window, grotesque and vaguely familiar with its parchment-yellow shine. 'Rats,' said Dip, his head muffled up in his cloak. 'The rats are eating me out of house and home.'

'Here. One drop of this will finish them off. Have it for free.' The ancient apothecary must have had the poison in his pocket, for he dropped it down at once, into Dip's outstretched hands. 'It couldn't be simpler,' he called as the boy hurried off to the inn. Dip bought three bottles of wine. Every last drop of the poison went into two of the bottles. The third he marked carefully to be sure of telling it apart. Then he was off to collect his rightful share of the golden hoard—every last coin of it.

In the pitch dark of late evening, he stumbled over Cut and Grab snoozing under the oak tree in the deep grass. 'Thought you'd forgotten us,' said Grab with a sort of grin.

'I wouldn't forget my two old friends, now would I?' Dip

opened his bottle of wine and took a swig. 'Have a drink, why don't you?' Cut and Grab knelt up and groped for the wine, their hands brushing Dip's face in the dark. They moved to either side of their good friend . . .

Along the road came the sudden noise of the plague cart rattling out of the town towards the lime pits in Ring-a-Rosey Hollow. They all three watched its creaking progress beneath the light of the coachmen's torches. Its white cargo of dead bodies joggled against one another like restless sleepers. A limp arm dangling through the cart rails swung to and fro, for all the world as if it were beckoning them . . .

'We took an oath to kill old Death,' said Cut, remembering.

'We'll get round to it some time,' said Grab, drawing his dagger. 'One thing at a time.'

He plunged the knife into the back of Dip's neck. It met with the seam of his hood, and the lad looked round in astonishment in time to make out the shape of Cut, outlined against the moon. Then Cut's sharp penknife caught him under the ribs and he sprawled, cursing, to his death, among the gnarled roots of the oak tree.

'It's done,' Grab panted, and his throat felt suddenly dry. 'Let's drink to our partnership, Cut. Where did he put the bottles?'

By feeling along the ground, they found the three bottles in the long grass. The opened one had emptied itself into the ground, but the others were intact. A bottle a-piece, Cut and Grab sat with their backs to the oak tree, and drank to their new-found fortune.

In the morning, Death came back for his pot of gold. He wrapped it in the miserable rags of his decaying cloak, close to his gappy ribs. The three corpses under the tree made no move to stop him, and he left them to a wealth of flies and crows before continuing his endless journey. The gold weighed light in his arms. Though his bones were dry and his muscles were like the withered tendrils of a grapeless vine, his strength was immense. He could carry off the biggest or strongest of men— even though, like any man or beast, he could never carry off himself.

The Cathedral Crypt

JOHN WYNDHAM

The past seems so close here,' Clarissa said, as though she thought aloud. 'Somehow it hasn't been allowed to fade into dead history.'

Raymond nodded. He did not speak, but she could see that he understood and that he, like herself, felt the weight of antiquity pressing down upon this Spanish city. Half unconsciously she elaborated:

'Most of our cities strive for change, they throw away the past for the sake of progress. And there are a few, like Rome, truly eternal cities which sail majestically on, absorbing change as it comes. But I don't feel that this city is quite like that. Here, the past seems . . . seems arrogant, as if it were fighting against the present. It is determined to conquer all the new forces. Look at that, for instance.'

A car, new and glossy, was standing before the cathedral door. A priest blessed it with upraised hand while he murmured prayers for the safety of the travellers.

'Commending it to the care of God, and the charge of St Christopher,' Raymond remarked. 'At home they say that the cars empty the churches; here they even bring the car to church. You're right, my dear, the past is not going to give in here without a battle.'

The car, with its celestial premium paid, drove on its way, and with it went all sign of the twentieth century. Late sunlight poured upon a scene entirely medieval. It flooded the cathedral's western face, turning it from grey to palest rose, showing it as something which was more than stone upon stone, a thing which lived though it rested eternally. The fragile beauty of living things was built into those Gothic spears which sped heavenward. Such traceries and filigrees, such magnificent aspiration could not absorb men's art and lives, and yet remain mere stone. Something of the builders' souls was swept up to live for ever among the clustered pinnacles.

'It's very, very lovely,' Clarissa whispered. 'It makes me feel small—and rather frightened.'

Over the dark doorways a row of stone saints in their niches stretched across the façade. Above them a rose window stared like a Cyclops' unblinking eye. Higher still, gargoyles leered sunward, keeping their ceaseless watch for devils. The cathedral was a fantasy of faith; spirit had helped to build it no less than hands: a dream in stone on a foundation of souls.

'Yes—that is beauty,' Raymond said.

He stepped towards the open doors. Clarissa, on his arm, hung back a little, she did not know why. Beauty can awe, but can it alone send a deeper prick of fear?

'We are going inside?' she asked.

Her husband caught the tone of her voice; he looked at her with a tinge of surprise. He would obey any wish of hers willingly. The world held nothing dearer than Clarissa; she had become even more precious in the three weeks since their marriage.

'You'd rather not? You're tired?'

Clarissa shook away her vague fears; they were a foolishness unworthy of her. Besides, Raymond obviously wanted to go in.

'No. Of course we must look at it. They say the inside is even more beautiful than the outside,' she agreed.

But as they walked about the huge, darkening place her uneasiness came creeping back. Ethereal fears clustered within and around her, clinging but impalpable. She fastened to Raymond and his firm reality, trying to share his pleasure in the pictures, shrines, and sculptures. Together they gazed up at the huge, shining crucifix slung from the distant roof, but her mind did not follow his words as he admired it. She was thinking how quiet, how lonely it was in this great place. Here and there one or two dim figures moved silently as ghosts, points of light shone in far, dark corners like stars in the blackness of space. There was a sense of peace, but not the peace of tranquillity . . .

They crossed to the side chapels where Raymond took a lengthy interest in the decorations and furnishing. Some time had passed before he looked up and noticed his wife's pallor.

'What is it? You're not ill, darling?'

'No,' she assured him. 'No, I'm quite all right.'

It was the truth. There was nothing wrong with her save only an overwhelming desire to get back to the familiarities of noises and people.

'Anyhow, we had better go. They'll be wanting to close the place soon,' Raymond said. They returned to the central aisle and turned towards the entrance. Now that the sun had set the western end was very dim. The lights were few and feeble, pale candles and a lamp or two; the rose window was no more than a blur; the shape of the doorway, invisible. With misgiving, Raymond hastened his steps. Clarissa clutched his arm more tightly.

'Surely they haven't—' he began, but he left the sentence unfinished as they both saw that the heavy doors were shut.

'They must have overlooked us when we were in that chapel,' he said with more cheerfulness than he felt. 'I'll try knocking.'

But the pounding of his fists against the massive doors was childishly futile. Sledgehammer blows could scarcely have been heard through those solid timbers. Together they shouted. Their voices fled away through the empty arches. The sound, flung from wall to wall, returned to them, a distorted, eerie travesty.

'Don't,' implored Clarissa, 'don't shout any more—it frightens me.'

Raymond stopped at once, but he did not admit in words that he too had felt fearful of the echoes, as though he were disturbing things which should be left to sleep.

'Perhaps there is a smaller door open somewhere,' he suggested, but with little hope in his tones.

Their heels clicked sharply on the flagstones as they searched. Clarissa fought down an absurd impulse to walk on tiptoe. Each door they tried seemed equipped with a more loudly clattering latch and more raucously grinding bolts than the last. A few opened, but none of these led into the open.

'Locked,' said Raymond disgustedly as they reached the main door once more. 'Every single entrance locked. I'm afraid we're prisoners.' Half-heartedly he hammered again on the wood.

'But we can't stay here.'

There was a piteous sound in Clarissa's voice, like a child imploring not to be left in the dark. He put his arm round her and she pressed thankfully closer.

'We must. There's no help for it. After all, it might be worse. We're together and we're perfectly safe.'

'Yes, but—oh, I suppose it's silly to be afraid.'

'There's nothing to be afraid of, darling. We can go back into that little chapel and make ourselves as comfortable as we can in there so that we'll forget that all this outer part exists. There are cushions on the benches, and we can use hassocks for pillows. Oh, we might be far worse off.'

Raymond woke suddenly at the slight movement of Clarissa in his arms.

'What is it?' he mumbled sleepily.

'Sh— Listen!' she told him.

She watched his face as he obeyed, part fearful lest he should not hear the sound, but in greater part hoping that he would prove it an hallucination. He sat upright.

'Yes, I can hear it. What on earth—?' He glanced at his watch; it showed half-past one. 'What can they be doing at this time?'

They listened in silence for some moments. The confused sound down by the entrance clarified into a chant of massive solemnity. No words could reach them, only harmony rising and falling like the surge of long, slow waves.

Raymond half rose. Clarissa seized his arm, her voice imploring:

'No . . . no, you mustn't, it's—' She stopped, at a loss. There was no word to express her sensation. But it touched him, too, like a warning. He relaxed and dropped back to the seat.

The voices approached slowly. The chant rolled on. Occasionally it would rise from its ululation to a paean and then sink back again to its woeful monotony.

The two in the chapel crept forward until only one high-backed bench hid them from the nave. There they crouched, peering out into the dimness.

The slow procession passed. First the acolytes with swinging censers, behind them a cross bearer, then a single, robed figure leading a dozen brown-habited monks, chanting, their faces uncertainly lit by the candles they carried. Then the Sisters of some black-robed Order, their faces gleaming, white as paper out of their sombreness. Two more monks, holding by ropes a lonely nun . . .

She was young, not ageless like the rest, but the beauty of her face was submerged in anguish. Bright tears of fear and misery poured from her wide eyes, trickling down upon her clothes. She could not brush them away nor hide her face, for her arms were tightly bound behind her back. Now and then her voice rose in a frightened call above the chanting. A weak, thin cry which choked in a tightened throat. She darted glances right and left, twisted to look behind her in hopeless desperation. Twice she hung back, writhing her arms in their cords. The two monks before her pulled on the ropes, dragging her forward. Once she fell to her knees and with lips moving, gazed up at the immense cross in the roof. She implored mercy and forgiveness, but the tugging ropes forced her on.

Clarissa turned horrified eyes to her husband. She saw that he also had understood and knew the rite which was to follow. He murmured something too low for her to catch.

The deliberate procession with its spangle of candles approached the altar. Each row genuflected before it turned away to the left. Despair seemed to snap the last stay of hope in the nun as she passed it, drooping. Raymond leaned further out of the chapel to watch the file disappear into a small doorway. Then he returned to his wife and took her hand. Neither spoke.

Clarissa was too deeply shocked for speech. A nun who had broken her vows—she knew the old punishment for that. They would put her—she shuddered and clutched Raymond's hand the tighter. They couldn't . . . they couldn't do that! Not now. Centuries ago, perhaps, but not today. But the thought of her own words came back to her: 'The past seems so close here,' she had said. She shuddered again.

Sounds stole out of the little door into the cathedral.

A short, weak scuffle; something between a gasp and a whimper; a voice which spoke in heavy, sonorous tones:

'*In nomine patris, et filii, et spiritus sancti—*'

A muffled clash. The ring of the trowel on the stone. Clarissa fainted.

'They're gone,' Raymond was saying. 'Come quickly!'

'What—?' Clarissa was still uncertain, bemused.

'Come along. We may be in time to save her yet. There must be a little air in there.'

He was pulling Clarissa by the wrist, dragging her after him, out of the chapel, towards the small door.

'But if they should come back—?'

'They've gone, I tell you. I heard them bolt the big doors.'

'But—' Clarissa was terrified. If the monks found out that there had been witnesses . . . What then?

'Hurry or we'll be too late.'

Raymond seized a candle from its altar and pulled at the small door. For its size it was heavy, and swung back slowly. He ran down the curving flight of stone steps beyond, Clarissa at his heels. The crypt below was small. One candle sufficed to show all there was to see. The two side walls were smooth, it was the one opposite at which they stared. It showed the shape of two niches long filled in, three more niches, empty and darkly waiting, and one lighter patch of new stones and white mortar.

Raymond set down his candle and ran to the recent work, one hand fumbling for a knife in his pocket. Clarissa raked at the damp mortar with her finger nails.

'Just enough to let us get a hold on this stone,' he muttered as he scraped.

He clenched his strong fingers on its edges. At his first heave it loosened, a second pull, and it fell with a thud at his feet.

But there was another sound in the crypt. They whirled round to stare into the expressionless faces of six monks.

In the morning, only one niche stood empty and darkly waiting.

One Chance

ETHEL HELENE COEN

It was the terrible summer of 1720. The plague hung darkly over shuddering New Orleans. Its black wings beat at every door, and there were few that had not opened to its dread presence. Paul had seen his mother, father, sisters, and friends swept down by its mowing sickle. Only Marie remained for him —beautiful Marie with her love for him that he knew was stronger than any plague—the one thing in all the world that was left to sustain him.

'Let us fly from this accursed place,' he pleaded. 'Let us try to find happiness elsewhere. Neither of us has a tie to bind us here —is not your sister to be buried this very day? Ah, Saint Louis has seen many such scenes in this last month—we will fly to Canada and begin all over.'

'But, my darling,' she protested, 'you forget the quarantine: no one is allowed to enter or leave the city; your plan is hopeless.'

'No . . . no . . . I have a plan—such a terrible one that I shudder to think of it. Here it is—'

While he rapidly sketched their one desperate chance Marie's face blanched, but when he finished, she agreed.

The daughter of the mayor had died that morning. A special dispensation had been secured to ship her body to Charleston for burial. The body rested in its casket in Saint Louis cathedral and was to be shipped by boat that night.

At six o'clock that evening the cathedral was empty save for its silent occupants awaiting burial. The tall wax tapers glimmered fitfully over the scene of desolation. Paul and Marie crept in and went to the casket of the mayor's daughter. Paul rapidly unscrewed the wooden top, removed the slight body, put it into a large sack; and Marie, nearly swooning from terror, got into the coffin.

'Here is a flask of water,' Paul whispered, 'and remember—not a sound, no matter what happens. I shall sneak aboard the boat before it sails at nine. After we are out for half an hour I will let you out of this. It is our only chance.'

'Yes, I know,' Marie whispered chokingly. 'I shall make no sound . . . now go . . . the priests will soon be back, so one last kiss, until we are on the boat.'

He kissed her passionately, then loosely screwed the top on the casket.

Stealing with his awful burden to the yard in the back of the cathedral he remembered a deep, dried-up well in one corner of the yard. Just the place to dispose of the body.

God rest the poor girl's soul, he thought; she, wherever she is, will understand that I meant no sacrilege to her remains, but this is my one chance of happiness . . . my only chance.

His task ended, he climbed the iron wall and walked rapidly up Pirates Alley and wandered over the Vieux Carré until eight-thirty. Thank God—it was time to try the success of their daring venture. His head whirled and his heart beat like a trip-hammer as he slipped on to the boat unobserved by any but the dock hands, who probably considered him one of their number. He secreted himself in a dark corner and waited. After centuries had passed, or so it seemed to him, the boat started moving. It would not be long now. He did not stop to think what would happen when they were caught—that would take care of itself.

Ah—voices, coming nearer and nearer. From his corner Paul could distinctly see the silhouettes of the two men who were approaching.

'Yes,' said one, 'it is sad. The mayor is broken-hearted—we were going to take her body to Charleston—but the mayor had her buried from Saint Louis just after the sun went down.'

The Secret of City Cemetery

PATRICK BONE

O nly kids believed City Cemetery was haunted. But that changed the Hallowe'en night fourteen-year-old Willard Armbruster disappeared. His body was never found.

Willard was a bully. He had no friends. There wasn't a kid in school who would play with him. But Willard didn't mind. He liked being a bully. The older he grew, the better he became at it.

Once, he told Wylma Jean Kist that her mother had been run over by a subway train. It took Wylma Jean weeks to get over Willard's *joke*. That didn't bother Willard. It just made him want to invent meaner pranks to play on people.

That's why he was beside himself with glee when he saw city workmen digging graves at the edge of the public cemetery. They were paupers' graves, intended for persons whose families couldn't afford the fancy plots near the centre of the cemetery. Several graves were dug before winter frost would make digging difficult. Willard knew they would be filled in as needed.

He was clever enough to see that the part of the cemetery where the graves had been dug was located next to the playground of Mark Twain Middle School. The sidewalk leading into the school playground and up to the front entrance ran beside the freshly dug graves. There was no way a kid could go in or out of the playground or school building without passing by the graves.

When weather permitted, smaller neighbourhood children always played in the schoolyard till dark. Willard didn't believe in ghosts. But he knew most of the kids did. He counted on that.

One evening, just before dark, he snuck into the graveyard next to where some kids were playing catch on the school playground. Fall had set in, and the days were growing darker. Willard hid near the freshly dug graves. At sunset the kids started to leave. Dark clouds hovered overhead. Wind whistled eerily through the trees.

'Perfect!' he snickered as he lowered himself into one of the graves, using a small stepladder he had stolen for the occasion. As the kids walked near the graves, he moaned in a pathetic, pleading voice, 'Help me! I'm still alive! Nooo, nooo. I'm alive! Please help me!'

The kids screamed all the way home, where they told their parents that someone was buried 'alive' in one of the graves.

At first none of the parents took them seriously.

'Ghost stories,' they all agreed. 'Overactive imagination,' some said. But when Willard played the trick again, a few parents called the police. Willard was long gone when they went out to check. After a while no one paid any attention to the kids. Police stopped checking, and the students at Mark Twain got used to the trick. They decided no one was actually buried alive. It was the ghost's way of haunting them from the graveyard.

Willard had fooled everyone. At least, that's what he thought.

One evening just before the cemetery closed, Henry Grasmick, the graveyard caretaker, saw Willard sneaking into the cemetery again. Henry always ignored the occasional kid who ran in and out of the graveyard to tempt the ghost and brag about it. But what Willard had been doing was not only tempting, it was cruel. So Henry crept up behind Willard and whispered, 'I know what you're up to, boy.'

Willard jumped as if a spider had crawled up his pants. When he saw it was Henry, he didn't act as if he was afraid. 'Get away

from me, you ugly old man,' he said, and spat right at Henry's shoes.

Henry wasn't intimidated. 'You don't know what you're getting into, boy. It ain't no good to mess with the ghost.'

Willard laughed. 'What ghost? I never saw any ghost. Even if one does exist, he can't do anything to me. Ghosts are spirits, old man. They can't touch me. But I can touch you'—he raised his fist—'which is exactly what I'll do if you snitch on me!'

Henry ignored the threat. 'Don't mess with the ghost,' he repeated. 'He does exist. He has his ways. Since I was a boy I worked here, and he left me alone. But I never messed with him.' Henry turned as if he were about to leave. 'You don't have to worry about me telling on you, young man. You only have to worry about what the ghost is going to do to you if you keep coming here.'

Henry's warning had some effect, because Willard did stop his tricks at the cemetery for a time. But he stayed busy elsewhere.

He almost got away with some vandalism at school, but became too sure of himself and was caught and placed on a week's detention. He got bored. On his last day of detention he flushed a cherry bomb down a third-floor toilet, shattering the commodes on every floor below. School psychologists had to be called in to counsel the kids who happened to be sitting on the pots when they exploded.

Willard was proud of his pranks, but he could never forget the excitement of playing dead in an open grave. He was soon to get the thrill of his life.

Hallowe'en night the middle school had a haunted house. To Willard, that meant one thing. Most of the kids would be there. He was delighted. Everyone who came would have to walk down the path past the open graves. *No more small-time tricks,* he thought to himself. *This time I scare all the kids.*

He arrived early at the cemetery and lowered himself into one of the graves, staying low so no one would see him. He even put his stepladder on the ground under him to make sure it was out of sight.

The sun set. Willard watched the darkness close over his grave like a shroud. He shivered and cursed the cold. It had rained earlier. He smelled the mouldy mud squishing under his feet. Suddenly he heard footsteps. He was about to scream out, 'Help me! I'm still alive!' But he realized the footsteps were coming from *inside* the cemetery, and not *outside*, on the children's path.

He froze, not from the night chill.

Is it the police, he thought, *or someone else who has discovered the tricks I've been playing?*

Now *he* was afraid, and the fear of being discovered was more than he could take. So he huddled there, as far down in the grave as he could, hoping whoever it was would go away without finding him. But the footsteps didn't go away. They got louder, and closer.

Maybe it isn't the police, he thought. *Maybe it isn't . . . even human? Or maybe . . .* He didn't want to consider that maybe he had gone too far in mocking the dead.

In his mind Willard could hear the old caretaker's warning: '*Don't mess with the ghost, boy. The ghost has his ways.*'

The footsteps were closer now. They were heavy steps. Soon Willard realized there were several sets of footsteps, coming directly to his grave. He was too terrified to scream. All he could do was stare up at the mouth of the grave and wait. Suddenly, just above the grave, he heard groans, heavy breathing, shuffling, and grunting sounds.

That's when he saw it. Something long and large and black hovered over him, then inched towards him into the grave.

It took Willard a split second to realize *It's a coffin!* and less than that to scream, 'No! Please! I'm down here!'

All four gravediggers reacted the same way. They dropped the ropes holding the coffin and ran for help. The coffin fell like dead weight, directly on Willard—*thump*—knocking him cold.

Minutes later the cemetery superintendent showed up with the gravediggers to inspect the grave.

'There's nothing down there but a coffin,' he said. 'Boys, I ain't got time for ghost stories. The only spirits in this graveyard are the ones you've been drinking. Now, why don't you just bury that body.'

When Willard came to, he discovered the 'trick' was on him.

Every Hallowe'en since, school children have claimed they could hear the muffled screams of the Ghost of City Cemetery, begging to be released.

'Help me! Please help me, I'm alive! Noooo, noooo. I'm alive! Pleeease! Don't leave me here!'

The Helpful Undertaker

ROBERT SCOTT

She went to the undertaker's to see the body of her husband as he lay in the Chapel of Rest.

'Oh, you've made him look really nice!' she said, then hesitated a moment. 'There is one thing, though.'

'Please, madam, if we can be of any help . . .?' The undertaker paused.

'Well, you see, I know I said I would like him to be in a brown suit but I rather think now that grey would have been better. He always looked good in grey. More distinguished, if you know what I mean.'

'I do indeed, madam. If you prefer grey, of course, we can easily make the change. I'm sure it wouldn't do if he were to feel at all uncomfortable once he has passed over.'

When she saw her husband the next day she was well satisfied. 'So very much better,' she said. 'So very much more suitable. I'm only sorry I put you to such trouble.'

'Oh, no trouble, madam, no trouble at all. As it happened we had a gentleman with us dressed in grey and as his good lady said she would really have preferred brown we made the exchange. Quite convenient, as you might say.'

'You are very kind. Whatever you say, I'm sure it must have been very difficult changing all those clothes.'

'Oh, no, madam,' said the undertaker. 'We just changed the heads!'

The Davenport

JACK RITCHIE

How long has your husband been missing?' Detective Sergeant Whittier asked.

Mrs Brenner had angry dark eyes. 'Since this morning at ten o'clock.' She pointed to the davenport upon which Whittier sat. 'He has Wednesdays off and he was lying right there, like he always does. I went downstairs to get the mail out of our box in the vestibule. When I got back, he was gone.'

Whittier put that down in his notebook. 'Have you checked with friends?'

'Of course. None of them have seen him. Besides, I went over his things in our closet. All of his clothes are still there. All of them. It's freezing outside and he certainly wouldn't go out without taking at least his topcoat and hat.'

She indicated a pair of shoes beside the davenport. 'Besides, those are his shoes. He certainly wouldn't leave the building without them, and none of his other pairs is missing.'

Whittier found himself stifling a yawn. Strange, he thought, I wasn't the least bit sleepy when I came here, but now I can hardly keep my eyes open.

He forced his mind back to Henry Brenner. Very likely Henry had yielded to a sudden impulse to walk out on his wife. Stocking feet and all. The odds were that he'd be back as soon as whatever money he took with him ran out. 'Would you know how much money your husband carried with him?'

She shrugged. 'Henry didn't believe in carrying a lot of cash with him. He always gave me his pay-cheque and if he really needed anything, all he had to do was ask for it and usually I'd see that he got it. He *wanted* it that way.'

Of course, Whittier thought. He stifled another yawn. 'Could you give me a description of your husband?'

'He was about average size. Thinning at the top. A little overweight. He was wearing one of his old white shirts and brown slacks.'

'Have you talked to the building superintendent? Perhaps he's seen your husband.'

'He hasn't. We even searched the laundry room, the storage locker, and the whole basement. Henry isn't anywhere.'

'Couldn't he have dropped in at one of your neighbours? Somebody in the building?'

She rejected that. 'We don't know anybody in the building more than to nod to. We mind our own business and they mind theirs. Something's happened to Henry. I just know it.'

Perhaps he has friends you don't know about, Whittier thought. Maybe he's in a poker game somewhere in the building and forgot about the time. Maybe there's even another woman.

Whittier stirred, vaguely uneasy. Somehow he had the strange impression that Henry was close. Very close. 'Have you searched this apartment?'

'Yes. I thought he might just be trying to frighten me. But he isn't anywhere.' She glared at the davenport. 'The minute Henry got home from work, he'd take off his shoes and just lie there. Most of the time he didn't even bother to look at television or even to read. He just went to sleep. I wonder what he ever saw in just lying there day after day. Sometimes I thought he'd turn into a davenport himself.'

Whittier touched one of the cushions beside him. Yes, it was really quite a comfortable piece of furniture. One had the overwhelming impulse to lie down. The davenport felt almost as though it were a living contented thing.

Mrs Brenner moved closer and stared narrow-eyed. 'That's not our davenport.'

Whittier looked at the cushion again.'It isn't?'

'It *looks* like our davenport. But it's different. I can feel it. It's not ours. Where did it come from?'

Whittier sighed. Why not outer space? It's a creature invading the earth disguised as a davenport. Perhaps there are thousands of them now on earth. No home is complete without one.

Whittier smiled at another thought. Suppose that Henry had for some reason wandered out into the hall and returned to what he *thought* was his apartment and was even now waiting for his wife to come back with the mail. Or sleeping on some strange couch. After all, these were furnished apartments and all of them probably looked somewhat alike.

Mrs Brenner seemed to think of something. 'Do you suppose that Henry might have left a note or something explaining everything in our mailbox downstairs?'

'It's a possibility,' Whittier said. 'Why don't you look?'

Whittier watched her leave and then yawned. There was something incredibly soporific about this davenport. You felt that you really must lie down. He stretched out and closed his eyes. It was delightful just to lie here and think of nothing at all. Nothing at all.

His breathing slowly deepened and after a few minutes more he fell asleep.

A minute passed. Another.

The back of the davenport slowly extended itself and folded gently over another sleeping man.

And quietly ate him.

Every Litter Bit Hurts

MICHAEL AVALLONE

The Impala gleamed shiny and red on the sloping drive-way. Bobby ran towards it, eyes twinkling, clapping his hands. He and Daddy were going for a ride! He paused, a bit puzzled, while his father lifted the hood and studied the engine carefully, peering at the electrical terminals of the starter to be sure no new wires had been added, wires which could connect to a dynamite bomb.

Jamison hadn't been that careful, and Jamison had been killed.

Bobby, of course, had no way of knowing the reason for his father's action, nor did the thought remain with him long. All he knew was that he and his father were going for a ride! And Daddy had strapped on his gun, even. Right under his coat in that dark leather holster.

The large man closed the hood, satisfied with his inspection, smiling at the boy.

'Remember,' Daddy was saying, 'don't ever throw anything out of the car. Understood? It's not nice. Especially when Daddy's driving fast on the highway. It just isn't *nice*, Bobby. You could hit another Daddy in the eye and cause an accident. *Do you understand?*'

Bobby nodded, tugging at the big Impala door.

'Good boy. I knew you'd understand once you knew the reason. Mommy will be proud of you when I tell her.'

Bobby smiled. The words were running around in his head like happy puppies. *Mommy. Proud. Good boy.* When you are only five years of age, those words are glowing beacons of progress and love.

But above all, progress. The march forward, the long trip towards that mysterious land of Growing Up.

'Where are we going today, Daddy? Police station again?' When Daddy took his gun, it almost always meant the police station.

'Daddy's got to go to Elmira,' Robert Black, Sr. said, a funny glint in his eye. 'Part of the job, too. I have to go to the District Attorney to hand over some papers. You know. I told you. We'll meet Mommy there and then maybe we'll take in a movie. Would you like that?'

He paused, lighting a cigarette from the dashboard lighter. Bobby watched him, bursting with ride-fever and pride. He liked the sure look of the strong hands, the keen profile of his father. Sharp, like the face on a coin, under a porkpie hat. Daddy had told him that once and he had remembered. What a funny name for a hat! Maybe Porky the Pig wore porkpie hats, too.

'Mommy's in town?' Bobby prodded with that unswerving curiosity of the young.

'That's right. Shopping. She took the bus. You were sleeping—'

'I miss Mommy.'

'So do I. But we'll see her soon enough.'

Daddy did some things with the dashboard and the wheel, and the car motor roared. Bobby liked that sound. It always meant going places and doing things. Though not very often with Daddy. Daddy was always away—packing bags, calling on the telephone from far-away places like Washington, DC, and hardly ever having time to play games or go walking in the

woods. Bobby wasn't too sure what Daddy did—he didn't go to work like the fathers of his friends, or leave the house in the morning and come back the same day for supper, or play catch—no, nothing like that.

Bobby only knew that the big man's work had something to do with the shiny badge he had seen pinned inside the black wallet that was sometimes left on the bureau in the bedroom. That and that scary gun he sometimes saw when Daddy was putting on his jacket. He remembered he had once tried to pick it up, and his father had been very cross with him for it. Bobby knew he'd never to do *that* again!

Robert Black, Sr. patted his son affectionately on the cheek and released the emergency brake. Bobby knew what he was doing. The brake always made a funny sound when Daddy touched it with his hand.

'Now, Bobby—what is it you're going to remember?'

'Not to throw anything out of the car window.'

'Right. So if we stop for candy or gum, you'll fold up the wrappers neatly and give them to me, and I'll put them in the ashtray. OK?'

'OK.'

'You know last time when you tossed that paper bag out of the car window, it blew all the way back against the windshield of the car right behind us. The man couldn't see where he was going or what he was doing. He might have gotten hurt and you wouldn't want that, would you?'

'No, Daddy.'

'Good boy. Well, we're off.'

Daddy backed the Impala down the driveway. The line of trees looked so pretty in the sunlight. The big man turned the car around, heading it out towards the highway, his thick wrists relaxed, his large hands holding the wheel lightly. Bobby recognized the big school building with the American flag flying above it; next year he'd be going there like the rest of the kids.

He sank back happily against the soft seat and folded his arms. It was nice going someplace with Daddy for a change, instead of Mommy. Mommies were nice and fun, too, when they went to stores and places, but Daddies were better.

And Daddies never cried, while Mommies did. Like last night—

'Daddy, who was that man on the phone last night? The one who said something to make Mommy cry? Was it the man who got hit with the paper bag—did he want you to spank me?'

Robert Black, Sr. smiled, but it was a humourless smile, a grim smile.

'No, son. It was a bad man. It was a man who thought he could keep me from doing my job if he threatened—' Robert Black, Sr. suddenly closed his mouth. 'It was just a bad man, son. Forget it.'

'Why did Mommy cry?'

'I told you to forget it, Bobby. The man wasn't very nice. Like the big bad wolf in Red Riding Hood—'

'Or in the Three Little Pigs?'

'That's right. Don't worry. He won't call any more. Not after these papers are delivered in Elmira.'

Robert Black, Sr.'s mind was on the road and the traffic; Robert Black, Jr. was thinking of all the things he could tell Mommy that happened that morning after she left. About the loose front tooth, the striped kitten he had found wandering in the back yard, that nest of chirping sparrows in the carport.

And the wonderful breakfast of French toast with syrup that Daddy had made. Daddies could cook good, too, just like Mommies.

'Daddy?'

'Yes, son?'

'What's FBI mean?'

Robert Black, Sr. chuckled. 'Who told you that?'

'I was watching television with a couple of the other kids, and they said you were a FBI man. Are you, Daddy?'

'Billy and Gary, I imagine. The neighbourhood stool pigeons. What we need are about eight guys like them available to the Department. Well, they were telling you the truth, Bobby. I'm an FBI man.'

'What's that? Some kind of policeman?'

'That's right. It means the Federal Bureau of Investigation. That's my job. You knew I was some kind of a policeman, didn't you?'

'I guess so.'

The Impala zipped ahead, going around a flying big blue car. Daddy drove like a race-car driver. Bobby beamed proudly.

'Is Mommy glad you're a FBI man?'

Robert Black, Sr. shook his head, amused. 'Sometimes I wonder, son.'

'She gets—*afraid*? Like last night?'

'Sometimes. Women are like that, son. But it's a man's job, you know. And somebody has to do it.'

Bobby nodded his head wisely.

'I wouldn't be afraid. I'm proud you're a FBI man. Honest to Pete, I am.'

'Thanks, Bobby.'

Robert Black, Jr. glowed, glanced at his father, and was surprised to see the smile on the sharp features suddenly change to a frown. His mind searched for a reason for the obvious displeasure.

'What's the matter, Daddy? I didn't throw anything out of the window.'

His father's attention returned to the highway, a smile on his lips despite himself. 'No, but you did something almost as bad. You didn't fasten your seat belt. You always said you were big enough—'

'I *am* big enough!' Bobby's voice was stout.

He pulled the buckle from its place between his father and himself and then reached down between the seat and the door for the spring-retractable tongue that wound itself up into its holder when not in use, like that turtle Gary used to have, pulling its head in whenever you touched it.

His fingers found the end of the seat belt and he tugged it. It seemed to be stuck. He tugged harder without success and then leaned over, peering into the dim recess between the seat and the door.

A strange egg-shaped object was lying there where nothing had been before, apparently pulled from beneath the seat by his efforts, and now firmly wedged.

Bobby bent lower, working it loose, bringing it to his lap together with the end of the seat belt to which it was attached. He blinked at it, fascinated.

Robert Black, Sr., guiding the car along the highway at 60 miles an hour, wasn't looking anywhere but straight ahead. His profile was just like those policemen Bobby saw on television. Bobby sighed and returned his attention to the egg-shaped thing in his lap. He had never seen anything like it before.

It was made of metal and was heavy, and it had odd squarelike bumps all over it and a funny round pin in its top, held to the end of the seat belt by a thin strand of wire. He was sure Daddy would be interested, but first he had to obey his instructions. He tugged at the egg shape; it came away from the tongue of the seat belt, separating also from the little pin which now dangled comically. Bobby held the egg shape in his lap and latched the belt.

'Daddy—'

'Yes, son?' Robert Black, Sr. turned his head. And stared.

His face went white.

Bobby could never remember Daddy's eyes seeming so big or so *scary*. His face was all screwed up, like he had a toothache.

The roar of the car motor drowned out something that Daddy was yelling. There were so many other cars racing by, thundering, bulleting along the highway. Bobby whimpered in sudden fright.

His father's right arm shot out, flailing. Bobby recoiled, thinking for one awful second that Daddy was going to hit him.

He hugged the egg-shaped thing to his chest and shrank against the car door to make himself smaller.

Cars were hurtling forward, zooming ahead in a race for the sun and the horizon. A car horn blasted, frightening Bobby even more.

'Bobby!' Robert Black, Sr. screamed. 'Throw that thing out of the car!'

The flying trees, the ribbon of road, the thundering motors, and four vital seconds had fled.

'*Bobby!*'

'But, Daddy,' Robert Black, Jr. protested, his small face crumpled in confusion, 'you said never to—'

Cop for a Day

HENRY SLESAR

They had eighteen thousand dollars; they couldn't spend a nickel. Davy Wyatt spread the money on the kitchen table, in neat piles according to their various denominations, and just sat there, looking. After a while this got on Phil Pennick's nerves.

'Cut it out, kid,' the older man said. 'You're just eatin' your heart out.'

'Don't I know it.'

Davy sighed, and swept the bills back into the neat leather briefcase. He tossed it carelessly on to his bunk, and joined it there a minute later, lying down with his fingers locked behind his head.

'I'm goin' out,' Phil said suddenly.

'Where to?'

'Pick up some sandwiches, maybe a newspaper. Take a little walk.'

The kid's face paled. 'Think it's a good idea?'

'You got a better one? Listen, we can rot in this crummy joint.' Phil looked around the one-room flat that had been their prison for two days, and made a noise that didn't nearly show his full disgust. Then he grabbed for his jacket and put it on.

'It's your neck,' the kid said. 'Don't blame me if you get picked up. With that dame playin' footsie with the cops—'

'Shut up! If they get me, they'll have your neck in the chopper ten minutes later. So don't wish me any bad luck, pal.'

Davy sat up quickly. 'Hey, no kidding. Think you ought to take the chance?'

The older man smiled. The smile did nothing for the grim set of his features, merely shifted the frozen blankness which was the result of three prison terms. He put a soft fedora on his grey head and adjusted it carefully.

'We took our chance already,' he said as he opened the door. 'And as far as the dame goes—you leave that up to me.'

He hoisted the .38 out of his shoulder-holster, checked the cartridges, and slipped it back. The gesture was so casual, so relaxed, that the kid realized once again that he was working with a pro.

Davy swallowed hard, and said, 'Sure, Phil. I'll leave it up to you.'

The street was full of children. Phil Pennick liked children, especially round a hide-out. They discouraged rash action by the police. He walked along like a man out to get the morning paper, or a packet of cigarettes, or to shoot a game of pool. Nobody looked at him twice, even though his clothes were a shade better than anybody else's in that slum area.

Davy's last words were stuck in his thoughts. 'I'll leave it up to you . . .' It was easy enough to reassure the kid that the old pro would work them out of trouble. Only this time, the old pro wasn't so sure.

They had planned a pretty sound caper. Something simple, without elaborate preparations. It involved one small bank messenger, from a little colonial-style bank in Brooklyn, the kind of messenger who never seemed to tote more than a few grand around. Only they had been doubly surprised. The bank messenger had turned out to be a scrapper, and the loot had turned out to be bigger than they had ever dreamed. Now they had the money, and the little bonded errand boy had two bullets in his chest. Was he dead or alive? Phil didn't know, and hardly cared. One more arrest and conviction, and he was as good as dead anyway. He wasn't made to be a lifer; he'd rather be a corpse.

But they had the money. That was the important thing. In twenty years of trying, Phil Pennick had never come up with the big one.

It would have been a truly great triumph, if the cops hadn't found their witness. They hadn't seen the woman until it was too late. She was standing in a doorway of the side street where they had made their play. She was a honey blonde, with a figure out of 52nd Street, and a pair of sharp eyes. Her face didn't change a bit when Phil spotted her. She just looked back, coldly, and watched the bank messenger sink to the sidewalk with his hands trying to block the blood. Then she had slammed the front door behind her.

The kid had wanted to go in after her, but Phil said no. The shots had been loud, and he wasn't going to take any more chances. They had rushed into the waiting auto, and headed for the pre-arranged hide-out.

Phil stopped by a news-stand. He bought some cigarettes, a couple of candy bars, and the *Journal*. He was reading the headlines as he walked into the tiny delicatessen. The hold-up story was boxed at the bottom of the page. It didn't tell him anything he didn't already know. The honey blonde had talked all right. And she was ready to identify the two men who had shot and killed the bank's errand boy. Shot and killed . . . Phil shook his head. The poor slob, he thought.

In the delicatessen, he bought four roast beef sandwiches and a half-dozen cans of cold beer. Then he walked back to the apartment, thinking hard.

As soon as he came in, the kid grabbed for the newspaper. He found the story and read it avidly. When he looked up, his round young face was frightened.

'What'll we do, Phil? This dame can hang us!'

'Take it easy.' He opened a beer.

'Are you kidding? Listen, one of the first things the cops'll do is go looking for you. I mean—let's face it, Phil—this is your kind of caper.'

The older man frowned. 'So what?'

'So what? So they'll parade you in front of this dame, and she'll scream bloody murder. Then what happens to me?'

Phil took his gun out and began cleaning it. 'I'll stop her,' he promised.

'How? They probably got a million cops surrounding her. They won't take any chances. Hell, no. So how can you stop her?'

'I got a plan,' Phil said. 'You're just going to have to trust me, kid. OK?'

'Yeah, but—'

'I said trust me. Don't forget.' He looked at his partner hard. 'This wouldn't have happened at all—if you didn't have a jerky trigger finger.'

They ate the sandwiches, drank the beer, and then the older man went to the leather briefcase and opened it. He lifted out a thin packet of bills and put it into his wallet.

'Hey,' Davy said.

'Don't get in an uproar. I'm goin' to need a few bucks, for what I've got in mind. Until I come back, I'll trust you to take care of the rest.' Phil put on his jacket again. 'Don't get wild ideas, kid. Remember, you don't leave the room until I get back. And if we have any visitors—watch that itchy finger.'

'Sure, Phil,' the kid said.

Phil had a hard time getting a taxi. When he did he gave the driver the Manhattan address of a garment house on lower Seventh Avenue.

There was a girl behind the frosted glass cage on the fifth floor, and she was pretty snippy.

'I want to see Marty Hirsch,' Phil said.

'I'm sorry, Mr Hirsch is in conference—'

'Don't give me that conference junk. Just pick up your little phone and tell him a good friend from Brooklyn Heights is here. He'll know who it is.'

The girl's nose tilted up, but she made the call.

The man who hurried out to see Phil was short and paunchy. He was in shirt-sleeves, and his sunset-coloured tie was hanging loosely round his neck.

'Er, hello,' he said nervously, looking towards the switch-board. 'Look, Phil, suppose we talk in the hallway? I got a customer inside.'

'What's the matter, Marty? Ashamed of your friends?'

'Please, Phil!'

In the hallway, the garment man said, 'Look, I told you never to come here.' He wiped sweat from his face. 'It doesn't look good, for both of us. We should do all our business by phone.'

'You don't understand,' Phil said. 'I ain't got nothin' hot for you to buy. I'm out of that business, Marty.'

'Oh? So what is it then?'

'I just want a little favour, Marty. For an old pal.'

The small eyes narrowed. 'What kind of favour?'

'You got a big uniform department. Right?'

'Yeah. So what? Army and Navy stuff. Things like that. So what do you want?'

'A uniform,' Phil said easily. 'That's all. A cop uniform. Only it's gotta be good.'

'Now look, Phil—'

'Don't give me a hard time, Marty. We got too long a friendship. I want to play a joke on a friend of mine. You can fix me up with something, can't you?'

The garment man frowned. 'I'll tell you what. I got here some stock models. Only they're not so new and they ain't got no badges. And no gun, you understand.'

'Don't worry about that. I got the potsy. Will this uniform pass? I mean, if another cop saw it?'

'Yeah, yeah, sure. It'll pass. I'm telling you.'

'Swell. Then trot it out, Marty.' The man looked doubtful, so Phil added, 'For the sake of a friend, huh?'

Phil walked out into the street with the large flat box under his arm, feeling that he was getting somewhere. Then he waved a cab up to the kerb, and gave him the cross streets where Davy Wyatt had killed the bank messenger.

It was chancy, but worth it. He didn't know whether the blonde was cooling her high heels in a police station, or just knee-deep in cops guarding her at her own apartment house.

He knew the answer the minute he stepped out of the cab. There was a police car parked at the opposite kerb, and two uniformed patrolmen were gabbing near the front entrance of the blonde's residence.

He looked up and down the street until he found what he was looking for. There was a small restaurant with a red-striped awning. He walked up to it briskly, and saw it was called ANGIE'S. He glanced at the menu pasted to the window, then pushed the door open.

He surveyed the room, and it looked good. The men's john was in a hallway out of the main dining-room, and there was a side exit that would come in handy when he made the switch in clothing.

There weren't many customers. Phil took a table near the hall, and placed his package on the opposite chair. A bored waiter took his order. After being served, Phil chewed patiently on a dish of tired spaghetti. Then he paid his check and went into the john.

He changed swiftly, in a booth. Then he put the clothes he'd taken off inside the box and tied the string tight. He pinned the badge to his shirt, and dropped the .38 into the police holster.

Leaving by the side door, he dropped the box into one of the trash cans near the exit.

Then he crossed the street nonchalantly, heading straight for the apartment house.

'Hi,' he said to the two cops out front. 'You guys seen Weber?' Weber was a precinct lieutenant that Phil knew only too well.

'Weber? Hell, no. Was he supposed to be here?'

'I thought so. I'm from the Fourth Precinct. We got a call from him a while ago. We picked up somebody last night, on a B and E; might be one of the guys you're looking for.'

'Search me,' one of the cops said. 'What do you want us to do about it?'

Phil swore. 'I don't know what to do myself. Sendin' me on a wild goose chase. He was supposed to be here by now.'

'Can't help you, pal.' The other cop yawned widely.

'Dame in her apartment?' Phil asked casually.

'Yeah,' the second cop answered. 'Lying down.' He snickered. 'I wouldn't mind sharing the bunk.'

'Maybe I better talk to her. I got the guy's picture. Maybe she can tell me something.'

'I dunno.' The first cop scratched his cheek. 'We ain't heard nothing about that.'

'What the hell,' the second one said. He turned to Phil. 'She's in 4E.'

'OK,' Phil said. He started into the house. 'If Weber shows up, you tell him I'm upstairs. Right?'

'Right.'

He shut the door behind him, stood there long enough to let out a relieved sigh. Then he stepped into the automatic elevator, punched the button marked 4.

On the fourth floor, he rapped gently on the door marked E.

'Yeah?' The woman's voice sounded tired, but not scared. 'Who is it?'

'Police,' Phil said crisply. 'Got a picture for you, lady.'

'What kind of a picture?' Her voice was close to the door frame.

'Guy we picked up last night. Maybe the one we're lookin' for.'

He could hear the chain being lifted: the door was opened. Close up, the blonde wasn't as young or lush as he had imagined. She was wearing a faded housecoat of some shiny material, clutching it around her waist without too much concern for the white flesh that was still revealed.

Phil stepped inside and took off his cap. 'This won't take long, lady.' He closed the door.

She turned her back on him and walked into the room. He unbuttoned the holster without hurry, and lifted the gun out. When she turned round, the gun was pointed dead centre. She opened her mouth, but not a sound came out.

'One word and I shoot,' Phil said evenly. He backed her against a sofa, and shot a look towards the other room. 'What's in there?'

'Bedroom,' she said.

'Move.'

She co-operated nicely. She stretched out on the bed at his command—and smiled coyly. She must have figured he wanted something else besides her death. Then he picked up a pillow and shoved it into her stomach.

'Hold that,' he said.

She held it. Then he shoved the gun up against it and squeezed the trigger. She looked surprised and angry and deceived, and then she was dead.

The sound had been well muffled, but Phil wanted to be sure. He went to the window that faced the street and looked down.

The two cops were still out front, chewing the fat complacently. He smiled, slipped the gun into the holster, and went out.

The cops looked at him without too much interest.

'Well?' the first one said.

'Dames,' Phil grinned. 'Says she knows from nothing. Weber's gonna be awfully disappointed.' He waved his hand. 'I'm goin' back to the precinct. So long, guys.'

They said, 'So long,' and resumed their gabbing

Phil rounded the corner. There was a cab at the hack stand. He climbed into the back.

'What's up, officer?' the hackie grinned. 'Lost your prowl car?'

'Don't be a wise guy.' He gave him the address and settled back into a contented silence, thinking about the money.

It was dusk by the time he reached the neighbourhood. He got off some four blocks from the tenement, and walked the rest of the distance. Some of the kids on the block hooted at him because of the uniform, and he grinned.

He went up the stairs feeling good. When he pushed open the door, Davy shot him once in the stomach. Phil didn't have time to make him realize the mistake he was making before the second bullet struck him in the centre of his forehead.

On the Sidewalk, Bleeding

EVAN HUNTER

The boy lay bleeding in the rain. He was sixteen years old, and he wore a bright purple silk jacket, and the lettering across the back of the jacket read THE ROYALS. The boy's name was Andy, and the name was delicately scripted in black thread on the front of the jacket, just over the heart. *Andy.*

He had been stabbed ten minutes ago. The knife had entered just below his rib cage and had been drawn across his body violently, tearing a wide gap in his flesh. He lay on the sidewalk with the March rain drilling his jacket and drilling his body and washing away the blood that poured from his open wound. He had known excruciating pain when the knife had torn across his body, and then sudden comparative relief when the blade was pulled away. He had heard the voice saying, 'That's for you, Royal!' and then the sound of footsteps hurrying into the rain, and then he had fallen to the sidewalk, clutching his stomach, trying to stop the flow of blood.

He tried to yell for help, but he had no voice. He did not know why his voice had deserted him, or why the rain had suddenly become so fierce, or why there was an open hole in his body from which his life ran redly, steadily. It was 11.30 p.m., but he did not know the time.

There was another thing he did not know.

He did not know he was dying. He lay on the sidewalk, bleeding, and he thought only: *That was a fierce rumble. They got me good that time*, but he did not know he was dying. He would have been frightened had he known. In his ignorance, he lay bleeding and wishing he could cry out for help, but there was no voice in his throat. There was only the bubbling of blood between his lips whenever he opened his mouth to speak. He lay silent in his pain, waiting, waiting for someone to find him.

He could hear the sound of automobile tyres hushed on the muzzle of rainswept streets, far away at the other end of the long alley. He lay with his face pressed to the sidewalk, and he could see the splash of neon far away at the other end of the alley, tinting the pavement red and green, slickly brilliant in the rain.

He wondered if Laura would be angry.

He had left the jump to get a package of cigarettes. He had told her he would be back in a few minutes, and then he had gone downstairs and found the candy store closed. He knew that Alfredo's on the next block would be open until at least two, and he had started through the alley, and that was when he'd been ambushed. He could hear the faint sound of music now, coming from a long, long way off, and he wondered if Laura was dancing, wondered if she had missed him yet. Maybe she thought he wasn't coming back. Maybe she thought he'd cut out for good. Maybe she'd already left the jump and gone home.

He thought of her face, the brown eyes and the jet-black hair, and thinking of her he forgot his pain a little, forgot that blood was rushing from his body. Someday he would marry Laura. Someday he would marry her, and they would have a lot of kids, and then they would get out of the neighbourhood. They would move to a clean project in the Bronx, or maybe they would move to Staten Island. When they were married, when they had kids . . .

He heard footsteps at the other end of the alley, and he lifted his cheek from the sidewalk and looked into the darkness and tried to cry out, but again there was only a soft hissing bubble of blood on his mouth.

The man came down the alley. He had not seen Andy yet. He walked, and then stopped to lean against the brick of the building, and then walked again. He saw Andy then and came towards him, and he stood over him for a long time, the minutes ticking, ticking, watching him and not speaking.

Then he said, 'What's a matter, buddy?'

Andy could not speak, and he could barely move. He lifted his face slightly and looked up at the man, and in the rainswept alley he smelled the sickening odour of alcohol and realized the man was drunk. He did not feel any particular panic. He did not know he was dying, and so he felt only mild disappointment that the man who had found him was drunk.

The man was smiling.

'Did you fall down, buddy?' he asked. 'You mus' be as drunk as I am.' He grinned, seemed to remember why he had entered the alley in the first place, and said. 'Don' go way. I'll be ri' back.'

The man lurched away. Andy heard his footsteps, and then the sound of the man colliding with a garbage can, and some mild swearing, and then the sound of the man urinating, lost in the steady wash of the rain. He waited for the man to come back.

It was 11.39.

When the man returned, he squatted alongside Andy. He studied him with drunken dignity.

'You gonna catch cold here,' he said. 'What's a matter? You like layin' in the wet?'

Andy could not answer. The man tried to focus his eyes on Andy's face. The rain spattered around them.

'You like a drink?'

Andy shook his head.

'I gotta bottle. Here,' the man said. He pulled a pint bottle from his inside jacket pocket. He uncapped it and extended it to Andy. Andy tried to move, but pain wrenched him back flat against the sidewalk.

'Take it,' the man said. He kept watching Andy. 'Take it.' When Andy did not move, he said, 'Nev' mind. I'll have one m'self.' He tilted the bottle to his lips, and then wiped the back of his hand across his mouth. 'You too young to be drinkin', anyway. Should be 'shamed of yourself, drunk an' laying in a alley, all wet. Shame on you. I gotta good minda calla cop.'

Andy nodded. Yes, he tried to say. Yes, call a cop. Please. Call one.

'Oh, you don' like that, huh?' the drunk said. 'You don' wanna cop to fin' you all drunk an' wet in a alley, huh? OK, buddy. This time you get off easy.' He got to his feet. 'This time you lucky,' he said. He waved broadly at Andy, and then almost lost his footing. 'S'long, buddy,' he said.

Wait, Andy thought. *Wait, please, I'm bleeding.*

'S'long,' the drunk said again. 'I see you aroun',' and then he staggered off up the alley.

Andy lay and thought: *Laura, Laura. Are you dancing?*

The couple came into the alley suddenly. They ran into the alley together, running from the rain, the boy holding the girl's elbow, the girl spreading a newspaper over her head to protect her hair. Andy lay crumpled against the pavement, and he watched them run into the alley laughing, and then duck into the doorway not ten feet from him.

'Man, what rain!' the boy said. 'You could drown out there.'

'I have to get home,' the girl said. 'It's late, Freddie. I have to get home.'

'We got time,' Freddie said. 'Your people won't raise a fuss if you're a little late. Not with this kind of weather.'

'It's dark,' the girl said, and she giggled.

'Yeah,' the boy answered, his voice very low.

'Freddie . . .?'

'Um?'

'You're . . . you're standing very close to me.'

'Um.'

There was a long silence. Then the girl said, 'Oh,' only that single word, and Andy knew she'd been kissed, and he suddenly hungered for Laura's mouth. It was then that he wondered if he would ever kiss Laura again. It was then that he wondered if he was dying.

No, he thought, *I can't be dying, not from a little street rumble, not from just getting cut. Guys get cut all the time in rumbles. I can't be dying. No, that's stupid. That don't make any sense at all.*

'You shouldn't,' the girl said.

'Why not?'

'I don't know.'

'Do you like it?'

'Yes.'

'So?'

'I don't know.'

'I love you, Angela,' the boy said.

'I love you, too, Freddie,' the girl said, and Andy listened and thought: *I love you, Laura. Laura, I think maybe I'm dying. Laura, this is stupid but I think maybe I'm dying. Laura, I think I'm dying!*

He tried to speak. He tried to move. He tried to crawl towards the doorway where he could see the two figures in embrace. He tried to make a noise, a sound, and a grunt came from his lips, and then he tried again, and another grunt came, a low animal grunt of pain.

'What was that?' the girl said, suddenly alarmed, breaking away from the boy.

'I don't know,' he answered.

'Go look, Freddie.'

'No. Wait.'

Andy moved his lips again. Again the sound came from him.

'Freddie!'

'What?'

'I'm scared.'

'I'll go see,' the boy said.

He stepped into the alley. He walked over to where Andy lay on the ground. He stood over him, watching him.

'You all right?' he asked.

'What is it?' Angela said from the doorway.

'Somebody's hurt,' Freddie said.

'Let's get out of here,' Angela said.

'No. Wait a minute.' He knelt down beside Andy. 'You cut?' he asked.

Andy nodded. The boy kept looking at him. He saw the lettering on the jacket then. THE ROYALS. He turned to Angela.

'He's a Royal,' he said.

'Let's . . . what . . . what do you want to do, Freddie?'

'I don't know. I don't want to get mixed up in this. He's a

Royal. We help him, and the Guardians'll be down on our necks. I don't want to get mixed up in this, Angela.'

'Is he . . . is he hurt bad?'

'Yeah, it looks that way.'

'What shall we do?'

'I don't know.'

'We can't leave him here in the rain.' Angela hesitated. 'Can we?'

'If we get a cop, the Guardians'll find out who,' Freddie said. 'I don't know, Angela. I don't know.'

Angela hesitated a long time before answering. Then she said, 'I have to get home, Freddie. My people will begin to worry.'

'Yeah,' Freddie said. He looked at Andy again. 'You all right?' he asked. Andy lifted his face from the sidewalk, and his eyes said: *Please, please help me*, and maybe Freddie read what his eyes were saying, and maybe he didn't.

Behind him, Angela said, 'Freddie, let's get out of here! Please!' There was urgency in her voice, urgency bordering on the edge of panic. Freddie stood up. He looked at Andy again, and then mumbled, 'I'm sorry,' and then he took Angela's arm and together they ran towards the neon splash at the other end of the alley.

Why, they're afraid of the Guardians, Andy thought in amazement. *But why should they be? I wasn't afraid of the Guardians. I never turkeyed out of a rumble with the Guardians. I got heart. But I'm bleeding.*

The rain was soothing somehow. It was a cold rain, but his body was hot all over, and the rain helped to cool him. He had always liked rain. He could remember sitting in Laura's house one time, the rain running down the windows, and just looking out over the street, watching the people running from the rain. That was when he'd first joined the Royals. He could remember how happy he was the Royals had taken him. The Royals and the Guardians, two of the biggest. He was a Royal. There had been meaning to the title.

Now, in the alley, with the cold rain washing his hot body, he wondered about the meaning. If he died, he was Andy. He was not a Royal. He was simply Andy, and he was dead. And he wondered suddenly if the Guardians who had ambushed him and knifed him had ever once realized he was Andy? Had they known that he was Andy, or had they simply known that he was a Royal wearing a purple silk jacket? Had they stabbed *him*, Andy, or had they only stabbed the jacket and the title, and what good was the title if you were dying?

I'm Andy, he screamed wordlessly. *For Christ's sake. I'm Andy!*

An old lady stopped at the other end of the alley. The garbage cans were stacked there, beating noisily in the rain. The old lady carried an umbrella with broken ribs, carried it with all the dignity of a queen. She stepped into the mouth of the alley, a shopping bag over one arm. She lifted the lids of the garbage cans delicately, and she did not hear Andy grunt because she was a little deaf and because the rain was beating a steady relentless tattoo on the cans. She had been searching and foraging for the better part of the night. She collected her string and her newspapers, and an old hat with a feather on it from one of the garbage cans, and a broken footstool from another of the cans. And then she delicately replaced the lids and lifted her umbrella high and walked out of the alley mouth with queenly dignity. She had worked swiftly and soundlessly, and now she was gone.

The alley looked very long now. He could see people passing at the other end of it, and he wondered who the people were, and he wondered if he would ever get to know them, wondered who it was on the Guardians who had stabbed him, who had plunged the knife into his body.

'That's for you, Royal!' the voice had said, and then the footsteps, his arms being released by the others, the fall to the pavement. 'That's for you, Royal!' Even in his pain, even as he collapsed, there had been some sort of pride in knowing he was a Royal. Now there was no pride at all. With the rain beginning to chill him, with the blood pouring steadily between his fingers, he knew only a sort of dizziness, and within the giddy dizziness, he could only think: *I want to be Andy.*

It was not very much to ask of the world.

He watched the world passing at the other end of the alley. The world didn't know he was Andy. The world didn't know he was alive. He wanted to say, 'Hey, I'm alive! Hey, look at me! I'm alive! Don't you know I'm alive? Don't you know I exist?'

He felt weak and very tired. He felt alone and wet and

feverish and chilled, and he knew he was going to die now, and the knowledge made him suddenly sad. He was not frightened. For some reason, he was not frightened. He was only filled with an overwhelming sadness that his life would be over at sixteen. He felt all at once as if he had never done anything, never seen anything, never been anywhere. There were so many things to do, and he wondered why he'd never thought of them before, wondered why the rumbles and the jumps and the purple jacket had always seemed so important to him before, and now they seemed like such small things in a world he was missing, a world that was rushing past at the other end of the alley.

I don't want to die, he thought. *I haven't lived yet.*

It seemed very important to him that he take off the purple jacket. He was very close to dying, and when they found him, he did not want them to say, 'Oh, it's a Royal.' With great effort, he rolled over on to his back. He felt the pain tearing at his stomach when he moved, a pain he did not think was possible. But he wanted to take off the jacket. If he never did another thing, he wanted to take off the jacket. The jacket had only one meaning now, and that was a very simple meaning.

If he had not been wearing the jacket, he would not have been stabbed. The knife had not been plunged in hatred of Andy. The knife hated only the purple jacket. The jacket was a stupid meaningless thing that was robbing him of his life. He wanted the jacket off his back. With an enormous loathing, he wanted the jacket off his back.

He lay struggling with the shiny wet material. His arms were heavy, and pain ripped fire across his body whenever he moved. But he squirmed and fought and twisted until one arm was free and then the other, and then he rolled away from the jacket and lay quite still, breathing heavily, listening to the sound of his breathing and the sound of the rain and thinking: *Rain is sweet, I'm Andy.*

She found him in the alleyway a minute past midnight. She left the dance to look for him, and when she found him she knelt beside him and said, 'Andy, it's me, Laura.'

He did not answer her. She backed away from him, tears springing into her eyes, and then she ran from the alley hysterically and did not stop running until she found the cop.

And now, standing with the cop, she looked down at him, and

the cop rose and said, 'He's dead,' and all the crying was out of her now. She stood in the rain and said nothing, looking at the dead boy on the pavement, and looking at the purple jacket that rested a foot away from his body.

The cop picked up the jacket and turned it over in his hands. 'A Royal, huh?' he said.

The rain seemed to beat more steadily now, more fiercely.

She looked at the cop and, very quietly, she said, 'His name is Andy.'

The cop slung the jacket over his arm. He took out his black pad, and he flipped it open to a blank page.

'A Royal,' he said.

Then he began writing.

Acknowledgements

Marc Alexander: 'Sweet Shop' reprinted from *Not After Nightfall* (Kestrel, 1985), Copyright © Marc Alexander 1985, by arrangement with Rupert Crew Limited. **Michael Avallone:** 'Every Litter Bit Hurts', Copyright © 1968 by Michael Avallone, first published in *Ellery Queen's Mystery Magazine*, 1968. **Ruskin Bond:** 'A Face in the Night' reprinted from *The Night Train at Deoli and Other Stories* (Penguin Books India, 1988) courtesy of the publishers (Penguin Books India Pvt Ltd) and the author. **Patrick Bone:** 'The Secret of City Cemetery', Copyright © 1994 by Patrick Bone, first published in *Bruce Coville's Book of Ghosts* (Scholastic Inc, 1994). **Anthony Boucher:** 'Mr Lupescu', Copyright 1945 by Weird Tales Magazine; Copyright © renewed 1972 by Phyllis White, first published in *Weird Tales Magazine* (Short Stories, Inc), reprinted by permission of Curtis Brown Ltd, New York. **Sydney J. Bounds:** 'Ghost Hunter', Copyright © Sydney J. Bounds 1981, first published in Mary Danby (ed.): *The 13th Armada Ghost Book* (Fontana, 1981), reprinted by permission of the author. **Ray Bradbury:** 'The Veldt' reprinted from *The Illustrated Man* (Rupert Hart-Davis, 1952), first published in *The Saturday Evening Post*, September 1950, published by The Curtis Publishing Co., Copyright © 1950 by the Curtis Publishing Co., renewed 1977 by Ray Bradbury, by permission of Don Congdon Associates, Inc. **Fredric Brown:** 'Voodoo', Copyright © 1954 by Galaxy Publishing Association, copyright renewed by Frederic Brown. **Ramsey Campbell:** 'Call First', first published in Kirby McCauley (ed): *Night Chills* (Avon Books, 1975), reprinted by permission of the Carol Smith Literary Agency. **John Christopher:** 'Paths', Copyright © 1984 John Christopher, first published in Peter Dickinson (ed): *Hundreds and Hundreds* (Puffin, 1984), reprinted by permission of Watson, Little Ltd on behalf of the author. **Ethel Helene Coen:** 'One Chance', reprinted from Robert Weinberg (ed.): *100 Little Weird Tales* (Barnes and Noble, 1994), by permission of Victor Dricks/Weird Tales Ltd. **John Collier:** 'Thus I Refute Beelzy' reprinted from *The John Collier Reader* (Souvenir Press, 1975) by permission of the Peters Fraser & Dunlop Group Ltd. **Roald Dahl:** 'The Landlady' reprinted from *Kiss Kiss* (Michael Joseph, 1960) by permission of David Higham Associates. **Richard and Judy Dockrey Young:** 'The Skeleton in the Closet' reprinted from *The Scary Story Reader* by Richard and Judy Dockrey Young (August House, 1993), Copyright © 1993 by Richard and Judy Dockrey Young, by permission of the publisher. **Evan Hunter:** 'On the Sidewalk, Bleeding', Copyright © by Evan Hunter. **Kenneth Ireland:** 'The Statuette' reprinted from *We're Coming for You, Jonathan* (Hodder & Stoughton, 1983), Copyright © Kenneth Ireland 1983, by permission of Jennifer Luithlen Agency on behalf of the author. **Gerald Kersh:** 'The Old Burying Place ...' reprinted from *Neither Man Nor Dog* (Heinemann, 1946). **Robin Klein:** 'We'll Look After You' reprinted from *Tearaways* (Viking, 1990), Copyright © 1990 by Robin Klein, by permission of the copyright holder Haytul Pty Ltd, c/o Curtis Brown (Aust) Pty Ltd, Sydney. **Geraldine McCaughrean:** 'Death's Murderers' reprinted from Geoffrey Chaucer's *The Canterbury Tales* (OUP, 1984) retold by Geraldine McCaughrean, Copyright © Geraldine McCaughrean 1984, by permission of Oxford University Press. **Richard Matheson:** 'The Near Departed', Copyright © 1987 by Richard Matheson. **Dannie Plachta:** 'Revival Meeting', Copyright © Dannie Plachta. **Alison Prince:** 'The Loony', Copyright © Alison Prince 1984, first published in *Nightmares 2* (Armada), reprinted by permission of Jennifer Luithlen Agency on behalf of the author. **Jack Ritchie:** 'The Davenport', first published in Helen Hoke (ed.): *A Chilling Collection* (Dent, 1980), reprinted by permission of the Larry Sternig/Jack Byrne Literary Agency. **Harold Rolseth:** 'Hey, You Down There!', first published in *Yankee Magazine*, reprinted by permission of the Larry Sternig/Jack Byrne Literary Agency. **Lance Salway:** 'Such a Sweet Little Girl' reprinted from *A Nasty Piece of Work and Other Ghost Stories* (Patrick Hardy Books, 1983) by permission of the publishers, Lutterworth Press Ltd. **Robert Scott:** 'The Meeting', 'The Talking Head' and 'A Hundred Steps', all Copyright © Robert Scott 1997, first published here by permission of the author; 'The Helpful Undertaker', Copyright © Robert Scott 1985, reprinted from Dennis Pepper (ed.): *A Book of Tall Stories* (OUP,

Acknowledgements

1985) by permission of the author; and 'Those Three Wishes', Copyright © Robert Scott 1997, retold, with Judith Gorog's permission, from her story 'Those Three Wishes' in *A Taste for Quiet* (Philomel, 1982) and *When Flesh Begins to Creep* (Gollancz, 1986), first published here by permission of the author. **Henry Slesar:** 'The Candidate' and 'Cop for a Day', both Copyright © Henry Slesar, reprinted by permission of the author. **T. H. White:** 'A Sharp Attack of Something or Other' reprinted from *The Maharajah and Other Stories* (HarperCollins) by permission of David Higham Associates. **John Wyndham:** 'The Cathedral Crypt' reprinted by permission of David Higham Associates.

While every effort has been made to trace and contact copyright holders this has not always been possible. If notified, the publisher will be pleased to rectify any errors or omissions at the earliest opportunity.

The illustrations are by:

Martin Cottam pp iii, 1, 9, 82, 93, 95, 97, 112, 119, 148, 158, 163, 168
Paul Fisher-Johnson pp 19, 26, 68, 101, 122, 126, 129, 131, 143, 177, 179, 189, 191, 204, 209, 213
Jonathon Heap pp 29, 33
Ian Miller pp 41, 47, 55, 64, 87, 91, 109, 144, 147, 180, 182, 186, 216
Brian Pedley pp 12, 16, 38, 56, 62, 71, 80, 99, 170, 175, 196

The cover photograph is by **Simon Marsden**

The Skeleton in the Closet

RICHARD AND JUDY DOCKREY YOUNG

One day some new kids at school were helping the janitor clean up down in the basement where the huge steam heating system was located. They went further and further back into the dark recesses of the basement and found a dusty door that looked like it hadn't been opened in years.

They took hold of the doorknob, which almost fell off in their hands. They pulled, but the door was stuck because the hinges had gotten rusty.

Finally, they pulled really hard and the door swung open. Dust poured out in a cloud. When the dust cleared, the kids saw a horrible sight.

There, slumped over against the wall, was a rotten skeleton.

They called the janitor, who called the police.

For a long time no one could figure out who the skeleton had been. Then, finally, they were able to identify the rotten tennis shoes, and knew who it was.

It was the 1954 school hide-and-seek champion.